D0020030

Advance Praise for *The Last Professional*

"With The Last Professional, Davis has done for American railroads what Kerouac did for American highways, and Steinbeck did for American nomads."

Jerry Cimino, Founder of The Beat Museum, San Francisco

"Wow, what an ending."

Don Bartletti, Pulitzer Prize Winner in Feature Photography

"With wonderful, lyrical writing that reflects author Ed Davis' own history of adventurous journeys on freight trains across the American landscape, *The Last Professional* captures the imagination. With his latest solid effort, Davis weaves an intriguing tale of mystery, sacrifice, and personal triumph. Compelling characters add to the literary mix, potentially positioning Davis as a fresh bright light among American fiction writers. Very well crafted."

D. C. Jesse Burkhardt, author of *Travelogue From an Unruly Youth*

"Lynden Hoover was a boy who had been abandoned and taken and abandoned again. Like a coda from a powerful song, he was coming full circle when he bolts a lucrative job and jumps a train 'to wherever'. Onboard a box car in the heat, he meets The Duke, a hobo royal who guides him through the violent and cinematic survival. Finally, a father figure appears from the rough skids of tramp life. Along the way, Lynden becomes 'Frisco Lindy', but who is The Last Professional? The last act of Frisco's enlightenment comes in a hobo jungle worthy of a raw Quentin

Tarantino awakening. Blood. Love. And a man's self-respect—fashioned by the force of Ed Davis and the rough poetry of life on the rails."

Viola Weinberg, Poet Laureate Emerita & Glenna Luschei Fellow

"Davis's wordsmithing is masterful. He evokes another time in modern times, deftly defining the wilderness of America's railways and building characters—teacher and student—whose complex stories unfold in moments lit by starlight and fueled by baking powder biscuits, and in quick jolts, screeching like metal wheels on rails."

Tracy Salcedo, National Outdoor Book Award winner

"*The Last Professional* invites us to take a leap, hang on, and discover a secret world far from our comfortable lives. In this beautifully written story, Ed Davis draws readers into the shadows to discover a vanishing brotherhood who, despite their raw, gritty, and sometimes desperate ways, elicit our respect for their absolute commitment to freedom. You will never see a passing freight train the same way again."

Fran Braga Meininger, author of *The Years Beyond Youth*

THE LAST PROFESSIONAL

A story of the River of Steel

By Ed Davis

Illustrated By Colin Elgie

Artemesia
Publishing

ISBN: 978-1-951122-25-6 (paperback)
ISBN: 978-1-951122-34-8 (ebook)
ISBN: 978-1-951122-40-9 (audio)
LCCN: 2021941115
Copyright © 2022 by Ed Davis
Cover Illustration © 2022 by Colin Elgie
Interior Illustrations © 2022 by Colin Elgie

Cover Illustration and Design: Colin Elgie
Cover Layout: Geoff Habiger

Names, characters, and incidents depicted in this book are products of the author's imagination or are used fictitiously. Any resemblance to actual events, locales, organizations, or persons, living or dead, is entirely coincidental and beyond the intent of the author or the publisher.

This book contains descriptions of trauma, violence, sexual abuse, loss, and suicide that may be disturbing to some people.

All rights reserved. No part of this book may be reproduced or transmitted in any form or by any means, electronic or mechanical, including photocopying, recording or by any information storage or retrieval system without written permission of the publisher, except for the inclusion of brief quotations in a review.

Artemesia Publishing
9 Mockingbird Hill Rd
Tijeras, New Mexico 87059
www.apbooks.net
info@artemesiapublishing.com

First Edition

Brother, have you seen starlight on the rails? Have you heard the thunder of the fast express?

Thomas Wolfe

Not all those who wander are lost.

J.R.R. Tolkien

Dedication

For Zuke
This *is* what we were meant to do.

Acknowledgements

Imagine you're in a boxcar, sidetracked somewhere near Watsonville, California, so the Coast Starlight, hours overdue, can pass. It is the tail end of the 1970s. Night has overtaken you and the Southern Pacific local that is slowly ferrying you southward. You are riding alone, your canvas rucksack your only companion. You use it as a pillow whenever you can catch a few ZZZ's, and as a cushion to soften the ride. It carries your change of clothes, and the hardening bread and harder cheese that are left over from your last meal.

Inside that rucksack is your spiral notebook. You fish it out. The notebook's cardboard covers are creased from hurried, careless folding, its pages smudged with road grime but little else. Your twenty-nine cent Bic ballpoint is stashed safely in the wire coil. You take the pen in hand, and by the light of the Amtrak streamliner that finally passes, you write: *Somewhere a hobo is waiting.*

Forty years will pass before those words, and the tens of thousands of others that they inspire, finally appear together in print.

But on that night, those five words are enough.

When that boxcar began to move, this novel began to take shape. In the years since, it was sidetracked many times, and traveled a twisting route no publisher would have envisioned. Yet, it continued to roll—drawn forward by the power of the people who believed in it.

The faith of friends and family kept it going. And I had

the good fortune to know a man named Frank Ward, a gambler, writer, and trainer of Australian Sheep Dogs. He was my first reader, editor, teacher. His long letters helped *me* believe.

In the mid-1980s the manuscript made its way to Hy Cohen's Manhattan literary agency, then to Chicago's Fine Arts Building, and finally to the dusty, book-strewn offices of Jane Jordan Browne, a legend in publishing. It was she who gave me tea, advice, and her best efforts to find a publisher. But a narrative about hobos proved to be a hard sell.

Time passed.

Decades.

Then the wheels began to turn again. In 2013, I published *Road Stories*, a travel collection that included four short pieces from the languishing novel.

New literary agents looked—and passed. Some said that *The Last Professional* was too short, others that it was too long. One suggested that I find a different word for *hobo*.

The world of literary fiction had changed since the 1980s. Self-Publishing released a floodtide of creativity but diminished my novel's odds of breaking through.

I sought editing help to make the novel more accessible to contemporary readers and got it from two industry pros. David Colin Carr helped me define the protagonist, and Aviva Layton helped me reimagine the plot.

But it was Vince Zukowski who helped me rediscover the spark. Zuke is a great editor who pointed me towards possibilities within my work and myself that I did not know were there. This book is dedicated to him.

And I have been blessed to find a publisher in Geoff Habiger, a man who loves the words, the work, and the writers who keep him burning the midnight oil to get it just right.

It was Stephen King who famously said, "Writing is a lonely job. Having someone who believes in you makes a lot of difference. They don't have to makes speeches. Just believing is usually enough."

Unlike that night in the boxcar outside of Watsonville, I did not always ride alone. Occasionally my path would coincide with a stranger's for a few miles, a few hours, a few days, though we always maintained the respectful distance required of the road. But two people not only shared the rails with me, they shared my life. Since high school, Richard Yonash has been in my corner. Whether ditching class, or dodging railroad bulls, or devoting ourselves to a business we can be proud of, I could not have asked for a truer friend. And my greatest adventure began when I met Jan Davis. We were just kids, newly in love, when together we hopped freights across Canada. She has been my partner ever since.

With these two, *just believing* has meant everything.

Ed

Chapter One

So pay attention now my children
And the old story I will tell
About the jungles and the freight trains
And a breed of men who fell.
                                    Virginia Slim

Until the railroad arrived virtually at their door-steps, most people lived within a day's walk of where they were born. America was smaller. Horizons meant something. The span of a life was measured out in strides.

A desire for more, a restlessness of the soul, always lay in wait.

It was a gnawing in the gut that comfort would abate for most, and conformity could subdue for others. Yet, in the hearts of some, the compulsion to wander was so irresistible that they had no choice but to follow. On horseback, on a raft, or on the last of their shoe leather, they would eventually leave everything they knew, seek solace in movement, and go in search of themselves.

These pilgrims, who longed for a different path, found that a river of steel had burst to life at their feet. Surging from the midst of the sprawling cities to the smallest ham-lets, its tributaries traversed defiant mountain ranges, spanned impossibly vast prairies, and linked the remotest reaches of the country.

Hobos these pilgrims were called, phantoms of the

road, and except to one another, they had no names.

The river of steel still flows through the land, but it is a changed land and a changed river. Its tributaries no longer reach into every corner, its currents are no longer inviting. The hobos that once were, are no more, having "caught the westbound" long ago. At the time of this tale, late in the last century, their golden age was a distant memory, their legacy known to but a dwindling few.

* * *

The country east of Roseville, California is a gentle plain of grassland and houses, tilting steadily upwards toward the Sierra Nevada. It's a gradual climb that an automobile wouldn't notice, but the eastbound freight labored at it, all six power units throwing thick black smoke into the afternoon sky.

In their boxcar Lynden and the old man stood like sailors on a rolling deck—hands clasped at their backs, feet wide apart for balance, faces thrust forward into the wind. Their car was like an oven from a day's worth of sun, so they had pushed back both doors to catch a cooling breeze. On either side, the great brown landscape peeled by. Hills sloped into the long valley. Palisades defined the hollows of the grasslands. The open doors framed the passing scenery like a movie screen, a private showing just for them.

Lynden remembered his first time on a train—fifteen years earlier, when he was only eleven. It was summer, and the hot metal side of the boxcar had stung his hand. Inside, the car had smelled of grain and warm wood.

He remembered the pasture behind his house in Auburn, Washington, and the railroad tracks just beyond the back fence-line—a line he knew he should never cross. He remembered the trains he often saw there. He'd learned to read the names on the cars, and he'd said their numbers aloud.

Occasionally the trains stopped. He'd see men riding in the cars. Sometimes he'd lean against that fence and talk to them. Sometimes he'd cross it. When the trains pulled away, the men would wave, and he'd shout back, his chest tight when they were gone.

His father was gone. "He's not dead. Just gone," his mother would say, until he stopped asking. Lynden remembered them fighting, remembered hiding in the darkest corner of the chicken coop until it was over—until his mom would bring him in for the night.

When his dad left, the fighting ceased, and they were alone.

The train Lynden would never forget stopped behind his house the summer after sixth grade. Since then, everything around him had changed, everything but that train. Time had not faded it, nor improved it, nor altered it. The train was too strong. It went forward, always in his dreams forward, all the cars linked and bound, the great length tied and whole. The train was real. Its attraction was real. It had been calling him across all his days.

His favorite tramp was on it, one he had talked to many times. He'd told the man how much he missed his father. The man listened and seemed to understand. Then, on that day, as his train started to move, the tramp had reached down from his boxcar and pulled Lynden in.

He could remember exactly what he'd felt at that instant: surprise, fear, excitement—hope. Maybe the tramp was taking him to find his father.

The tramp was just taking him.

From nowhere the smell of sweet tobacco overwhelmed his senses. That scent, mingled with sweat, grime, saliva, was so primitive, so raw, it clung in his memory even now. The tramp had rolled his own cigarettes—his fingers reeking of that pungent smell as they fondled him, probed him, held him if he tried to pull away. But he didn't try, not really. For the three weeks they were together he did not resist.

He did not fight back.

For the fifteen years since, he'd been haunted by that fact. If he'd been drowning, he would have struggled for air; if slipping, he would have strained for any handhold that might arrest his fall.

But on that train, he'd drowned, he'd fallen.

After three weeks of it, the tramp had abandoned him—just like his dad.

Lynden never learned the man's name. "The Tramp" was how he thought of him, and he thought of him often—of punishing him for what he had done. What he hadn't seriously considered, until yesterday, was doing something about it.

Only yesterday he'd been offered a promotion that would have made the business section of the Mercury News. "Data Dynamics, pegged as one of 1983's fastest growing tech firms, today named Lynden Hoover, age twenty-six, head of Product Development. Hoover becomes one of the youngest Silicon Valley programmers to hold such a post, and possibly the highest paid."

There was no *possibly* about it.

There was also no story.

Instead of saying yes, he'd said goodbye.

His coworkers, who did not know him well or understand him at all, were sure he'd quit because of the added pressure. Either that or as a ploy for more money. But it wasn't about money or pressure. He loved programming. Circuits were like barricades for Lynden, equations like battlements. When he brought them together with code, they created a fortress, a realm that was entirely his own—one he could control. He understood every inch of that world, just as prisoners know every inch of their cells.

As long as he was in self-imposed solitary, he could

convince himself that he was fine.

But when Derek Zebel, the new VP and his immediate supervisor, had cornered him in the men's room—right after he'd offered him the promotion—it was like discovering his cellmate was a rapist. It pushed him over the edge. Not the breakdown edge or the bughouse edge. Just the quitting edge. He'd done it before. Hell, others at his level had done it before. All programmers were a little crazy, and all the good ones knew when to bail.

Until yesterday, Lynden had been holding it together. The new design was going smoothly, and the prototype of the DD 2000—Double Dildo the techies were calling it— was fifty percent locked down. But it wasn't the Double Dildo that had toggled him from a one to a zero.

It was Zebel, and the confidence in his voice when he'd said, "I *know* you've been saving it for me." The squeeze of his hand on Lynden's crotch, not a caress but a vice-like *squeeze*, was a statement of control, of possession, and a declaration that he could and would do anything he wanted.

Anything at all.

And behind Zebel, fifteen years behind, was The Tramp.

From nowhere the smell of sweet tobacco came to Lynden's nostrils and he saw the glint of sunlight on polished brass. Zebel seemed amused when Lynden shoved him away, a reflex so strong that he could not have restrained himself. "Go ahead... play hard to get," his new boss grinned, "but you're not fooling anybody, and we both know it." Lynden heard him, and though he *didn't* know it, the question plagued him. And it wasn't Derek Zebel's voice that he heard, or Derek Zebel's face that he saw.

It was The Tramp's. The Tramp, standing over him. Not a face or a body or anything clear, but there was no mistaking it for anything, or anyone, else.

And he felt, what? Dread? Shame? Longing? Maybe all of those. Or maybe just the hole they left behind.

Fifteen years, and he still wasn't sure.

Small problems you walk away from, he thought. He'd been doing that most of his life. *But from big ones, you run.*

He'd sprinted through the plant, tossed his I.D. badge at the guard as he hit the door, and didn't stop until he'd grabbed his backpacking gear from his apartment, hiked to the nearest onramp and stuck out his thumb.

It may have been an accident that the first ride he'd hitched ended in Roseville. He could accept that. But going down to the freight yards was a decision he'd been wrestling with for fifteen years. His Tramp might still be out there. Lynden pictured the man standing over him. After all this time he wasn't sure he trusted the image, but the emotions it stirred remained clear and raw—always ready to ambush him when he least expected it, or when they would do the most harm.

The scent of sweet tobacco. The gleam of polished brass.

And in the background, all this time, that deep deadly rumble.

Beckoning. Fearsome.

The sound of the trains.

Now he was on a train again, the first he'd ridden since he was a boy. He'd jumped aboard as it was rolling out of the Roseville yard—an awkward and clumsy catch with the heavy pack strapped to his back. Somehow he got on, scrambling into what he thought was an empty boxcar. It was only when he was safely inside, catching his breath and shucking off his pack, that he realized he wasn't alone. From the darkest corner of the car he saw a silver glint on a long steel blade, and the shadowy shape of the man holding it.

* * *

The Duke was not accustomed to being scared.

For two weeks now he'd been glancing over his shoulder, and every time his gut jumped a little. In fifty years on the road, bulls had pistol-whipped him, jungle buzzards had knifed him for the change in his pockets, and the killing wheels of the freights had always been there, ever sharpening themselves on the whetstone of the rails. He had seen men die beneath those wheels, seen them sucked in and ripped apart, but none of it had derailed him. Not until two weeks ago. Not until that mess in the jungle outside the Colton Yards.

Not until Short Arm.

Now he was running.

That night in Colton he'd snagged the first freight he saw—anything to get away. Turned out it was a Southern Pacific shuttle, so he rode it to the old LA yard, then ditched and lay low. He was sure nobody had seen him, but on the Coast Express next morning he'd stayed hidden anyway.

Countless times that coastal had carried him from LA to Oakland. Usually, he stood in a boxcar door watching the ocean and the sand dunes and the broad blue sky. This trip he watched nothing, crouching in the car's darkest corner, listening. He dreaded the moments when the train slowed down.

He'd made it through Santa Barbara and the crew change at San Luis Obispo. By Paso Robles his nerves were shot. What if somebody saw him when they set out cars at King City? What if the bull at Watsonville stripped the train? And if he made it to Oakland—what then? He was "The Duke," and if some Sixth Street stew-bum recognized him, that was it.

Paso Robles might be safe, he'd thought, at least until things blew over. Only local freights stopped there anymore. In steam days there'd been a water tank at the south end and next to it a hobo jungle where some home-guard boys were still holding it down, their riding days long past.

When the coastal had slowed for the grade south of town he left it. Twenty miles per hour, yet he hit the grit running and stayed up—not bad for an old man.

A week in the Paso jungle, and nothing. Part of another week and all he'd seen were rum-dumbs by the jungle fire and freight trains working up and down the grade. He started to relax, to tell himself that he'd never been afraid. He was Profesh, damn it. In a lifetime on the rails he'd faced every kind of danger the road could throw at him.

All without fear.

Then, one afternoon when he was coming back from the Sally, one of the home-guard boys slipped him word, one of the few who still knew the score. "Some yegg came through lookin for you. A Johnson if you ask me, though I ain't seen one of those evil rat bastards since Hector was a pup. Big guy with a wing missin."

That was three days ago.

He'd fled north. First on foot, then by thumb, but finally back to the freights. No place on the coast was safe for him now. That left the East, or maybe Canada, though Short Arm might still give chase. Most yeggs and jack rollers wouldn't leave their home turf and worked a circuit where the law and the routes and the easy prey were all familiar.

But Short Arm was different, the last of his kind and crazy at that.

There was no predicting what he would do, only what he wouldn't do.

He wouldn't stop.

Since before dawn The Duke had been in Roseville, working not to be noticed. Though he hadn't eaten in two days, he avoided the Salvation Army soup kitchen. The

Sally was the first place Short Arm would look. Same with the last remaining hash house down on the main stem, and the watering hole next to it, both too well-known in their ever-shrinking universe to be safe. In any case, he told himself, he'd need what little money he had for the long trip ahead.

He snatched a couple of over-ripe pears from a neglected tree in an untended back yard, devoured them down to the seeds, and licked his fingers clean.

The next northbound left at four o'clock, the next eastbound not long after. The Duke had ridden both many times before. Unless he wanted Short Arm to catch him and kill him right there, he'd have to flee town, and flee the state, on one of them.

While he waited, he stayed clear of the yards and the rescue mission and the park where a few bums dozed in the shade. He changed his usual mackinaw and work pants for a dispatcher outfit. His slacks, old suit jacket and yellowing white shirt turned him into a retired railroad employee. He would think like a side-tracked dispatcher, act like one, and go to all the places a retired railroad stiff might burn time. Since hitting town he'd spent a few hours in the library and a few more down at the mostly empty Roseville depot swapping lies with the custodian.

At half-past four—freights can always leave late, and often do, but never early—he'd ducked between some broken-down bad-order tankers parked on a dead-end siding and hit a string of boxcars just as the power units began to move, pulling slack out of the couplings, the sound coming to him like slow thunder from the head end of the train. He found an open boxcar and tossed his road-worn leather satchel into the darkness inside. He followed after it, with a grace and ease that belied how complicated the movement was, and suspended, for a moment, his terror that Short Arm might be waiting for him inside.

* * *

"I've seen prettier catches." The stranger stepped into the light.

Lynden flashed on the last time he'd been with a man in a boxcar. The fear, the excitement, the shame—all of it switched on in an instant. But there was no cunning in this voice, no threat. Only wariness.

"What do you figure that backpack of yours weighs?" The hobo was a compact old man, a foot shorter than Lynden and well north of sixty years old—the rugged features of a life lived outdoors imprinted deeply on his face. He wasn't brandishing the knife, just making sure Lynden could see all of its twelve-inch length.

"Forty pounds, forty-five maybe." In the hobo's other hand Lynden saw a battered valise. "How about that bag of yours?"

"Ten pounds." The hobo considered. "Hell, eight pounds. And there's times I got nothin but my wits and my walkin stick. Seein all your gear, I don't guess you'll be wantin mine." He opened his bag and placed the hunting knife inside. "This here's my boxcar, but you're welcome to share it, long as you behave."

"I'll do my best." Lynden felt himself begin to relax, enough to offer a hint of a smile along with his answer. "Where's this train heading, do you know?"

"Wherever the hell she takes us." The old man stepped to the open door. "If she swings north up here, then it's Dunsmuir and on to Oregon. If she holds straight east, then it's over the hump to Reno and Sparks. You goin somewheres in particular?"

"No. Just like you said, wherever the hell she takes us."

* * *

In the fifteen years since he'd been hauled into that first freight, everything in Lynden's life had changed completely. Yet, out the door in front of him now, a familiar watery image of a shadow train shimmered dimly beside them. He remembered that from before, it was all just the same. Silver wheels honed and polished themselves on the anvil of the rails, the air filled with their raw, steel scent. He knew the smells—diesel and rust—and a roar like the ocean in a shell. His feet vibrated with the strain of a hundred thousand tons and the surging of the air lines and the flexing of the springs. Doors banged, metal slapped, dust flew. This was the train that threaded through his dreams, The Tramp's train. It pulled him, relentless as gravity, but onward.

Their freight headed east at the switch, then climbed a ridge rising gradually above the valley floor. Lynden scanned the wide, sweeping land of ranchettes and open range that spanned to the south below. A row of palm trees undulated over the rolling hills. Not far from the tracks, billboards blared at the heedless freeway traffic speeding by. Horses grazed in dry pastures. On larger country estates, the unreal blue of swimming pools glittered like cold gems sewn into the fabric of the warm, brown plain. As the track curved, Lynden could see the full length of the train. *This thing's more than a mile long.*

Fifteen years long.

Within an hour they were deep into the Sierra Nevada. Pines and huge cedars crowded close against the tracks; cars moved at a walker's pace. The old man stepped back from the doors. Lynden remained in the waning light, and watched the hard-edged landscape soften into pastels— evening's gossamer veil layering mystery over the meadows, suggesting secrets in the forest glens.

Night, and still he watched. High in the mountains a harsh wind bit his face. The cold and dark enlivened him. Moonlight illuminated the great rock faces rolling by, close enough to touch. Tunnels and snow sheds. Patches of snow like icing on the ground. They were crossing a trestle over a deep canyon. The snow in the bottom, a hundred feet below, glowed as if lit from within. He imagined himself stepping off the edge of the car and falling towards it—the thrilling release, the wind in his hair, the gentle embrace as he sank into the snow.

The last sheer face of Donner Summit rose, menacing and ghostly, before them. The rock's cold white fingers reached into the obsidian sky. A snow shed opened, and one after another the cars were sucked in, as if the mountain were inhaling.

Magnifying the train's roar, the snow shed grew darker, eclipsing light and shadow when it became a tunnel. Lynden clutched the edge of the door. He touched his palm to his nose. His eyes searched the car, at the noise from the opposite door, then to where the old man hunkered down. Blackness. He inched his head outside and looked toward the front of the train. A hot wind coursed roughly over his face—the smell of diesel and damp and mold. His eyes watered from the wind and blowing grit. Nothing to be seen.

He closed his eyes and rubbed them hard. He could see then, but no more than familiar colors swimming behind his eyelids.

Lynden floated, weightless, sailing through a shapeless void, unable to sense the train's direction except when it lurched. As he had watched the foothills in the daylight, and the forests of the mountains at dusk, he settled back and watched the absolute darkness.

The train emerged beneath brilliant moonlight and stars that, after the darkness, were as shocking to his eyes as a million small suns.

"Tunnels been known to eat greenhorns like you." The hobo was standing beside him, moon glow playing across his face. "Me and some boys rode through the Moffat tunnel with this young fella one summer and damned if we didn't lose him. While we were inside, the fool got up to relieve himself—relieved himself right out the door."

The train's character shifted as it plunged down the eastern slope. After hours of plodding, pleasant and harmless, it was gathering speed, uncoiling into a rolling threat. Lynden's feet picked up the tension as a thousand brake shoes engaged spinning steel. The air filled with the hot metallic smell of friction.

Soon the boxcar began pitching wildly from side to side, its wheels at odds with the rails.

"You scared kid?"

"Yes... you aren't?"

"I was, when I was like you."

The rapid waters of the Truckee River threw darts of silver light back at the sky, and a hot wind came whistling through the boxcar doors. They were flying down the mountain, rushing and swinging, hurtling toward the great flat desert below.

Whether it lasted minutes or hours Lynden wasn't sure, but finally the train began to slow onto the flats, its frantic spell broken.

In the distance, like a beacon, the pulsing glare of Reno drew them steadily closer.

Track #1
On the Fly — To catch a moving freight.

Before we took a break to eat and tend the fire, you were talking about the truth, remember?

Was I?

You said it's all that counts. *Strip away the good and bad, and what's left is the truth.* Those were your exact words.

Good words. Seems a guy will say almost anything for a drink of whiskey and some hot chow.

Maybe, but I don't think you'll lie to me.

Won't I?

When we began, it's the way you said you wanted it.

I guess I did.

The truth, then. Let's start with who you are.

I'm a hobo, a stiff who rides trains. That's true enough. You might see me waving out a boxcar door when you're stopped at a crossing, waiting... if you see the freight at all that is. Or cooking up in a camp by the tracks like this one here... a *jungle* we call it... cause it's usually tucked away in the bushes and trees. Maybe even walking down the street next to you. I'm not the sort you always notice, but I've been around. Just a colorful character from the old days, like in the folk songs. *Listen to the steel rails hummin', that's the hobo's lullaby.*

That sounds like who you think I *want* you to be... not who you are.

Then maybe you oughta get your ears checked.

The truth, remember.

Whose... yours or mine?

You think there is more than one kind of truth?

Don't matter what I think. You want the painless truth, the awful truth, or the final truth? You want the preacher's truth, the lawyer's truth? Maybe the lover's truth is what you're looking for. There are as many kinds of truth as there are kinds of people. You can pick truth off the rack like a suit of clothes.

We're after the real truth, aren't we?

That can be damn hard to find. Harder to face.

I'm willing if you are.

You may not like it.

Chapter Two

Seeing the raveled edge of life
In jails, on rolling freights
And learning rough and ready ways
From rough and ready mates.
Harry Kemp

Lynden stood between the open boxcar doors, his eyes shifting from the anxious faces on the sidewalks to the neon brilliance of Reno all around them. The old man rode quietly and watched from the shadows.

Casinos glittered on either side of the tracks. Crowds waited for the slow rolling freight to pass on its way to the Sparks yard just east of town. Some gamblers, frustrated with the train's interminable length, were so eager to try their luck at the next gaming palace that they scrambled clumsily across the couplings—risking more than a few dollars.

"Yard's starting," the old man said softly.

"What?"

He pointed outside. They were still in the midst of the casino district, but a siding had appeared next to them, and another next to it, like the branches of a candelabra springing from its stem. Glare from the first of the freight yards many blinding floodlights, perched atop their fifty-foot towers, filled the car. Lynden slipped back into a corner.

The rhythmic dirge of the freight beat slower with every turn of the wheels. Lynden and the old man watched the yard slip by. To their left a web of sidings splayed out, to their right a wide gravel area with trucks and sheds. They passed a string of power units idling on a spur. The yard office came into view, then the depot, and then both slid back into the night.

"She'll change crew here. When she rolls out again, we can snag her by the overpass down at the east end."

"We have to get off?"

"There's desert to cross tomorrow. How much water you carryin?"

"A full canteen."

"Yeah, we have to get off."

The tempo slowed till the rocking motion stopped. With a dull clanking the boxcar came to a stone silent halt. The quiet was so intense that neither man spoke.

A burst of air blasted from under the car.

"Christ!" Lynden froze.

"It's only the air release." The old man grabbed his bag off the floor. "You comin?"

Lynden shouldered his pack and stepped into the open doorway.

"Don't move." The hobo's sudden grip on Lynden's shoulder stopped him. A few sidings over a low white sedan was cruising left to right, tires stepping clumsily over the rutted access road.

"Did you tangle with a yard bull in Roseville today?"

"Tangle? No... a guy chased me out of the yard. Told me to stay out. When he was gone, I snuck back in." Lynden had liked the thrill of it, of disobeying. "Why?"

The sedan came to a stop.

Nothing moved. Boxcars ceased banging in the yard, engines quit their droning.

The sedan inched forward again.

"Maybe he didn't spot us." Lynden's eyes were fixed on the car.

"Like hell." The cruiser pulled out of sight. They heard it accelerate as it hit the city streets. "Get your I.D. yanked twice on the same line, you get thirty days in county." The old man was scanning the open yard. "Guards will shake you down for everything you've got, and you'll end up with a boyfriend if you're lucky... ten if you ain't. With that backpack on, can you run?"

"Can you?"

They jumped down from the car and broke into a sprint.

Lynden *could* run—Bay to Breakers every year, and three miles before work most mornings. But burdened by the pack he was no match for his companion.

A hundred yards and no sign of the bull. A hundred fifty and still no sign.

The old man ran past the service road that marked the yard boundary, and kept going.

Lynden stopped there, feet numb, shoulders raw. He shifted the pack to relieve pressure, then heard a sound. He looked back.

The white sedan was almost on him.

The hobo was gone, hidden in the bushes. Lynden dashed to the first opening he could find and dove in. It was a tunnel through the thicket, branches and brush all around. His pack snagged. He lurched, broke free, and tumbled into a hollow of weeds and blackberry brambles.

"Where the hell you been?" The old man, crouching beside him, had his knife drawn.

"Jesus Christ!"

"Save your prayin for later."

"What's that thing for?"

"Him," he answered. They heard the bull's car pull to a stop in front of them.

"Look... it's not worth it, even if we go to jail."

"No?" The old man spat on the blade, polishing it with

the heel of his hand.

Through the bushes, just yards away, they could see the bull's legs and hear the snap as his holster opened.

"You can't use that thing on him!" Lynden, against the rising panic of what he thought was about to happen, tried to whisper, matching the old man's intensity.

"Watch me."

Beams of yard-light glare filtered through the bushes. The old man held his knife in one of them and flashed its blade toward the tracks. "I've never stuck this thing in nobody, but I've never had reason to. Right now, he's wondering if it's worth it. Chances are we're leaving his town. Chances are he won't ever see us after today. But he knows what he'll see if he comes in here." He flashed the knife in the light again.

They watched the legs take a step forward.

"All right," the bull's voice, loud but lacking conviction, made them both jump, "I know you're in there."

Lynden opened his mouth as if to answer.

The old man stopped him with a hard look.

Stillness.

"Don't let me catch you in my yard again!"

The legs took a step backward. The holster snapped shut.

Moments later the car pulled away.

Lynden was lying against his pack, heart still sprinting. "Are you nuts?"

"He had your I.D." The old man reached into his battered leather valise, took an undershirt from the bag, and wrapped the knife. "It was on your account I run him off. You got a thing for getting busted?"

"I've got a thing for not getting shot!"

"Did you?"

They glared at each other. A light wind carried the smell of creosote, hot gravel, and rusting iron. Back in the yard a switch engine groaned on the hump.

Minutes passed.

The old man put his knife away.

"You hungry?" Lynden pulled his pack open, not sure if the tension between them was broken yet, or ever would be.

"Guess I could eat... if you're offerin." The hobo managed to sound disinterested, even as his stomach growled.

Lynden began to pile food on the ground. Cans of corned beef hash, stew, beans. Some coffee, fruit, a sack of beef jerky. "I stocked up... thought I might be gone awhile." He yanked out a folding stove and a can of Sterno. Mess kit, silverware, salt, pepper. Even a dented pot for coffee. "I camp a lot. The stuff accumulates."

"I camp too." His companion began to lay out the contents of his valise. A thin blanket, tightly rolled and bound with a belt. A mackinaw and work pants. A denim shirt. Shaving gear, the knife, something wrapped in a kerchief. That was all. He undid the belt and rolled out his blanket. "You got half the grocery store in that balloon of yours. Bring your wardrobe too?" The old man slipped off his old suit jacket, laid it carefully on the blanket and pressed it flat with his hands.

"Some of it. A couple pair of Levi's, some shirts. Just what I grabbed on the way out." He held up a can of hash. "This all right with you?"

"It's your grub."

"And some coffee?"

"You're fixin it."

The hobo removed his shirt, folded it, then shucked off his pants. "This here's all I carry." He rolled up his town clothes in his blanket, so tight it was hardly bigger than before. "Keeps em pressed, in case I gotta look good." He cinched the belt. "Whole thing don't weigh more than a promise."

"Why so little?"

"Why so much?" He pulled on his road clothes and pointed at the pack. "You actually expect to catch trains with that on your back?"

"Unless you want to carry it for me."

* * *

As the kid prepared their meal, the Duke watched. Whenever there was a sound from the yard, he could see his new companion stop, listen. The Duke listened too. He knew the sounds, knew them so well he hardly heard them anymore. *The kid seems to know them too*, he thought, *but different.*

The Duke recalled a Christmas in Kansas City when the Salvation Army put on a symphony show for the bums. He hadn't heard that kind of music since back in Cumberland, back before he left home. His mother had a gramophone that she played sometimes, mostly when she was feeling low. It was symphony music she played, and that Christmas at the Sally in KC, The Duke listened and remembered. *That's how the kid looks right now, like he's remembering something.*

* * *

When Lynden reached to hand him a plate of food, the old man grabbed his wrist and held it. "What the hell's your story? This isn't some camping trip. People die on these rails."

"I know that." Lynden looked him in the eye and held his gaze. "When I was eleven years old, I ran away from home and met up with a tramp. We rode trains."

"When you were eleven?" He released his grip.

"That's what I said." Lynden hesitated. *We rode trains*, he thought. *That makes it sound so simple.* "After a few weeks we split up. I went home."

"Just like that?"

"Just like that."

"What are you doin out here now?"

"Just looking. Want to see if it's like I remember."

"And that stiff... you lookin for him?"

"I don't remember him." Sweat stood out on Lynden's forehead. "He was just a tramp." *A tramp? The Tramp. Whose hands smelled of sweet tobacco. Whose boots were laced with wire.*

"Did he hurt you?"

"No!"

Lynden watched the old man studying him, and felt revealed.

* * *

Half an hour later they were sitting on the sidewalk in front of an all-night grocery and laundromat. Each of them was drinking beer from a can in a brown paper bag, absently watching the comings and goings in the parking lot. Since leaving their hiding place they'd said almost nothing.

"Data Dynamics..." The old man nodded toward Lynden's logo tee shirt. The company gave them away to programmers who were usually too preoccupied to dress themselves in anything else. "That's computers, right?"

"You've heard of Data Dynamics?"

"Just cause I sleep under newspapers sometimes don't mean I can't read em."

The store lights illuminated the parking spaces in front of them like a stage. A car pulled up. They both watched as the old lady behind the wheel got out, skirted past them, and disappeared into the store.

"What were you gonna say to that bull... if I hadn't stopped you?"

"I don't know."

A man in his thirties came out of the store, the two little girls with him carrying dripping Popsicles. The man nodded as he walked past. The kids flashed red Popsicle smiles.

The old lady came out carrying a carton of milk, a loaf of bread, and a smell that reminded Lynden of moth balls, only sweeter.

"You computer guys used to doin just what you're told?"

"I guess it depends on who's doing the telling." Lynden thought of Derek Zebel, and the way he seemed so sure that Lynden would do *exactly* what he was told.

"Yeah, I guess it does." The old man drained his beer and crushed the can. "There ain't many I'll step aside for, and that bull isn't on the list. What he don't seem to know is that I own these rails."

"Is that right?" Lynden considered him. "Unless I was imagining things back there, what *he* owns is a gun."

"Ownin and usin ain't the same... we just seen that."

"Maybe. Or maybe we got lucky."

Another car pulled up—a fifty-seven Chevy, polished and gleaming. A hard-edged high school boy, seventeen at most, sat behind the wheel. Hair combed perfectly; tee shirt so white it glared. His girlfriend at his side.

"Listen... you probably got enough dough to buy a ticket out of here. I don't buy tickets."

"Meaning what?"

"I've been run outta yards plenty of times. I've never *stayed* out. I'm going back there and catch me a train."

Inside the Chevy the boy stared straight ahead, one hand on the steering wheel. His girlfriend stared at him. Lynden could see their lips moving. "Going back is stupid." Lynden's eyes were locked on the scene in the car. "Why don't I buy us bus tickets to the next big town... assuming we want to stick together. We can pick up a freight there. I don't even know where we're going."

"We're goin east. I'm goin by train. And if you hadn't

just cooked me dinner, I'd take it personal... you callin me stupid. What the hell's your name anyway? I'm not used to getting insulted by strangers."

"Lynden. Lynden Hoover. Until a couple of days ago I worked at Data Dynamics. Now, I don't know what the hell I'm doing... or who I'm doing it with."

"Them that knows me... and there's damn few that still do... they call me The Duke," the old man offered his hand. "I ride trains."

The boy in the car turned his head, and the couple kissed. No hands, no holding, nothing but their two mouths stamped together. She arched toward him; her arms were pulled back at her sides as if pinned. Lynden could see the curve of her chest straining beneath her blouse. The tip of her breast brushed against her boyfriend's flexed bicep, hard within the sleeve of his bleached white tee shirt.

Lynden saw her freeze there. She seemed to be giving herself to him, but she was also taking. He guessed that it was exactly the sensation she was after, the touch of lips and breast against the hardness of her man. She moved against him now, only touching him there and there, only taking what she wanted to take.

"Like I asked before, what the hell are you doin out here?" The Duke said, breaking Lynden's spell. "If you can buy a ticket, why are you on the rails?"

Lynden reluctantly pulled himself away from the scene in the car, the girl in the Chevy having lain back against the seat, for the moment appearing satisfied.

"I'm here to ride trains, too."

"Sure, but there's a bull in every goddam yard. You gonna run from all of them?"

Lynden stared at him. "I'm sorry I called you stupid."

"What?"

"I'm going with you."

It was The Duke's turn to stare. "Are all computer guys

light on ballast? Or is it just you? Hell, I don't care. If we're gonna do this thing, let's do it."

In a dumpster behind the laundromat The Duke found an empty plastic bleach jug with the cap still on. He rinsed and filled it from a dripping hose bib on the back of the building, water for the desert trip.

When they walked back across the parking lot, the Chevy was gone.

* * *

A four-lane highway passed over the Sparks yard at its eastern limit. The highway bridge had pedestrian spirals at each end and a jump-proof fence all across both sides. From mid-span, looking west, Lynden and The Duke could see the entire layout—freight cars hulking in the darkness, car-knocker's lanterns bobbing like fireflies as they checked the couplings. A switch crew was making up a train at the west end, and on the main line a string of power units waited, ready to roll.

"That'll be our ride." The Duke pointed at the engine marker lights. "Chances are she's the same one we drug in on."

"How long till it leaves?"

"Could be anytime. That engineer will hit the horn, then goose the throttle. After that, it's up to us."

"And the bull?"

"He's out there. And we won't see him until he wants us to. But once we're on that train, we're gone. I ain't seen em stop a freight to catch a hobo in better than thirty years."

"And if we don't get on?"

The Duke wasn't listening. His ears were tuned toward the yard, toward a sound he could hear that Lynden didn't. Then a change in the monotonous droning of the engines, a shift in pitch more than volume. He saw that Lynden could hear it too.

"Is that us?"

The lead engine's tracer light flashed on, its swinging beam splashing against the overpass. An unseen hand moved on the throttle. As one machine, three giant power units revved their huge engines.

Triple columns of hot smoke and spark shot up into space.

The diesel horn cried out, then again and again.

A low, vibrating groan. The engines lugged, caught, and the train began to roll.

"That's us. Just watch me. Stay close, and we'll grab this sucker by the tail."

The kid made ready to run.

"Easy," The Duke cautioned. "There's nothin to ride on the head end anyway, and no sense tippin the engine crew we're around."

They walked off the bridge and ducked under it, watching as the power units rumbled by.

"When do we go?" The freight was picking up speed, and already moving faster than at Roseville.

"Don't worry, there's still plenty of train."

Seconds ticked past. The cars began rocking gently back and forth, each faster than the last. Lynden watched them anxiously, watched The Duke.

"You ready, kid?"

"Ready!"

"There's our car." A gondola was coming up fast. "Make for the front ladder on that gon and run like hell!"

They raced forward, Lynden and The Duke side by side.

A wide concrete bridge support separated them from the tracks. The kid dodged quickly around it and out to the cars.

Behind him, The Duke stopped. Some crude writing on the support caught his eye, some chalk scribbling on the face of the concrete slab.

He was almost past when the letters had connected in his mind, connected to form words, a name.

Short Arm.

Beneath the name was a date, two days old, and under it an arrow. Short Arm was eastbound. How was that for hobo luck? The man he'd been running from for the last two weeks, the man who meant to kill him if he caught him—his old partner—had slipped by and was now waiting somewhere out across the desert. The Duke had seen it play out like this before. Sure, it was a wide country, but the rails were narrow and connected—a steel ribbon that always wound back on itself. No matter how hard you ran, if you stayed on those rails long enough, your past would catch you.

He hadn't seen Short Arm in more years than he could remember, was sure he was dead. Then two weeks ago in that jungle outside the Colton yard, there he was—still alive, but changed. Short Arm had been glad to see him. That was a surprise, considering the way they'd parted. And his old friend was eager to demonstrate a new talent—something he was sure The Duke would appreciate. That demonstration ended with one man murdered, and The Duke running for his life.

The old hobo couldn't move. Two days earlier and Short Arm would have caught him right there—would have stepped out from behind that pillar and ended it. Somewhere ahead he was waiting. In the dark, in the shadows, waiting. The Duke's skin was pimpled with cold. He could head back west again, maybe south to Mexico. Anywhere but right on Short Arm's heels and he'd be safe, at least for a while.

He turned to leave.

* * *

Lynden reached the train, looked around, but the old man was gone. He glanced frantically both ways on the tracks.

The Duke was nowhere in sight.

What he did see was a pair of headlights bouncing violently as they sped straight at him out of the yard.

The gondola rolled by. He could still catch something, maybe, or search for The Duke, or face the bull and his gun.

"Fuck!"

He didn't move.

* * *

The Duke burst out from behind the pillar, saw the headlights coming, the train going, and Lynden caught motionless in between. "Go for the flat!" he yelled, then yelled again to be heard over the freight noise. He saw Lynden turn toward him, looking confused. "That flat right there!" He pointed to a flatcar just a few lengths up and coming fast.

Lynden saw it, faced it, and broke into a run.

Twenty cars back the caboose was clearly in sight, the bull's headlights seconds behind it.

Both men hit the flatcar's front ladder at the same time.

Lynden grabbed hold.

The Duke faded back, going for the rear ladder. Rapidly the car slid by him. He wasn't going full speed yet, but he knew what full speed was, and knew he'd need all of it.

The car was halfway past when he quickened his pace. The lumber flat had headboards at both ends and the rear board was almost on him. Between strides he tossed his bag up, then the bleach jug, and saw them roll to a stop at the back of the car.

With his hands free he hit full speed, his body balanced and natural. Fifty years of chasing trains had taught him how to run. Arms reaching, legs stretching, hands clawing the air, running flat out.

It wasn't enough.

The train was going too fast.

He saw his gear sliding by. The ladder was just above his shoulder. His only chance.

Surging forward he reached out and grabbed.

The shock was so stiff it popped all his knuckles.

His arm jerked tight. His shoulder stretched.

He held on.

The tips of four fingers were all that gripped. He reached with the other hand, found something to grasp, and instinct took over. His legs still ran, his feet still hit the ground, but with each step his strides grew longer and longer till he was leaping, yards at a time. Then a spring and a pull.

The Duke was on.

* * *

Lynden wasn't on.

He had the ladder with both hands, but his feet were moving so fast he couldn't push them off the ground.

Out the corner of his eye he'd seen The Duke hoist himself onto the train. He tried it, stumbled, caught himself.

He had to get on, let go, or run until his legs gave out.

The train was flying. He concentrated. Took an extra-long step.

As he pulled up, the searchlight hit him.

The bull was abreast of their flatcar, hacking the blackness with the blinding beam. It hit Lynden like a blow, shocking him at the instant he jumped.

The coarse gravel roadbed seemed to shift beneath him, pulling his feet away.

For a second, he hung in mid-air.

Then, instead of running, he was being dragged.

His hands slipped, held—then slipped again.

At the bottom rung he hung on, his body suspended inches above the scouring gravel. Feet skittering across the rocks and ties, screaming muscles stretched tight. The hungry jaws of the flatcar's huge wheels were pulling him in. A whisper away.

The bull's spotlight carved jaggedly through the rushing dark.

A hand grabbed Lynden's forearm.

"Pull yourself up!" The old man was leaning out over the ladder, the bull's light slashing across him. "Use your arms! Forget about your feet!"

Lynden's arms wouldn't move. He hung there, his backpack swinging from his shoulders like an anchor.

"Let it go! Let the damn thing go!"

It was the only way.

He released the ladder with one hand and his body dropped down even lower. The pack jerked violently. He twisted, shucking off a strap. He switched hands to free the other arm. The pack caught the ground, and shoved him head first toward the pounding wheels.

He closed his eyes.

The backpack bounced free, flew up, then was sucked under the train and was gone.

Both hands on the ladder again, Lynden began to climb.

The Duke reached down, grabbed his shirt, and pulled him onto the car.

The last the bull saw of them, Lynden and The Duke were hugging, screaming, and beating each other's backs as they disappeared into the Nevada darkness.

Track #2
Profesh — A professional hobo, bound by a code.

Why do you ride freight trains?

Because it's faster than walking.

So is a bus. So is a plane. You don't ride those. Why not?

Can't afford to.

Why go anywhere? Why not stay in one place?

And do what?

What other people do. Live, work, have a family, a home.

I've got a home. You're in it.

We're in a hobo jungle. It's not yours... not really.

Nothing's mine or yours or anybody's... really. We use it for a while, sure, but it isn't ours for long. What if I did own a house? It wouldn't be much good to me once I caught the westbound, would it? Some other fella's gonna move in, and it won't matter a bit that I spent my whole damn life trying to keep the weeds down and the mortgage paid.

You don't think much of the American Dream, do you?

Hell, I *am* the American Dream. I've got everything I want. A train to ride, food to eat, and more country than a body could ever see. All that's mine. I look at it, own it while I'm in it, then turn it loose for the next guy.

And the trains?

I've got to get around to see my holdings, don't I?

That's the only reason you ride them?

I ride them... I'll always ride them... because I have to.

Chapter Three

Gently, but with undeniable will,
Divesting myself of the holds that would hold me.
I inhale great draughts of space,
The east and the west are mine,
And the north and the south are mine.

Walt Whitman

The eastbound stretched itself across the waiting desert.

Sheltered from the wind by the flatcar's forward headboard, they sat side by side. A wide country disappeared into the blackness around them, and a brilliant spread of stars fanned out overhead. To the west they watched the lights of Reno fading as their train drew steadily eastward. The limitless American night deepened, the desert's sleeping heat slowly cooling as the wheels rolled rhythmically over the rails and the miles clicked by.

When Lynden dozed off, The Duke shook him gently. "Swing around and get your feet up tight to this headboard before you nod out. Do it the other way, and you'll smash your noggin if she stops quick." He rapped his knuckles for emphasis. "I expect you've had enough smashin for one night."

Lynden spun around, too tired to speak. His last thoughts were of his backpack. There would be time to miss it later, it and everything it represented. Now he was just remembering it, and the places it had taken him, and the weight of it that sometimes held him down and held him back. A memory that, like his wakefulness, surrendered effortlessly to sleep.

* * *

For a long time The Duke watched him sleep. The night layered itself over them. The air chilled. Carefully the old man wrapped his blanket around Lynden's shoulders, tucking it in so it wouldn't blow away. He wedged himself against the headboard, crossed his arms tight over his knees, and closed his eyes.

* * *

Just after dawn their train stopped on a siding somewhere east of Winnemucca. Lynden woke, all his joints aching, and struggled to sit up. His face, already crusted, became crustier when he touched it with a grimy hand. Hair like a brush, stiff with dirt, his fingers stuck when he tried to run them through it.

Inventory time. There was this ex-G.I. back at Dynamics who did a little check-list every time he left the john. "Spectacles, testicles, wallet, and comb," he'd say. Seemed like a good place to start.

Spectacles?

He didn't wear any.

Testicles? Wallet?

Both safe and sound, but he felt for his wallet just the same—the credit cards and cash it contained were his fallback ticket home.

Comb?

That's in my backpack.

He heard that sound again, the sound as it was sucked under the train.

What was left to check? Jacket? Same as the backpack, gone but not forgotten. Or did he have the wrong cliché? Shouldn't it have been *There but for the grace of God go I*? For an instant he thought about the *go I*, then pushed it aside. The jacket was gone, he wasn't.

Then he noticed the blanket.

Dirty, crumpled, frayed at the edges. *This isn't mine*, he thought, wrestling himself fully awake. *It must be The Duke's.* He looked again.

He saw himself—eleven years old—cold, exhausted, a little afraid. It was a night fifteen years earlier on a train, riding through the mountains. He was with The Tramp. It was summer, but their boxcar was frigid inside. They didn't have blankets. The Tramp made a bed for him of cardboard and paper. Lynden remembered the tearing sound as it came off the walls. "Thousand-mile paper," The Tramp called it, as he stacked layers on top of him. Heavy, crinkly, smelling of tar.

Lynden liked the smell of tar.

There was only enough scrap for one bed. The Tramp had gone without. The Tramp—a label he'd made up because he didn't know what else to call the man. Except for the few details he was certain of, like thousand-mile paper, like the strange belt buckle The Tramp wore—like the things he *tried* to forget but couldn't—Lynden didn't trust any of his memories.

Yet here he was, looking for a trail that might not exist, looking for a man he probably wouldn't recognize.

And the man didn't even have a name.

Lynden stood up and tried to turn his neck. It wouldn't move. His shoulder joints had filled with grit, his feet turned to clubs.

"You don't look so hot." The Duke was awake, twisting out his own kinks. "Ain't this railroadin fun?"

"Yeah, fun. The only thing I didn't bruise last night was my voice. Where are we?"

At each side of the train a low, barren ridge ran off toward the horizon. Old tire tracks crisscrossed the crusty surface and a row of crumbling fence posts stood wireless, abandoned. Telephone poles stretched backwards and forwards as far as Lynden could see. The air was hot and still, and nothing within it moved.

"We ain't in Reno and we ain't in jail." The Duke popped his back loud enough to echo off the car. "We must a caught a red light on the main line." He motioned forward. "I'd put us somewhere this side of Carlin. You ever been in the desert before?"

"Never."

"Figures." He took a drink from the plastic jug, spit, then passed it over. "That's all our water, understand? Sometimes a train'll sit in a 'hole' like this for a couple minutes, sometimes all day."

"What about the caboose, or the power units?" Lynden drank, handed back the jug. "They've got water, don't they?"

"If it gets hot enough, we'll be begging it off em. After that business with the bull last night, I expect they've got word to be watching for us, so I'd just as soon leave em be."

"You think they'd search the train?"

"Would you? Probably too scared of facing two desperados like us."

"Desperados? All I'm desperate for is some food and a place to wash my hair."

"You want a salon car you boarded the wrong damn train. No dining car neither. Nothin but sand till this old iron decides to roll."

"Got it." Lynden stared out across the emptiness. "Look, since we're stuck here, how about teaching me some things?"

"What things?"

"Like how to keep from doing what I did last night."

"Stay away from the freights... that's how."

"You don't much like me, do you?"

"This time a day, after a night like last night, I don't like anything." He stepped to the side of the flatcar and pissed into the sand. "Give me a couple a minutes."

"You awake enough to answer a question?"

"No, but you're gonna ask anyway."

Lynden hesitated. *This will sound crazy. It probably is crazy.* "When I was eleven years old, I rode trains with this older guy, this tramp."

"That's what you said. Was he some kind of friend of yours?"

"I thought he was. I went with him because I wanted to find my—"

"Let me guess," The Duke stopped him. "You were lookin for your father. Or maybe your brother, right? Now you're lookin for this tramp fella, and you're wondering if I've seen him or know him or if I AM him. Listen kid, it doesn't work like that."

Lynden studied the old man. "I *was* looking for my father. And you're right, I didn't find him. Now... I guess I'm looking for the tramp I rode with. I thought you might have—"

"Known him? Maybe. And maybe I knew a thousand guys who were hobos back then. What of it?"

"I'd like to know his name."

"The hell, you say."

"He was a big man, at least six feet tall, and—"

"When you were little I woulda looked six foot tall."

"—and he wore a belt buckle in the shape of a fist."

The old man stopped talking.

A gust of wind, smelling of sage and creosote, blew through. Undaunted in its wandering course across the parched landscape, it was heedless of the flat car, the men standing and facing each other, and the silence that hung between them.

"A fist. Brass, I think, and polished," Lynden went on,

aware that something had changed, but not sure what. "It reflected the sun in my eyes when..." He saw The Tramp standing over him, saw what they'd done.

"What else?"

No words.

"What else!"

"Nothing else." He fought his way back from the memory. "He was a big man, and he wore that buckle... that's all. I was only eleven."

"Did the guy have a bum leg, or a go-funny eye? Maybe a scar? You remember somethin like that?"

"There was something about his eyes. I can't be sure. Why? Did you know him?"

"I don't know shit."

"Then why'd you ask? Was it the belt buckle? If you knew him, tell me. Please."

"What if I did? What if I knew a lot of guys with them buckles?"

"Not like this one. It was a fist, polished brass, and it looked like—"

"Like it was gonna hit you any second," The Duke finished for him. "Like it was gonna jump off the guy's belt and smash your face?"

"You did know him."

"Probably not, but I knew that buckle. It meant he was one of The Johnson Family."

"A family?"

"That's what they called themselves. They got rollin in the early days. Safe crackers, mostly. Later there were lots of reasons for wearin the buckle, none of them good."

"And the hobo who traveled with me?"

"He wore the buckle—that means he was a Johnson. They didn't abide pretenders, and they'd grease the tracks with any man they caught wearing one if he hadn't earned it."

"Earned it?"

"Usually by killin somebody."

"I don't believe this."

"That they'd kill for it?" The Duke studied him. "What don't you believe… that there are bad men out here on the rails? There are. Always have been."

Lynden seemed not to be hearing him.

"The Johnsons weren't all killers. Most were jack rollers, hijacks, and jockers. You've heard of jockers?"

"I've heard." He had more than heard and sensed that The Duke knew that.

"They'd catch punk kids and take em under their wing, sometimes just for company, usually more. Prushins they called em. You must a been a prize when you was eleven. Leastways now I know why you're out here." The Duke was looking at him differently. "You're figurin to settle a score."

"Maybe… I really don't know. But if I could talk to him, I might—"

"You might what?" the old man challenged. "Don't you get it. He was a *Johnson*. If you found this yegg—or if he got wind you were lookin for him and found you first—he woulda been just as likely to throw you under a train as talk to you."

"Would have been?"

"He's dead." The Duke's voice was flat. "The Johnsons are dead. Killed each other off. Fifty years ago there might have been a hundred Johnsons ridin. When you were a kid, maybe a dozen. But now," he paused, "now they're all gone. Looks like you come back too late."

"How can you be certain?"

The Duke stooped and reached into his valise. "Two weeks ago, I was down in Colton. A jungle buzzard traded me this for some food. He was a big guy, coulda been that fella you're looking for."

The Duke extended his hand. It held a tarnished hunk of metal. Tarnished but unmistakable.

A fist.

"It's the first I've seen in better'n ten years." He wrapped the buckle in a kerchief and slipped it back in his bag. "That guy I got it from was no Johnson. They'd sooner starve than trade their badge."

"What if that was my tramp?" Was it excitement or dread Lynden heard in his own voice? He couldn't tell. "Maybe he traded somebody for the buckle, back before we rode together. I need to find him. Where do you think he is now?"

"Caught the westbound."

"He's dead?"

"Took a load of buckshot in the belly not ten minutes after making that trade. He didn't even get a chance to eat. There was this fight. Your boy lost."

"You're sure?"

"I saw him go down spoutin blood, and he didn't get up. If he was a Johnson, he was the last."

"Who killed him?" Lynden asked vacantly, not that he cared—not now.

"Just some bum," The Duke lied. *Is it to protect the kid, or protect myself?* he wondered, then realized that with Short Arm after him, the answer didn't matter. "A bum with one arm."

Track #3
Rank Cat — The lowest form of bum

What's the worst thing you've done to survive on the road?

Why would I tell you that?

Are you ashamed?

Shame's a luxury I can't always afford.

You think shame is a luxury?

I think it's a fine you charge yourself every time you do something you know you shouldn't. But instead of money, you pay it off with a chunk of your soul. It's like a speeding ticket for how you behave. Yeah, it costs you... but it doesn't always stop you from doin it again.

Do you ever give yourself that ticket?

Sometimes it gives itself. If it's a difference between being dead or being ashamed, well, I'm here ain't I? Those tickets, and what they cost, are the price of stickin around.

Sounds like you think your survival justifies your actions.

Hell yes that's what I think. You do, too... only I'm guessing you'd prefer not to look at it that way, not in your own life anyhow. One winter, when I took a coat off a guy who was freezing and probably gonna die anyway—took it so I didn't freeze along with him—was that justified? Or when I see a guy getting the shit beat out of him by a bunch of yeggs—and I don't help him because I don't like the odds? Or all those times I've swiped milk off somebody's porch, or food out of their pantry, and told myself it was okay because I was hungrier than they were?

Do you think it makes a difference that those situations are life and death, or could be?

Everything is life or death. Like cheating on your taxes, if the extra dough will let your kid go to college. That's gonna change that kid's life, ain't it? Or driving away from a hit-and-run if you've been drinking, because losing your license will mean you couldn't put food on your family's table. Or letting some other guy take the rap for a fuckup you made at work, so you don't lose your job. Or padding an insurance claim. Or taking the disability money, even if you ain't disabled. Or looking away when a bunch of cops have got a guy down and they're putting the spurs to him. Just because your world's different... you think your choices are different. They aren't. Someday you've gotta square yourself with yours, just like I gotta square myself with mine.

And have you?

What do you think?

I look at the lines in your face, and the wear and tear on your body, and the way you choose to live—away from society, away from anybody who might judge you—and I don't see a man who's come to peace with his choices. I see a man who is running from them.

You've got it half right... I'll give you that. I'm not running—this is the way I live. But have I come to peace with my choices? No. It's *owning* my choices that put these lines on my face. Ignoring yours is how you keep your face smooth.

Chapter Four

For a long, long stretch we've rambled, Jack,
With the luck of the men that roam,
A backdoor step for a dining room,
And a boxcar for a home.

A. L. Kirby

"There's nothin with a flanged wheel I haven't ridden." Hardly a hollow boast, yet it felt hollow. Everything he'd said since they'd talked about the fist buckle sounded empty. "There isn't a car rollin that you can't ride on somewhere. But waiting for a good one's better'n dyin on a bad one." More truth, only the kid wasn't listening. "Your smart tramp will mostly ride the boxes, and them he picks pretty close. But there's times, times like last night, when you gotta take whatever you can get a mitt on. I'd say you done pretty good, considerin." A compliment, but no answer.

Their train had started rolling again just after they woke up, just after the buckle came out. For a desert ride it wasn't bad—early enough not to be too hot, clear enough to see a thousand miles if there was anything to look at. Later in the day, if they stayed on that flatcar they'd be frying, and the heat haze would shut the blue right out of the sky. The Duke knew what was coming, but at the moment he didn't care. Getting this kid to talk, after lying to him, was suddenly more important than anything.

"You wanted me to teach you? All right, I'm teachin."

"Save it." Lynden wasn't looking at him, but after an

hour of nothing, at least it was a start.

"You figure you don't need any help, is that it?"

"I don't need anything out here. Don't waste your breath."

"Right, your tramp is dead, so you're gonna go back to your computers. Stupid as you're acting... you've got no business bein on the road."

Lynden stared hard at him. "I called you stupid last night and I apologized. I'm in no mood to be insulted, so take it back."

"And if it's true?" The Duke wasn't sure where this was heading, but he preferred it to silence.

"Listen, you washed up old son-of-a-bitch, I'm the best there is at what I do, and it's a hell of a lot harder than riding a train. There's nothing you could teach me that I couldn't learn on my own."

"You're afraid."

"What's that supposed to mean?"

"You came out here to find yourself, or some bullshit like that, only you couldn't find your asshole without a road map. And when things don't go just like you figured, what's your first move? To turn tail and run. That's why you're stupid. You can't run—"

"Shut up, old man."

"—cause you don't know what the fuck you're running from."

"SHUT UP!"

"Make me!" The Duke challenged, grinning at the childish sound of his dare.

Lynden came at him.

* * *

Punching a keyboard was second nature, but punching a man was all new. Lynden lunged forward, and stuck out a fist. The Duke ducked. He swung again, but the old man stepped aside. The Duke moved in close, went for a bear hug, and Lynden landed a glancing blow to his shoulder.

"You fight like a punch-drunk Palooka." Before Lynden could strike again the old man tagged him with three stiff ones to the stomach.

Lynden charged, but didn't swing. He grabbed. The Duke tried to spin free, but Lynden had him.

"Who's afraid?" They were staggering like sailors, fighting for balance on the swaying car.

"You are and..." The train swung into a curve, throwing them to the car's edge. They struggled to keep their footing, all the while maintaining their grip on each other.

"Hold on!" Lynden grabbed for the headboard as they teetered. The Duke, staring down into fifty mile per hour sand, was about to fall. "Hold on, damn it!" He tightened his grip on the old man. A choke hold.

"You're fuckin strangling me!" The Duke flailed backwards with an elbow that caught Lynden hard in the ribs, and Lynden let go of everything.

They went down, but their car was on straight track again, so they tumbled onto each other instead of off the side.

"You crazy bastard." The Duke was on his feet.

"Crazy? I just saved your neck!"

"It don't feel saved." As they squared off again, the train braked sharply, tossing them against the headboard, then dumping them into a tangle of elbows, knees, and curses as they scraped across the rough wood deck.

"You give up, old man?" Lynden landed on top.

"Not till you do." He didn't sound very defiant with his face smashed against the floor.

"All right, I give." Lynden pulled himself off, winded. "Do I really fight like... what was it... a punch-drunk Palooka?"

"Just like one." The Duke sat up, pushing his neck back into place. "And there's nothin tougher than a punch-drunk Palooka."

Davis

"Or an old hobo." Lynden was testing his ribs. "What the hell did we just do that for?"

"Conversation."

* * *

It was still early morning when their train slowed at Carlin. For over an hour they'd been tracing the edge of a shallow, brown river—its snaking course the desert's single distinctive feature. But near Carlin things began to change. Fences, trees, shacks looking as dry and barren as the land around them. Clusters of weathered house-trailers—whole camps of them gathered beneath scrappy riverbank willows. The train lurched as it slowed. Up ahead the town came into view. No skyline, no distinguishing feature. Wide dusty streets, low windblown bungalows, a forest of bristling antennas. Life, however hardscrabble, finding purchase in the hardscrabble American soil.

The Duke got to his feet and stretched. "You too sore to eat?"

"Probably, but I'm too hungry to care. Let me buy us some breakfast. Lots of breakfast."

"We ain't got time. This train's a hot-shot. We'll be stuck all day if we lose her."

"So?"

"Either we eat on the fly or we don't eat."

"Goodbye sausage and eggs. Damn."

"We only gotta stay with the train, not on it. We'll do the cinder dick waltz up here to keep from gettin pinched, but we should be able to grab a lump at the cook shack."

"What the hell did any of that just mean?" Lynden gave him a sidelong look. "Cinder Dick Waltz? Next, you'll be calling yourself a Knight of The Road, telling me you palled around with Jack London."

"It means we gotta get off the train, steer clear of the bulls, and grab something to eat before we catch her again at the other end of the yard," the old hobo explained, mak-

ing no attempt to hide his exasperation at Lynden's igno-
rance. "About London... can't say I ever met the man. Rode
with a Jack name a Kerouac once. You probably never
heard a him."

"Right."

As the train came out of a long turn, they could see the
yard. The Duke motioned Lynden to the front ladder and
mounted the back himself. On his signal, they dropped off
together and cut sharply away from the tracks. A moment
later they were hurrying up a side street. There was no
indication they'd been noticed.

To their left was a row of small, forlorn houses,
sprinklers sputtering on front lawns, dark shapes moving
behind screened doors. A slight woman sweeping her
porch looked up as they passed, glad for a reason to pause
in her work.

The Duke tipped his hat to her.

Lynden nodded.

The woman smiled.

* * *

A freight yard is a perplexing maze, a landscape of
hulking cars on curved sidings that twist and cross, branch
and disappear over the oiled, gravelly earth. A slow-mo-
tion maelstrom.

The Duke headed straight for it.

"I could tell right away that you'd ridden before," he
said. They were walking fast, not looking at each other.

"Tell? How?"

"It's like sex."

"Like what?"

"Sex. Once you done it, no matter how long it takes till
you do it again, you don't ever forget how."

They crossed a rusty fence at the yard limit, passed a
"No Trespassing" sign, and stepped behind a string of broken-down refrigerator cars that looked like they hadn't

moved in years. The next string they climbed through, and the next, until they disappeared among intertwining canyons of steel boxcars arrayed so close that they blocked out the sun. In the narrow spaces between the cars the air was cool, like inside a cave. There were few sounds, just the crunching of gravel beneath their feet and the rumbling of power units somewhere off in the distance.

The Duke felt at home in the yard, even with Short Arm after him. Everything about this place was familiar. The hump that sent single cars noiselessly coasting, a hundred tons of silent rolling death if you got in the way. The flood lights, useless during the day, but at night watching the whole incredible landscape with their pale unblinking eyes. The control tower's green windows glowing like jewels, its disembodied voice barking orders though scratchy speakers that were scattered about like forlorn, colorless calla lilies. Gandy dancers and car herders, brakies and switchers, the drone of refer cars, the stink of crude oil tankers. All part of a system that produced the greatest rolling machines on the face of the earth.

A system he understood and had mastered in a way that few others ever would.

For Lynden the yard was a foreign landscape, visited once in a distant memory. He might actually have been here fifteen years ago. Or Stockton or San Jose. It didn't matter—he was here now, out among the boxcars, bums, and rails. Feelings were returning. At least the memory of feelings. Fear, excitement, a sense of danger. A sense of loss. The Tramp had left him with other feelings that weren't so easy, some he couldn't even name.

In front of a grubby orange shack they saw a handful of railroad men—one in a grimy easy chair, the others on a sagging bench. Some wore overalls. All wore striped engineer hats with the bills pulled low against the morning sun. The man in the chair smoked the nub of a cigar.

The Duke had a theory about railroad men—all men, really. Tell them the pure truth or a pure lie, chances are they'll believe you.

"Morning, gents." Heads turned as he approached. "Damn hot day for railroading." He raised a hand to block the sun.

"Damn hot," a man on the bench agreed.

"Where to, bo?" the cigar smoker asked, curious but not very.

"East, on that hotshot," The Duke motioned to the train they had come in on, several sidings away and snaking slowly through the yard, "if we can snag her again."

"They'll pull a crew change. You've got fifteen minutes." He glanced at his companions. "That is, if the bulls don't snag *you* first."

"We were hoping to maybe tuck into a second power unit. Gets mighty damn brutal out across that desert there."

Cigar man got up from his chair. "Even though there usually ain't crew in those second units, that's a dumb idea for a smart old man." He shifted the stogie and spat between his teeth. "After that deal down in the jungle the other day, our yard dicks are itching to bust somebody. Anybody."

"What deal in the jungle?"

"Two days ago. Some fuzzy tail came through and was roughing up the home-guard. Put one of the boys in the hospital. The tough guy only had one arm the way they tell it."

"They catch him?"

"Our bulls? Hell, no. I say let him go. One stiff thumps another stiff, that's their business."

The Duke was silent.

"I was you guys, I'd go for an open box." Cigar man's tone was conspiratorial now, more an adviser than an adversary, and for the first time he included Lynden in the dialogue, sizing him up as he spoke. "There's bound to be a few on this hotshot. Right, Louie?"

"Right," Louie answered from the bench, "least half a dozen."

"She won't pull out at more than five miles per, so just hustle on down there to the far end and pick the one you want."

"I'm kinda new at this." Lynden guessed the role the man had selected for him. "I don't know... catching one on the fly... isn't that pretty dangerous?" He aimed his words at the brakeman, but his attention was focused on The Duke, mute at his side.

"Hell, yes, it's dangerous." Cigar man spat again. "What are you, scared? Jesus, I rode all over this country when I was a kid like you. Didn't do me any harm, did it?"

Someone on the bench snickered. "Just rattled your brains is all."

"I'll rattle your ass, Thompson!" he said over his shoulder. "Now, you two, get outta here. And if they pinch you, don't be telling em we talked. They'll know you're lying. And if I find out, you'll be spittin teeth. Understood?"

"Understood." Lynden nodded, and started to walk away.

"You get what I said, old man?"

The Duke had not moved, and seemed not to hear.

"Hey!"

"Yeah, understood."

* * *

In the yard their train moved slowly forward. Ahead, the control tower loomed. Across from it stood the crew's barracks in identical buildings painted railroad orange and diesel gray.

Men moved from the barracks to the tower, clean men with freshly scraped faces and slicked-back hair. From the yard came other men, smudged and tired, who climbed the barracks steps with lead feet, waving to friends with lead hands. Shift change. Breakfast time.

Lynden watched his companion, not sure what had just happened, or what their next move would be.

"You did good with that blowhard... read him good." The Duke seemed to come back into himself, as if shaking off a dark thought, or something darker still. "You just as good at mooching?" They were nearly to the barracks, walking with their heads down, ignoring stares from the railroad men.

The smell of hot coffee and frying bacon wafted up to them. "I don't know much about mooching, but for some of that, I'm willing to try."

"All right then. The trick's in knowing where to hit and where to pass up. Look there." He pointed to markings on the corner of the first barracks—three horizontal scratches crossed by four vertical.

"A hobo sign?"

The Duke nodded. "Means stay away, and that's just what we're gonna do. This next one oughta be more encouraging." On the second barracks they found a misshapen oval with three dashes in the middle.

"Looks like a loaf of bread."

"Or a baked potato. Either way it means we got a chance."

"A chance?"

"Depends on how good you are."

"Who put those scratches there. They look ancient."

"They should. I put em up better'n ten years ago."

The kitchen door was around back, a small bare light bulb and row of fuming garbage cans marking it unmistakably. "I'll do the talkin, you chuck a dummy. That damn near always works."

"Chuck a dummy?"

"Act dumb," he said under his breath, then stepped up and knocked on the greasy screen door. "Slobber or something."

A face appeared behind the gummy screen. "Yeah?" He was a short man, greasy himself, suspicious. "What is it?"

"This guy's sick in the head, mister. It ain't nothin to me, but I saw him wandering out in the yard there, so I asked him what he's doing. All he says back to me is 'Denver,' only kind of stupid like."

Lynden tried to make a noise in his throat.

"What's he saying'?"

"Den-f-furre" Lynden stammered.

"See, that's all I can get out of him. Like I say, it don't mean nothin to me, but I saw him with no eats and figured, what the hell. I brought him over thinking maybe you could feed him. I'd stake him my own self, only I ain't got enough to do a big guy like him much good."

"Brea-f-fust!" Lynden blurted.

"You see."

"Ba-biss-kutts!"

"Shut him up, will ya?" The face behind the screen disappeared, but the door didn't close.

"Bac-ka-kon!"

"Pipe down, fella," The Duke said, full voiced. Then, in a whisper, "Pretty talkative for an idiot."

"My mouth was too dry to slobber. What was I supposed to do, have a seizure?"

"Might have been smarter than askin for 'bac-ka-kon.'"

There was movement behind the screen door. "It's all I could scrape up." The man shoved a greasy brown paper bag at them. "I got work to do."

"Thanks, mister."

The door closed.

They looked at each other, nodded, then sprinted for the east end of the yard. In a few minutes they were rolling out into the desert in a boxcar with both its doors slid open, scarfing down baking powder biscuits and strings of fat link sausage.

* * *

Riding, talking, sleeping. Watching the miles roll by. The Duke kept his promise about teaching.

"A good box—like this one—is your first choice, but you catch the best ones with your ears, not your feet. Listen as it rolls up. If she's thumpin, that means some engineer locked the brakes and ground a flat spot on the wheels. A car like that'll knock you silly on a long ride. Don't go for the rattlers either. Any noise you hear from the outside is a fuck of a lot louder inside.

"But when your good box comes along, chuck your gear in nice and easy so it doesn't sail out the other side. Then either chuck yourself in or tell your stuff goodbye. It's goin down the tracks, even if you ain't."

"And to actually catch the thing... more gracefully than I did back in Roseville?"

"Run till the back edge of the door comes up, then reach out with your near hand and grab ahold. Don't try grabbin the front edge of the door... it's pulling away, so you'll end up grabbin air instead of steel. But once you latch onto that back edge, just push hard with your outside foot, pull like hell, and dive right in on your belly."

"You call that graceful?"

"Hell no. I've seen plenty of guys try for graceful... them that ain't born to it. Mostly they end up standing out in the weeds, watchin the train pull away, and wondering what happened. Push with your outside foot, pull with your inside arm, hug that floor. Once you get a hand on her, you're gone."

Hoppers and gondolas, flats and piggyback cars, there was a smart way—and a wrong way—to ride them all.

"Don't never ride with a load." The Duke pointed to a

flatcar of milled lumber a few lengths up. "I knew a hobo name of Kamloops Dave got smashed flatter'n day old beer by a load like that. The engineer dumped the air, the load shifted, no more Dave. If you got no choice, at least ride the tops. That way you don't get squashed, you just get thrown off."

They were stopped on a siding somewhere east of Elko when an Amtrak express flashed by, a red, blue, and silver blur. "If a young guy like you was game," The Duke said, "and if you stuck to it long enough, one day you might be snagging those rail rockets. Nobody's riding em these days, but time was you could... I've done it plenty. With these new cars, the roof's your only choice for more'n a few minutes, and those top decks can be slicker than spit. But that doesn't mean a couple a guys like us couldn't do it in a pinch."

They rolled past Shafter and Wendover, out across the vast salt flats of Utah. The horizons on both sides were thin white lines. Salt drifts straddled the tracks. Brackish red water pooled in the low places. Ahead they watched a mirage shimmer and grow larger—until they were out on it, the Great Salt Lake. It smelled like an ocean, but not alive like the Pacific. Lining the roadbed, instead of pilings, half-submerged boxcars—rusted carcasses that had once graced the rails—were settling as a bulwark against the slow erosion of salt and time.

Lynden watched. The Duke talked.

He talked because of Short Arm, because Short Arm was about to win. And when that happened, he wanted to leave some trace of who he'd been. He didn't have an estate to pass on, he had what he'd learned in his life on the road. He didn't have a family. He had this misguided kid.

The kid would have to do.

Somewhere ahead Short Arm was waiting. Not searching. Just waiting, as if they had an appointment, as if it didn't matter what either of them did.

Short Arm would catch him.

And after that?

There would be no after.

He kept on talking.

They were across the lake and gliding on toward Ogden when The Duke stopped talking. He was assessing his chances at Pig Hollow, the jungle just outside the Ogden yard. In this season it would be full of men—home guarders, fruit tramps, maybe Short Arm. *Probably Short Arm*. He began to picture how it might be, how it might end.

He could run again, as he did in Colton and as he had started to last night.

He wouldn't.

He was Profesh, blowed-in-the-glass. It meant he couldn't give up.

Especially not to Short Arm.

As Pig Hollow neared, The Duke's resolve grew thin as smoke. The train slowed as they rolled into the outskirts of Ogden, every turn of the wheels bringing him closer to the truth.

Short Arm would be waiting. There was nothing he could do about it.

He stood in the doorway, rigid. Unable to think, or feel, or move. The kid, the train, everything bled away. He focused on the narrow strip of roadbed as it curved in toward the yard, as sidings branched out, as the big freeway overpass threw its black mid-day shadow on the ground. In that shadow were men. Twenty? Fifty? He couldn't tell, he couldn't see.

The train stopped, and in the shadows something moved, someone moved.

The Duke tried to pry back the darkness with his eyes.

Track #4

Single O. — Traveling alone by preference

What about friends?

I've had some.

Real friends?

What do you mean by real friends?

If you've had them, and I'm guessing that you have, you know what I mean. How many?

A man doesn't count his friends.

Why not?

It's not a contest. You don't count your days... you just have them. Same with friends.

And they have you?

How do you mean?

If you have them, then they must have you.

You said that, I didn't. True friends don't come with conditions.

No? How many people *have* you called friend?

You mean now, or ever?

Ever.

I don't know.

Ten, twenty, fifty?

I don't know. A few. Five or six.

At one time?

Total! How many more can you survive in one life?

That depends on the life.

It depends on the friends. Like the ones who slip the knife in... you can feel that stab every day. Or the ones you push away without meaning to, and they start to hate you, and there's nothing you can do to stop it. Then there's the ones who die, or just disappear. I *expect* to lose the sun every day. If I make it through the night, then I expect to see it again. Not so with lost friends.

You're alone then?

I'm alone. At least I don't belong to anybody.

And nobody belongs to you. You want it that way?

I've *got* it that way. And yeah, that's how I want it. At least that's what I tell myself.

Tell yourself? Why?

Cause the friends I'd give my life for are gone, and I'll never see their like again.

Chapter Five

I grabbed ahold of an old freight train
And around the country traveled,
The mysteries of a hobo's life
To me were soon unraveled
                                    T-Bone Slim

Lynden's eyes were better than The Duke's. Back in the shadows under the overpass were some thirty men, sitting, lounging, sleeping in tall dry grass. Hard-bitten traveling men like The Duke. Like... The Tramp?

Lynden's senses sharpened. He glanced from one man to the next, scanning, searching, looking. For hands? For boots?

For a dead man?

No.

He'd felt it since The Duke first told him, just as he'd felt it for the last fifteen years. Now, he knew. Maybe not under this bridge, maybe nowhere he'd ever be able to find. But somewhere, The Tramp was still alive.

His eyes were growing accustomed to the shadows.

He saw more. The crumpled hats and bright bandanas, the sunburned necks and pale chests, and the faces—leathery, hard, stamped with the imprint of the road. He recognized these men—loners, pairs, the group playing cards on the old, cracked suitcase.

But it wasn't each of them he recognized. It was everything about all of them. Newspapers spread like blankets on the ground. Wine bottles and beer cans scattered in the brush. Pouches and papers for rolling smokes, crusty plugs for chewing. Trash everywhere, butcher paper, grocery sacks.

It was all familiar, the bedrolls, the duffle bags, the lumpy bundles tied with wire. Even the muffled sounds of cars on the overpass, locomotives idling in the yard. And the smell of the place. The acrid odor of diesel-soaked gravel, blended with the rising aroma of the warming weed-clotted earth, both drifting to him like the scent of baking bread from an open oven door.

Lynden searched every face, every form, waiting for the snap of recognition. It didn't come. All he recognized were parts. Parts of The Tramp, parts of this life.

Probably not here, he thought, both disappointed and not. *Somewhere, but not here.*

Lynden jumped down.

He saw that The Duke didn't move.

"You see them tramps in the shadow there?" The old man was squinting, shading his eyes with his hand.

"I see them."

"I can't... and I'm not getting off this car till I can."

"You looking for someone in particular?"

"He's lookin for me." For the first time, Lynden saw strain on The Duke's face, and resignation, and what he might have recognized as fear if it hadn't seemed so out of character. "He's a big guy with an arm missing, and—"

"The bum from Colton?"

"Yeah, and I'm not anxious he should find me just yet. You see him?"

"Maybe." Lynden scanned the group again. There were two men shaving, taking turns holding the mirror, and one of them was missing a... "No. There's a guy without a leg, but it looks like everybody's got both arms. I don't think your man's here."

"You don't think?"

"Want me to go check while you wait?"

"Screw it, we'll both go."

They left the boxcar, Lynden striding, The Duke straggling.

"They seem harmless enough." Lynden was still sizing-up the group, looking not only for traces of his own Tramp, but for The Duke's one-armed bum. "Most of them look something like you."

The Duke grabbed him and spun him around. "Listen, you be ready to run. If somethin happens, get the fuck out and don't look back. Understand?"

"No... I don't understand. What the—" he began, but didn't finish. Someone was shouting at them from under the bridge.

"Hey, Duke!" The voice was lazy, friendly. "You looked kinda stiff jumpin down just now. Getting a little long in the tooth for catchin out, aye?"

"Bill? That you?"

"Ain't nobody else." Out of the shadows stepped a short, thin man wearing overalls and a painter's cap. A scrawny, scraggly-haired dog was tucked under one arm, in the other a dented grease bucket. "Thought maybe I'd give you a hand." He sat down on the bucket and slipped on a pair of ladies' sunglasses. "Rusty here figured we oughtn't to though, said you might get embarrassed. Ain't that right, Rusty?" The dog curled up at his master's feet.

"That dog always was smarter'n you." The Duke broke into a smile as he bent down to scratch Rusty behind the ears.

"Where's your manners, old man... who's your partner?"

"Ain't so old as to take too much of your guff... *old man.*" The friends were easy with each other in the way that disregards separations, no matter the duration. "Trainer Bill, this here's Lynd... this here's Frisco. Frisco Lindy."

The Duke shot Lynden a warning glance. "Frisco, this here reprobate's called Trainer Bill." Lynden nodded. Bill tipped his hat.

"They call me Trainer cause I always got some kind a critter along. Only I can't never train em to do nothin. Had me a parrot name of Felix one time. Duke... you remember Felix?" Bill looked at his friend, saw that he wasn't listening, and turned his attention back to Lynden. "I couldn't teach that bird to say one goddam word... not till the day he died. I give him a cup a Muscatel, cause he was actin sort of puny like. Old Felix, he sticks his beak down into that hooch, sucks it dry, then he turns his head to one side like this, and he says to me, 'Thanks sucker.' And he drops dead out, cleaner than a broke-dick dog. Now... I ain't never seen a broke-dick dog, but I know this for certain... if I did see one, I couldn't train him for shit."

Trainer and Lynden shared a smile. But The Duke, squinting again at the men gathered under the overpass, no more saw the smile than he heard the story.

"Bill, I need to know somethin. You been right here the last couple a days?"

"Been here the last couple a years, and it's a damn sight better than chasing around like you. Say Frisco, how's the touch down on Market Street these days? Used to be one of the best main stems going."

"The touch. Well... sure... it's good."

"Yeah? I ain't been out to the coast since seventy-three. Had me a run-in with some harness bulls—them rent-a-cops—down in San Jose, and I ain't found the energy to get back since. Could be I ought a give her a try. Where you boys headed?"

"We're—"

The Duke cut him off. "Ain't headed no place." Lynden bit his lip. The smile left Trainer's eyes. "Mostly we're just seein the sights."

"Mostly you're full a shit." Trainer bent down to pick up the dog, who nestled snugly into his lap. "I saw one of those sights you're looking for, only it was looking for you."

"When?"

"Two days ago. He stopped just long enough to ask some questions, start a dust-up with some of the boys, and throw his moniker on the wall yonder. Pretty handy... for a guy with just one hand."

The sound of rolling wheels on rails interrupted them. They looked up to see a string of cars being shunted toward them out of the yard, a car knocker in striped overalls riding the forward ladder. He stepped off as he neared a parked grain hopper, turned toward the switch engine, and slowly waved his arms in big inward circles, dropping them to his sides a few seconds before the cars met with a deep metallic thud—like a bag of anchor chain dropped on a concrete floor—the report of a perfect coupling. He stepped between them, connected the air line, signaled the switch engineer that the join was made, then stepped up onto the ladder again and rode back into the yard. It was a move he would duplicate scores of times in his shift, and one that every man in the jungle felt compelled to watch, no matter how often they had seen it.

"What'd you tell that one-armed fella?" The Duke asked, trying and failing to appear disinterested.

"Didn't say he had one *arm*," Bill considered him, "only you knew that already. And I didn't tell him nothin cause I didn't know nothin. He asks if I seen you, and I says no. He asks where you might be holding it down, and I says I got no idea. One of the other fellas mentioned something about Hubbard being down at Salt Lake there, so it's likely that's where your boy went. I ain't seen him since."

"You know who he is, don't you?"

"Course I know him. I thought all them boys were on the wrong side of the sod."

"They are. All but one."

Lynden suddenly understood. "You mean he's a Johnson? You said they were all dead."

"I lied."

"Then he could be—"

"Your tramp? Only if your boy was missin an arm. You told me he wasn't. That's why I figured it didn't matter."

"You figured!" Lynden turned to Trainer. "Which way did he go?"

Bill, still sitting on his bucket—Rusty now asleep—held his words

"Which way?" Lynden said, impatient and not trying to hide it.

"Caught the peg-leg to Salt Lake two days ago," the old hobo relented. "But I wouldn't be following him if I was you. Whatever you want with that kink—Johnson or no—it ain't worth it."

"It's personal," Lynden's face flushed as he said it. "How do I get to Salt Lake?"

"You don't... if you're smart. If you're going anyway, there's only three ways short of walking. You can hitch her, you can snag the peg-leg like he did, or—"

"Or you can come with me," The Duke broke in. "Peg-leg's already gone for today, and hitching's a crapshoot. Greydog's probably our best shot, wouldn't you say, Trainer?"

"That it is, only she'll run you three-fifty each, and she don't take no I.O.U.'s. I'd front you the fare," he said, "but me and Rusty ain't got six bits between us."

"Wait a minute!" Lynden turned to face The Duke. "You're running from this guy. I know you almost ditched me under that bridge last night when you saw his name. I saw it too. 'Short Arm'... right? Okay then. You don't have to follow me to Salt Lake."

"It's you that's following me."

"You think I can't find him on my own?"

"Bill, you tell him."

"Tell me what?"

"That without help you ain't got a snowball's chance of even *seeing* Short Arm if he doesn't want ya to," Trainer said. "He could find you, and he'd take you down if he had a mind. But a greenhorn... on your own? You won't never get close to him. I don't know why you'd want to."

"But you or The Duke could find him?" Lynden looked at the two old men. "Why am I supposed to believe that?"

"The Duke could. I'm too fuckin old. He is too—only he don't know it. We're profesh, Frisco, or leastways he still is. If you ain't heard the term, it means—"

"Look," Lynden cut him off, "whatever it might have meant once, it doesn't mean that anymore."

Bill smiled, but it was a hard smile. "It means you not getting your ass kicked. Or am I just wastin my breath?"

Lynden stared at him, then lowered his eyes, stifling his impatience.

"Used to be there was three kinds a men riding the freights." Trainer's smile softened. "Profesh, The Johnsons, and everybody else. Profesh, like me and The Duke, were at the top of the heap, the genuine article... *blowed-in-the-glass* like the old timers used to say. Johnsons were at the bottom. A guy could be damn near anything he wanted, from a gate-banger to a sign painter, and wouldn't nobody give a shit. But if you was aiming to be a Johnson, or aiming to be profesh, that was a different deal.

"Why was it different?"

"Hear me out. The Johnsons were crooks before anything else. They used to hit the small-town post offices cause there wasn't much heat, and cause doing federal time was easier than state if they got pinched. I seen a gang of em take a jerkwater obie once when the postmaster was closed for lunch, and they were just like a fucking army... even hijacked a freight train to make their getaway. Most anybody could tag along with The Johnsons, so there was punks and jungle buzzards thick as fleas wherever they went. But *being* a Johnson was something else. That meant wearing the buckle... and that you had to earn.

"I'm not saying all Johnsons were bad, or all profesh good, but that's pretty much how she ran. For profesh, like me and The Duke, the most important fuckin thing in the world was riding trains. Sure, we worked around some, and begged some, even stole some if we were hard-up. But whatever we did, it was to keep moving."

Bill looked at The Duke then, and Lynden saw an understanding in their eyes, born of their friendship.

Between the two old men in that moment, the bond formed by their lifetime thirst for roaming—and the meaning they found in quenching it from a grail cup of rusting iron and twisted steel—had never been stronger.

"Tell it, Bill." The Duke spoke in the reverent tones of a parishioner offering his pastor a respectful but encouraging Amen.

"Damn, but we did move..." Bill went on, losing himself now in the telling. "Three days coast to coast weren't nothing for Profesh. We knew every town, every jungle, and every way there was to snag a train. It was our road, Frisco.

"Only The Johnsons didn't see it that way. One-to-one, the best of them wasn't a match for the worst of us. But you couldn't get em one-to-one, or leastways not face-to-face. You'll never find this Short Arm if he doesn't want to be found. The Johnsons always pick their ground, and it always gives them the edge. Plenty of innocent bums—and not a few Profesh—ended up greasing the rails at their hands. Believe me, you don't want nothing to do with em."

"I *do* believe you," Lynden acknowledged. "But those days you're describing... Johnsons versus Profesh... died with steam engines. Nobody lives like that now, and I think you both know it. Here's what it's about for me." Lynden seemed to be coming to an understanding as he spoke the words. "I need to talk with this *one* Johnson. Maybe more than talk... I don't know."

The Duke said simply, "I still live that way."

"All right, but you're an exception. What about you, Trainer? When was the last time you caught a freight?"

"The last time I rode Old Dirty Face?" He paused to think. "Caught the peg-leg down to Salt Lake just last month," Trainer offered, making Lynden's point for him, and realizing it. "You're right, I ain't caught a real train since I shagged down from Spook-a-loo, and that's been better than five years."

"You used to be profesh, the top of the heap, and you haven't ridden in five years? I'm not claiming what you said wasn't true, but that it's history."

"Short Arm don't think so," Bill stated, not as opinion, but as fact. "Try to convince *him* that it's history and you're liable to end up under a wheel truck."

"Maybe, but first I've got to find him."

"And on your own," The Duke said, "you won't get close enough to see his dust."

"That's my problem, isn't it?"

"I'm offerin to help."

"Why?"

"Because Short Arm's a son-of-a-bitch. Because right now it's either him or me, and I've only got two choices. I can run, or I can chase. I'm tired of runnin. He's a Johnson, I'm profesh. It doesn't matter *what* you say... nothing has changed."

"He's right, Frisco. Guys like me don't count, but The Duke here's still a mainline hobo, and Short Arm's still a yegg. Either of them gives up, and they both stop being what they are."

Lynden stared at them, seeing in the two old men a nobility that had not been visible to him before. Whether he was perceiving an artifact of their past or a shared delusion, there was no denying the conviction of their belief, or his attraction to it.

"Can you really help me find this Short Arm?" he asked The Duke, no skepticism now, just an honest needing to know. "And... are you sure you want to?"

"I can," the old profesh said without hesitation, "and I am."

"Okay then. I've got two conditions. I get first crack at him."

"Be my guest."

"And no more lies."

"Who you callin—" The Duke began, then stopped. "Right. No more lies."

"Trainer," Lynden extended his hand, "it's been a pleasure, and an education."

"Likewise, Frisco."

"Bill," The Duke said, "if you should see that yegg again, watch your ass. I can assure you we'll be watchin ours."

* * *

They cleaned up in a yard washroom and walked into town to catch the evening bus for Salt Lake City. Lynden paid, even offered to buy dinner, but The Duke refused. "We'll eat in Salt Lake and get you some gear. Don't be so anxious to spend your dough, Frisco."

"Frisco? Why not just Lynden?"

"Because Lynden works with computers, he don't ride trains. He's got an apartment somewhere, and a job, and a wad of money in his jeans most likely. There's still plenty of jack rollers in the jungles... no need to paint a target on yourself. Frisco... now he's got nothing but the clothes he's wearing and a yen to travel."

"Who named you?"

"That ain't a question I've had to answer maybe ever. I did a good thing a long time ago, treated some guys royal, they figured. They hung the moniker on me and it stuck, that's all."

"What's your real name?"

"Only one person drawing breath knows, and I ain't tellin. I got an Arkansas I.D. in my pocket that reads T. Duke, if ever I need it. My advice, don't be asking names out here unless you want people asking yours."

Their Greyhound lumbered out of Ogden, and by the time it reached the freeway Lynden was asleep. The Duke watched him, envious, remembering a time when he could sleep no matter what. *Maybe it's part of getting old. Like runnin slower and breathin faster and bruises that don't go away. Like being scared.* He couldn't remember ever being scared when he was young, not like now.

And all that spiel with Trainer, when the kid asked if he could find Short Arm, and if he wanted to? *I can, and I am*? *Bullshit.* A hundred times in a hundred jungles he'd seen the same thing happen—a coward getting braver as his audience grew. But there'd be no audience when Short Arm caught up with him. They'd be alone, he knew that. And no amount of talk, true or not, would help him then.

Track #5

Midnight Creeps — A lone freight car rolling silently
through a yard.

What's it like to live without locks?

I wouldn't know. I've got locks all around me. Locked
yard gates, locked boxcars, locked jail cells if I don't watch
my step.

But out here, living the way you live, you don't have
any locks to protect you.

And you think you do? Oh, I get it. You're wondering
how I can sleep without a locked door between me and...
everything.

That's right. You run more risk in a single day than
most people do in a lifetime. Don't you ever feel vulnera-
ble? Exposed?

Yeah. That's the point. The kind a locks you're talking
about cut both ways. How you gonna wake up to moonlight locked safe and sound in your bed at night? How you
gonna swap stories if there's a deadbolt between you and
the next guy? And soon as you get one of those locks—it
doesn't matter how fancy it is—some fellas trying to pick
it. I'd just as leave do without.

You don't ever fear for your safety?

Not from anything a piece of hardware can stop. Sure,
I could get bumped on the head some night and wake up
dead. You could too. Only difference is... I'm not hiding behind some lock waiting for it.

Is wanting to feel safe a bad thing?

No. But tricking yourself into thinking that you are
sure as hell is. We've all got a private compartment wait-

ing for us on the westbound. You find a way to lock that sucker so I can't get in, I'm all ears. Only, there ain't no such lock, and I ain't gonna waste my time wishing that there was.

I'm not sure I believe you.

I'm not sure I give a shit.

Chapter Six

We are the true nobility.
Sons of rest and the outdoor air.
Knights of the tie and rail are we,
Lightly meandering everywhere.
Having no gold we buy no care,
As over the crust of the world we go.

Unknown

It was dusk when they stepped off the bus in Salt Lake City, the regular passengers—the laborers, the students, the old ladies clutching their handbags—eyeing them as they left the station.

"Where to?" Lynden asked.

"The Roper Yards."

"You think he'll be there?"

"I know he's *been* there. It's the first place he'd go. Being there's something else. A guy like Short Arm, he can be anywhere."

"But you can find him?"

"I can."

Lies sound better blunt, The Duke thought. Maybe he could find Short Arm, but he wouldn't. Short Arm would find him, he was sure of it.

They walked to the tracks and headed south, warm evening air buzzing around them—the clicking of hidden cicadas, the castanet calls of katydids. Lynden was out front, stepping lightly over the ties, sometimes walking on the rails. The Duke lagged. To their left Salt Lake City rose to the mountains. Sirens and car horns, grinding gears, and the ebb and flow drone of distant voices floated past them. City sounds.

Far up ahead, the blast of a freight train sounded. They both stopped to listen. Too far to tell if it was coming or going, too far almost to hear, but a freight for sure.

An hour after leaving the bus they were still walking, following the double-line track through the city, saying nothing. Under a wide street bridge The Duke stopped to rest at a steel door that led into the bridge's foundation. The door was padlocked shut. They sat in front of it, pressing their sweaty backs against the cool metal. A car thumped by overhead. They heard a train whistle again, closer than before. Night was thick around them now— black in the shadows, indigo in the open spaces. On the tracks in front of them, nothing and no one moved.

Then something did move. Lynden caught it out the corner of his eye, a low dark shape like a big dog, or a crouching man. He nudged The Duke. It was across the tracks from them, moving from one bridge support to the next, stalking. It moved closer, crossing the first track. At the second it dropped out of sight. There was a sound, a groan, then the thing stood erect and came at them, shouting. "Who the fuck's under my bridge!"

"That's tough talk for an old man, Hubbard."

"Duke?"

"*The* Duke to you." He stood as the newcomer emerged from the shadows. "What'd you do, trip?"

"Right on my ass." The man was brushing off his clothes, then saw Lynden and took a step back. "Damn, since when you travelin tandem again? Big stiff like him could scare ten years off a guy."

"Might be an improvement in your case." The Duke reached out and shook the man's hand. "This here's Frisco Lindy. And Frisco, this moth-eaten collection of bad habits is Hubbard the Gambler."

Even in the dim light Lynden could see that "moth-eaten" was accurate. Hubbard's brown road coat was missing its zipper and the stuffing was gone from its sleeves. Gray stubble covered his face and scalp as if beard and hair were all the same. At his waist a rope belt held up baggy pants, and his feet were encased in black salesman's shoes with the gum soles worn completely away. He was a little taller than The Duke, twice as thick through the middle, and his cheeks puffed out like sponges. A gambler? Maybe. A winner? Definitely not.

"How you keeping yourself?" Hubbard asked, pulling a cigar stub from his pocket. He struck a match on the concrete.

"Not bad for an old tramp. You?"

"Sixes and sevens," Hubbard shrugged. "Sixes and sevens." He offered to share his cigar, but got no takers. "What brings you down to see old Hubb? Ain't fixing to borrow no money I hope?"

"What money? This close to Nevada you can't get more'n a nickel in your purse without rushing right over and pissin it away."

"Says you," Hubbard protested, grinning. "Why, at this very moment I've got three hundred and fifty dollars under my own damned name up at the Rocky Mountain Savings and Loan. Ain't been to Wendover in quite a spell," he declared. "I've been on the Job Corps!"

"You don't mean you've been workin?"

"Job Corps ain't working. It's takin money to learn *how* to work, only I had that figured way ahead of em. Six hours a day I sit in them stupid classes and pretend they're teaching me something. But what that Job Corps gang don't know is that I've already learned it. If three-fifty an hour just for sitting ain't making a living, then I'll go screw a light socket for you!"

"You gone crazy, Hubbard?"

"Hell no, I gone smart. Three more months and they'll kick me off because they figure I should a learned something. And I have, too. Learned I can get the Job Corps for six months over the hump in Denver, six months up to Idaho Falls, and six months damn near anywhere else. Could be I'll end up teaching them classes, seeing I learned so quick and all."

"What's the big plan for this fortune you're saving, Hubbs? Still perfectin the system?"

"Every hour of every day. Tried it out on this roulette table over in Wendover a few months back, and damned if I didn't have em going. Run outta money too soon was all, but I'm saving this time, so I'll be ready. You fellas can come visit my penthouse after she hits."

"You've got a roulette system that works?" Lynden asked, unable to hide his curiosity, or his smile at the unlikeliness of the conversation—talking number theory with a hobo. "I know a bit about systems, but I've never heard of one for roulette."

"Cause you ain't never heard a mine," Hubbard winked. "Worked on her twenty years at least, The Duke can tell you. Next time I play she's gonna pop. Most guys ain't smart enough to understand, but I'll tell you the high spots anyways, if you promise to keep em to yourself. Tried explaining her to The Duke here once, only he ain't even smart enough to know how dumb he is."

The high spots of Hubbard's system had something to do with dividing a roulette wheel into sections like a big pie and betting the sections in a special sequence that even Hubbard wasn't too clear about. But the system's strongest feature wasn't its mechanics.

"Psychology's where you get em," He tapped his head for emphasis. "You know you're going to hit on your A and your C sections, and you've got them blacks and reds figured, so you just let the chips lay. Three or four spins and you got a big pile, but still you don't touch em. Then, when the time's right, you look that dealer square in the eye like you was gonna spit at him, and say 'Switch em,' but not a word more." Hubbard demonstrated for effect.

"If that dealer so much as flinches, then the table's yours. Last time over in Wendover I not only got that sucker flinching, the little weasel was wettin his pants. System worked too good I guess. Next time I'll know better. You get what I'm driving at, Frisco?"

"It's a masterpiece," Lynden affirmed. "I can see why most people don't follow it. Some ideas are just ahead of their time."

Hubbard beamed.

"Don't be encouraging him or he'll go runnin off to Wendover before inviting us in. We got some horse tradin to do, Hubbs, if you're still in the business. Some supper wouldn't hurt neither."

"Course I'm still in business." Hubbard fished a key from his pocket and clicked open the padlock on the steel door. "About that dinner... if you don't like my cooking, that just means more for me."

Hubbard pulled back the door and stepped inside.

Lynden turned to The Duke, and behind his hand mouthed, "He doesn't really live in there, does he?"

They stared into the dark hole.

A match, then a candle, began to illuminate the spacious cavern—walls were the concrete sides of the bridge, floor was sandy dirt, roof was the underside of the road surface. Another candle flared up. A bed, a legless couch, and two bicycles leaned against a wall. A third candle. A rock-lined fire-pit, a tripod with hanging pot, and the scattered cans and cartons of Hubbard's kitchen appeared. The cavern was a hundred feet long and easily fifty feet wide, *The Hall of the Mountain King* with Hubbard the

Gambler its unlikely master.

"Get in here and shut the door," Hubbard yelled. "Goddam hobos got no manners."

The air inside was cool, moist, old but not stale. "This place is incredible."

Hubbard overheard.

"Damn rights, Frisco. And I gotta fight like hell to keep it for myself. City guys are always trying to boot me out, and fucking visitors keep droppin in all the goddam time. Not you two, of course, but just the other day I—"

"Hold on, Hubbs," The Duke stopped him. "Frisco here needs some gear, and we could use a belly full of a grub a lot more than an earful of your troubles."

"Screw you." Hubbard took Lynden by the arm and led him across the shadowy hall. "Never could figure why I like that sum'bitch." Loud, so The Duke could hear. "Sure as hell ain't his disposition."

In a corner of the den Hubbard stooped and lit another candle. "Here's the goods." A mountain of clothing and tangled junk. "With the Job Corps and all, I ain't been collecting like I used to, but I still keep my hand in."

"Where does it all come from?" Lynden asked, making no attempt to hide his astonishment. Toasters, dishes, stacks of pants and shirts, a typewriter, records and a phonograph, several irons, and a litter of small tools and broken toys.

"I work the donation boxes in supermarket parking lots. Used to be half a dozen I'd hit real regular, but now I don't check em more than once a week. It's hard times... the quality of junk ain't what it used to be."

"Hubb's been eliminatin the middleman," The Duke had come to join them. "Folks put this stuff out for the needy. Hubb figures he's as needy as it gets."

Lynden nodded, his eyes scanning the heaps of cast-offs.

"Frisco got separated from his gear back at Sparks. We figured maybe you could fix him up."

"Can't nobody do it better. You just fish out what you want, Frisco. Me and The Duke will stir up some eats. We can dicker prices later."

The two old men went off to the fire-pit. Lynden's first find was a leather bowling bag labeled "Brunswick" on the side. Perfect for the necessities of the road.

One item at a time, he began to fill it.

* * *

Hubbard and The Duke sat silently by the small cooking fire, amber light flickering across their faces. A caldron of something that might have been stew was bubbling over the heat, its smell of potatoes and pepper and potted meat thick in the air around them. They listened to the muffled sound of cars passing on the bridge, and water dripping somewhere in the darkness.

"Short Arm was looking for you," Hubb said.

"When was he here?"

"Come two days ago, and stayed most of yesterday. Just stomped right in and sat down. Said he'd wait."

"What'd you say?"

"Told him you weren't here and weren't expected. But he wasn't having it."

"You know who he is?"

"It's been a long time, but yeah, I know. And I know what he is. You got business with him I should hear about?"

"I got business with him, and the kid does too, or thinks he does. What I need to know is where the fuck he's gone. I half expected he'd be waitin for me here."

"He would have been if I hadn't got sick of him. I come back from the Job Corps yesterday, and I tell him I run into Step-Down-Johnny up to the yard, which I did. I tell him that Step says he seen you that very morning, and you was catching out for Oregon. Everybody knows you and Step used to summer up Klamath Falls way. Sure enough, soon as I feed him my line he high-balls it. Course I knew he wasn't taking my word. Like I figured, he heads down to Roper and gives old Step the hard and nasty.

"Step tells him you was heading for Katy, just like me and him planned. By now I'd say Mr. Short Arm's up somewhere around Pocatello, running hard for K Falls. Could be if he gets side-tracked up there, we won't be seeing him till the snows on the ground."

Hubbard stirred the fire and smiled to himself.

The Duke stared into the flames.

"Hubbard?"

"Yeah?"

"Thanks. These are the first easy breaths I've taken in weeks. I ain't built for runnin. I owe you one."

"You don't owe me shit, except maybe some answers. Short Arm and you, I guess I understand that. But what's Frisco's part in this deal?"

"When he was a kid some Johnson snatched him for a prushin. He thinks Short Arm might be him or might be able to tell him who it was."

"Does he know a name or anything else about the jocker? Maybe we know him. We knew most everybody, on both sides of the tracks."

"He don't remember much except the buckle. But that ain't stoppin him. I told him all the Johnsons were dead, but he saw through the lie. Now he's chasing Short Arm. I'm going with him."

"To K Falls?"

"Not even close, only he doesn't know that." The Duke kept his voice low and checked to see that Lynden was still fully engaged on the other side of the cavern, sorting through the piles of junk to find the items he'd need for the road. "You steered Short Arm for me, now steer the kid. Somewhere way out east, Harrisburg maybe. Tell him that's where Short Arm was headed."

"I don't know, Duke. Lying to a yegg's one thing, but a greenhorn like Frisco? It ain't right."

"It's my fuckin life, Hubbs. I wouldn't ask otherwise, but I got no choice. Short Arm gave me one, and I couldn't take it. You know the stakes."

"Same as always... Johnsons and Profesh. I thought them days were gone."

"They are, except for this one last round."

Hubbard stared at him, then poked up the fire. "Tell me, this business you got with Short Arm... it got something to do with that empty sleeve of his?"

"Maybe."

"He's got somethin up there, don't he? Somethin secret? I've been around gimps all my life, but I never seen one hold his stump like that. What gives?"

"You don't wanna know. He'll kill anybody but family who finds out."

"Then how...?"

"Don't ask. Listen, Hubb, if that bastard comes back, you stay clear. If he comes at you, run. You did me a big favor, you and Step, and I won't be forgettin it. But pulling you any deeper into this Short Arm mess is no good. Your necks are too far out already."

"We didn't do nothin but what's expected." They gazed at each other. Once they'd traveled as sidekicks, then equals going their separate ways. Embers from a lifetime of campfires and jungles and freight trains were banked behind their eyes—a relationship with their way of life, and with each other, that words would never cover. "Time was when guys like Step and you and me, we had the whole damn show. You're the last still holding her down, the very last near as I can tell, but there's some of us that still remembers. We all pissed out the boxcar door."

* * *

Lynden joined them, the bowling bag tucked under his arm. "Got what I needed. You two talking about our friend?"

A knowing look passed from Hubbard to The Duke. "You wouldn't mean Short Arm, would you?"

"Yeah, where can I find him?"

"Now? Somewhere over the hump, over the Rockies most likely. He was making for Harrisburg. Harrisburg, P.A. Seemed he was looking for The Duke."

"Harrisburg? Why in the hell would he...?"

"Cause he's smart," The Duke broke in. "Enola Yard's in Harrisburg. The biggest yard and the biggest jungle east of Chicago. Short Arm was right to pick it. I didn't tell you, but that's where I was runnin to."

"And now?"

"Now it's us doing the chasing instead of the other way around."

* * *

Hubbard served the dark, steaming stew into blue speckled enamelware plates that displayed as many chips as speckles. They ate in silence—the old men concentrating on their food, Lynden concentrating on Harrisburg, on the fact that he didn't care how stupid the whole thing was. What were the odds of his finding Short Arm? Slim to none. And the odds of Short Arm being The Tramp, or knowing who The Tramp was—knowing anything? Slimmer still.

But that didn't matter. He had a goal—Harrisburg, the Enola Yard. If it was hopeless, so what?

His personal compass had lacked a true north for most of his life. Now, if not a destination, he had a direction. He had not yet found his way. But he sensed, for the first time, that he was no longer lost.

Hubbard picked his teeth with a bone-handled pocketknife, folded it ceremoniously, then cleared his throat for business. "Went for my best damn satchel, I see. Won't find a bag like that just anywhere."

"It was under a broken lawn chair and stuffed with moldy newspapers." Lynden could already see where this was going and warmed to the prospect.

"Course it was. I packed it special to hold its shape. That's genuine fake leather, you know, and there ain't a tear in it more than a inch long. You got a real eye for quality, Frisco."

"And you've got the balls of a burglar!" The Duke chimed in. "Quality? I've seen bottle bums carry better'n that. Frisco only picked it cause it's the best you got. Maybe he's too polite to say anything, but I'd be ashamed of toting that rag."

Hubbard eyed The Duke's ancient valise, a raised eyebrow sufficient retort. "Frisco, what else you got?"

Lynden pulled a tightly rolled blanket from the bag.

"Would you look there. That blanket's been my very own for more than six months. I only just took it off the bed when the weather turned warm. Ain't no way I could possibly part with it... that blanket was given to me by a very special lady friend down Vegas way. I know, business is business, but sentiment counts for something, don't it? Sorry Frisco, no sale on that one."

"He's right, Frisco," The Duke nodded, "if that blanket come from one of Hubb's ladies, she most likely gave him something else along with it. You can never tell, a blanket like that could eat a guy alive, or up and crawl away on you in the middle of the night. Better to go cold if you ask me."

Lynden's next item was a doll mirror with a pink plastic back.

"Funny you shoulda picked that particular mirror." Hubbard examined it. "You know, that's the only mirror I ever found that works worth a damn when I'm trimming my nose hairs."

"But he only trims his nose hairs when he's taking a bath. Which means he ain't used that hand glass in a year at least."

Lynden pulled out a dented mess kit. Hubbard couldn't part with it—patriotic reasons. A knit cap. Hubb needed it for winter. A red bandana. Hubb's favorite color. Hubbard invented reasons why he couldn't sell each item; The Duke invented reasons why Lynden shouldn't buy.

"I think that does it," Lynden said finally, his new gear spread out on the ground in front of him.

"It damn well better," Hubbard protested. "That's my best stuff you got there, and every item handpicked outta the finest sources in Salt Lake City."

"Don't say much for Salt Lake." The Duke surveyed Lynden's choices, and shook his head.

"That's right, you have your fun. Next I expect you'll be stiffing me out of this valuable merchandise like it wasn't worth nothing."

"Which it ain't. But we're not stiffing today, we're buying. With cash money." The Duke nodded to Lynden who took out his wallet.

Hubbard became very cool. "I figured we were talking trade," he said, just a little surprised. "But cash money, that's serious. I've got my nest egg to think of. I'm saving for the future."

"Meaning you want how much?"

"Seven-fifty, and that's my bottom price." The gambler set his jaw. "You can talk, but if it ain't for seven-fifty, I ain't listening."

Lynden opened his wallet.

The Duke exploded.

"You gone weak in the head, old man. There ain't three bucks worth here and you know it. But since you gave us dinner, we'll give you a five-spot, and I do mean give."

"Twenty years younger and I'd give you something.

But I'm too soft-hearted for my own damn good. A five spot it is."

Lynden paid, and Hubbard threw in a few cans of food for the road. "Riding old Dirty Face can be hungry work."

* * *

Outside Hubbard's door it was fully dark. Their host spoke, his tone soft and serious.

"Lotsa boys down to the Roper jungle these days," the gambler said, part observation, part warning.

"And a good many up at Pig Hollow," The Duke said, in the same hushed tones. "We ran into Trainer Bill and Rusty when we came though."

"Yeah, Trainer ain't left in a couple years. Probably figures on stayin put if they don't roust him out."

"What about you, Hubbard?" Lynden asked. "Looks like you're pretty comfortable here."

"It ain't a bad place, but it ain't the best I ever had. That was down in Vegas... The Duke remembers probably. Had me a whole damn house made out of tumbleweeds, all tied together and lined with gyp board. Nicest place a guy could ever live. Only thing, it was by the Santa Fe yard, and there was this big Paiute car knocker working graveyard shift. Every night about three this old boy would get the urge and take him a dump just outside my front door... must have liked doing his business under the stars, I guess. I put up with it long as I could, but finally had to pull the pin. Neighborhood starts going to pot like that, there's nothing a guy can do." The raised eyebrow again, and a wink to go with it.

"Thanks for everything." Lynden picked up his new traveling bag, so light compared to his backpack that it hardly seemed to weigh anything at all. "I'll take good care of your gear."

"Thanks, Hubb." The Duke extended his hand, all the important words between them already said.

"Hope you find your man. Sounds crazy to me, but I'm just an old tramp."

He waved them on their way.

"He's right, about it being crazy," The Duke said as they started walking down the tracks toward the Roper Yard, a cluster of milky lights in the distance ahead.

"You scared?"

"Hell yes, and you should be, too. Short Arm isn't just some fuzzy tail tramp with a bad temper. He's a Johnson, and mean like you've never seen before."

"But I have seen it, when I was eleven years old."

"Did he...?"

"What... hurt me? What do you think?" Lynden realized as he said it that he had never made that admission before, not even to himself. "It still hurts. That's why I need to find him."

"And do what, exactly?"

"I'm not sure. But I *am* sure of this... I'll know when the time comes."

* * *

A campfire burned near the Roper's north limit, flames silhouetting at least a dozen figures. Beyond the firelight there were many more—sitting, sleeping, passing wine bottles hand-to-hand. As they approached, several men hailed The Duke by name, two even stood to greet him.

"You know all these guys?"

"Don't know none of em except Step. They know me, or like to think they do. But that's a different story, ain't it."

They stopped outside the circle of light. "Don't ever just walk in on a fire." The Duke examined the men. "Take a good look first. If it don't feel right, then pass on by."

Lynden counted ten men near enough the fire to be seen. Half were lying on the ground, asleep. One was tending a coffee pot, three were passing a gallon jug. One leaned stiffly against the trunk of a tree. Very tall. Very thin. Almost frail. The bum with the coffee pot was talking to him, and when the tall man answered, his gray eyes shone in the firelight.

"You know him?"

"Long as I've known Hubbs." The Duke listened to the fireside conversation, and at a pause he stepped forward, Lynden a short pace behind.

"Evening, Step. Looks like you got some company."

"Always got company, Duke." No surprise in his voice. "Sometimes I invite em, sometimes they just come, but they're most always around. Got a few more than usual just now." He nodded toward the darkness.

"Hard times, I guess."

"Hard enough. Who's your friend?"

"This here's Frisco Lindy. Frisco, meet Step-Down Johnny." They nodded, but no handshake was offered.

"Just met another old friend of yours, Duke," Step-Down said. "Fella calls himself Short Arm these days. Said he was looking for you, so I sent him up to—"

"Harrisburg... *we* know," The Duke said, abrupt in a subtle way that Lynden missed, but Step-Down did not. "We just seen Hubbs. He told us the whole deal."

"He told you—"

"Said Short Arm is heading for Harrisburg," The Duke repeated. "You see, Frisco's looking for him. Enola Yard's where I figure he'll be."

Step was slow to reply. "Yeah, Enola Yard," he drawled, his eyes fixed hard on The Duke's. "Ain't none of my affair... but what's your business with this yegg, Frisco?"

"It's personal." Lynden met the man's gaze. "He may know someone I'm trying to find."

"Seems he knows most everybody, don't it? Kind of funny, you looking for him, him looking for The Duke. Could be quite a palaver when you all meet up. As I recollect, he don't much like crowds."

"Recollect? You mean you know him?"

"I knew him. Hell, time was we all knew him. Seems like some of us maybe forgot. Didn't The Duke tell you?"

"Tell me what?"

"About Short Arm." Step looked at The Duke, then at Lynden. "Before ol Dirty Face winged him, he went under a different moniker. And he was one of us. Short Arm used to be Profesh."

Track #6

Bad Order — A wrecked boxcar

Do you think this life attracts people who are more dangerous than most?

It's a dangerous life.

But the people, what about them? Jockers, jack-rollers, yeggs? You even have names for them.

Pedophiles, muggers, armed robbers... you've got names for yours, too.

But it's almost primal here, isn't it? Outside the law? Out of view?

Maybe. Nobody's watching all the time, if that's what you mean.

And with no one watching, are people freer to follow their true natures?

Sure, but that doesn't make them dangerous. It just makes them different.

And different... that's always okay?

No, not always. Some aren't just different. Some are bent, like they were made wrong.

Bent how?

Twisted inside. Bent where they should have been straight. Square where they should have been round. It ain't their fault. Or maybe they get bent somewhere along the way.

How does that happen, getting bent when you started straight?

Are you asking if *I'm* bent?

I don't know... are you?

Not so's you'd notice. Everybody gets dented, pushed

out of shape. Most spring back. Some don't.

Sounds like you have some sympathy for them... the bent ones, who won't or can't spring back.

Some. Same as I'd have for a rabid dog.

But we put rabid dogs down, don't we?

That we do. If they don't put us down first.

Chapter Seven

The fangs of hunger and disease
Upon his throat had left their trace,
The smell of death was in his breath,
But in his eye no resting place.
Arturo Giovannitti

Short Arm Johnson was thinking about his hand—the one he no longer had. He moved the fingers in his mind, opening and closing them, feeling the tendons stretch up through his wrist. He made a fist and smiled at the way his bicep bulged. But he had no bicep, no hand, no fingers—there was nothing below his right shoulder.

Almost nothing.

It was two days since he'd left Salt Lake and now he was heading back west, to Klamath Falls. His old friends had been afraid of him, the ones who remembered anyway. The others, too, he thought. Part of it, he knew, was the way he looked. The scars on his face—too many to count—and the set of his eyes—too deep and too narrow to look directly into—had *always* scared people. And the buckle? Though they might try to hide their reaction, those who knew what it meant couldn't hide their fear. He could see it, stamped across their foreheads in tightened and twitching muscles that telegraphed, like a Morse Code only he could read, their barely controllable dread.

Or was it his new secret they feared?

But no... they didn't know about that. Not yet.

Only The Duke knew.

That was why he had to die.

There were other reasons his former friend needed to catch the westbound, older reasons. But he had been willing to forgive those, even the loss of his arm.

None of that mattered now. The past didn't matter.

He hardly remembered his life from before the night his arm left him. That was how he thought of it, the arm had *left* him, betrayed him. Shock treatments and drugs had muddled his memory of the incident itself, of the wheel rolling over him like a butcher's blade, only dull and wide and slow. How many years had he been in the asylum? He didn't know. He was older now, there was gray in his hair, and his left arm was twice as strong from the years of struggling against his tormentors without the use of his right. But years? It could have been two. Or twenty.

Then, without any warning, it had all changed.

One day he was in the wardroom, taking Thorazine by the cupful.

The next day, free.

"Budget cuts," one of the attendants explained, the one who was least afraid of him. Even drugged, Short Arm could always measure the fear he sparked in a man and stoke or smother it to suit his needs. With this attendant he had smothered more than stoked. "It ain't right," were the man's parting words, as close to an apology as Short Arm would get, "them shoving guys like you out onto the street with nothing but a bag of pills and a fare thee well."

They can cut all the budget they want, Short Arm said to himself, in an inner voice that he preferred to actual speech, *if it means they're cutting me loose.*

In the morning they had discharged him from the Oregon State Insane Asylum in Salem. By afternoon he had tossed the pills and was on a southbound headed for California. At Dunsmuir an unsuspecting alki-stiff crawled into the boxcar with him, a played-out canned-heater with rotten teeth and wheezing lungs. Short Arm could feel the old familiar fear boiling off of the man like heatwaves from a glowing stove, and he was fired with the long-absent thrill of it as he dragged the bum to the door.

They were crossing a high trestle. He tossed the old man out—like a thoughtless driver might throw a sack of garbage from a car window—and watched with indifference as the body bounced against the rocks below.

* * *

In the asylum they had implanted the hook that would enable him to become, if not whole again, in some ways better than whole. Through the fog of his confinement, the idea had come to him with perfect clarity, and like a vision it sustained him. No clamp, no pincer, but a simple upturned hook, screwed right into his shoulder bone. *Useless*, they'd said at first. But he demanded it, and demanded it, and demanded it; not with his inner voice, but with a voice that he knew they all feared and could not ignore. "Strange as this hook idea may seem to us," the beleaguered psychiatrist had finally gone to the chief warden, "perhaps it will help Mr. Johnson cope with the loss of his arm in a more rational, effective manner. And," he had added, not very professionally, "it will shut him up."

The shrink had been half right.

It was *very* effective.

* * *

At a pawn shop in Sacramento he'd found it. The size, the shape, the fit, everything was just as he'd pictured. Unlike the appendage he'd lost, this one would never betray him.

* * *

In Colton, he'd used it for the first time. The Mexican had been playing cards with him one minute, was dead

the next. And The Duke was there to watch. He never would have shown anyone else, the secret would be spoiled if others knew. But The Duke was special.

All along there had only been two choices for him and The Duke. After Colton, there was only one.

Maybe it would happen in Klamath Falls. They all used to go there in the old days—good fishing in the lake, good sleeping out under the trees. If The Duke thought he could hide, fine. After so long away from the wind and the sun and the rails, it felt good to be on the hunt again.

Klamath Falls was only a day away, and a day later, maybe two, the chase would be over.

It was almost too easy, almost...

And suddenly he knew. He didn't understand how he knew, anymore than he understood the power he had over others. Anymore than a snake understands why it curls around an offered hand sometimes, and why sometimes it strikes.

The Duke wasn't headed for Klamath Falls. Step-Down and Hubbard had lied to throw him off the track. They had been scared, but not scared enough. Profesh sticking together. He wouldn't make that mistake again.

Like an ape he swung off the moving train, hit the ground running and turned back. It was five miles to the nearest siding, a dozen more to the nearest yard. He didn't care. He'd walk all the way, but he'd get there.

And when he did?

The absent hand began to itch. It always itched when he got angry, and he always reached to scratch it. In the hospital they'd belted his good hand behind his back so he couldn't move it.

But he found ways.

There were ways to do anything, if you wanted it bad enough.

There were ways.

Chapter Eight

Watch the curves, the fills, the tunnels:
Never falter, never fail;
Keep your hands upon the throttle,
And your eyes upon the rail.

A.E Abbey

At daybreak they awoke in western Colorado. They'd chosen a good boxcar—smooth riding, soft sleeping, melodic as it clicked over the rail joints. Rolling through the canyons of the Gunnison River Valley, Lynden watched the painted landscape reaching out for the sun. Crisp air and blue sky, sandy bluffs and the swift, sandy river.

"You'll be wantin to know about Short Arm." The Duke wasn't waiting for Lynden to ask. "Last night there wasn't time, but I figure you've got some questions."

"Who is he?"

"An old friend, just like Step said."

"Step also said that he used to be profesh."

"That's right. But he ran both sides of the track, and he wasn't the only one." The Duke paused. "Being a Johnson was tempting, and some guys had to see what it was like. Some switched."

"Short Arm switched. Why?"

"Most likely because of me."

"You? How?"

"Sometimes he used to wear the buckle, told me he killed a guy for it—I suspect he did. One time I caught him with it, fixin to kill this crippled wino who couldn't defend himself, and we had a fight."

"You lost?"

"I won. He lost his arm."

"Jesus."

"We were friends for maybe ten years before that. Most of the other boys didn't cotton to him... he was too wild. Probably why I liked him. Hell, I saw him sand the journal boxes—that's where the bearings are—on a whole train one time just because the conductor threw him off. Ten miles down the track that train seized up like an arthritic joint in January. You should have a seen old Short Arm laugh." The Duke caught himself smiling. "His name wasn't Short Arm then. Spooky we called him. There was something about his eyes that wasn't quite right. That, and those friggin scars. He'd lace into anybody. But big as he was, he didn't win much. Too batshit to fight smart, I guess. His face got the bare-knuckle bust-ups to prove it. Made him hard as hell to look at, kinda like that Notre Dame bell ringer guy."

"The hunchback?" Lynden, tried to picture this man they were pursuing, who might hold a key to his past, as a Quasimodo of the rails.

"Yeah... exactly. Old Spooky. Next to Bill and Hubbs, him and me were about as tight as you can get."

"You and Short Arm? And now he's chasing you?" Coming from a life where his most intimate adult relationships had been with computer code, Lynden struggled to grasp how a friendship that had been so close could have gone so wrong. "Tell me about his arm... about what led to..."

"There ain't much to tell. We were fighting in this yard, beatin the sense out of each other. Most Johnsons... they'd never go one-to-one—they don't like the odds. But that wasn't Spooky. We were down under this boxcar scratching like cats, and some switch crew kicks the string. Both of us were laid out across the tracks. When Spook saw that wheel coming, he shoved me out of the away. I got clear. He lost his arm at the shoulder."

"He was trying to save you?"

"He *did* save me. And now he's trying to kill me."

"Why?"

"Maybe... because I left him."

"You left him?" Lynden remembered what had happened under the bridge at Sparks, how The Duke had almost abandoned him, and began to wonder if it was something the old hobo would do again.

"I took him for dead, figured that train had finished him for sure. I didn't stick around to find out. Somethin like that, a guy don't recover from. I hadn't seen him in all the years since. Down at Colton I couldn't believe it was Spook at first. Then he killed this fella right in front of me. There wasn't no stoppin him, and he didn't fight batshit like before. Him being so calm and cool about it... that scared me like nothing I've ever seen." The Duke stopped, unable, for a moment, to hold back the fear that had come with the memory.

"Afterward," he knew he had to finish the story, that Lynden would not let him rest until he did, "Spook told me how they'd had him locked up in some crazy house since the last time I saw him. He said he was a Johnson now for sure and handed me the buckle to prove it."

"The buckle you showed me?"

"Yeah, the one I showed you." The Duke hesitated. Lynden wasn't sure why. "He kept it all those years in the looney bin, I guess. Since Hubb and the boys just saw him wearing one, seems like he must have had two."

"He really will kill you, won't he? This is no game."

"It's no game. He'll kill me if he can."

"Then we have to stop." Lynden realized that his return

to the rails—his revenge fantasy—had always seemed unreal, even over the last few days. A thought more than an act. There was nothing unreal about a maniac intent on murder. "I think we should go to the cops," he thought out loud. "Short Arm probably escaped from that hospital. The law must be looking for him."

"I expect that hospital is mighty glad he ain't their problem anymore. And the law won't get involved unless somebody that matters makes a riffle."

"So… you want to keep following him? That doesn't make any sense."

"You don't know this life, Frisco, not really. Me chasing him, him chasing me, it's all the same. Whatever else he is, Short Arm's the last Johnson. Him and me are gonna tangle again. It's only a matter of time."

"You're right," Lynden looked at him, "I don't understand."

"There's no shame if you want to clear out. Maybe you should. Short Arm probably doesn't know nothin about that tramp of yours. But… if you stick with me it's likely to get messy. I don't want to see you hurt. Sounds like you've already had your share."

"If I don't stick with you, you're going to face him alone."

"Yeah, sooner or later. At my age probably sooner. There might not be a later. If it makes any difference, when I *do* come nose-to-nose with that son-of-a-bitch, I'd sure feel better with a guy like you at my side."

It shouldn't make any difference, Lynden thought, as he stared at the old man beside him, a man he'd never seen until a few days ago. They gazed out the boxcar door in silence as the land turned from gray to gold around them.

And they both knew Lynden would be there.

* * *

At Grand Junction their train broke up. From the boxcar door they could see the jungle, a clutch of willow trees not far from the tracks. Thin smoke was rising above the canopy and with it, the smell of cooking.

Someone was there ahead of them.

"Morning folks," The Duke called out as they entered the jungle camp, addressing a large, nimble woman who was busy at the fire. An even larger man sat at the base of a willow, chin on chest, eyes closed as if sleeping. Two spotted hounds, Bluetick in their background, were sprawled at his feet. "Fine looking dogs."

The man raised a weighty eyelid, mumbled a single word, and instantly his dogs were on their feet, teeth bared, ears back. He mumbled again and they went limp. "Good dogs," he grunted. His eyelid drooped shut.

"Smells mighty good," The Duke ventured, watching as the woman sliced strips of bacon off a fatty slab across her knees. "You folks wouldn't mind if we use the fire when you're done?"

"Sit," the man said, aiming his chin at a fallen log half buried in the dirt.

The Duke leaned close to Lynden's ear. "Get out our food. Those cans Hubbard gave you."

A can of beans and one of sliced peaches appeared from the bowling bag. The Duke considered them a moment. Careful not to disturb her slicing, he placed them on a rock beside the woman, then took his place next to Lynden on the log.

When her bacon was sizzling in the crusted cast iron skillet, she wiped her hands on her skirt and turned to the cans. She gave each a shake and a thump, like testing a melon for ripeness, then deftly lifted her large body and padded through the dust to her campmate's side.

He didn't wake, so she tickled him with her toe, and set the cans next to him.

From a sheath on his belt, he pulled a hunting knife

of alarming length and thickness. With a swift thrust and twist he opened the can of beans in two lightning strokes, handed it back, and licked bean syrup from the blade. Again, the knife flashed and dove. This can he did not return, instead he raised it to his lips. In one long pull half the peaches were gone.

"Good?" The Duke smiled the question, and elbowed Lynden to stifle the protest he sensed was coming.

Their host smiled back, raised the can in a toast, and drained the other half.

At the fire, their beans were mingled with the tangle of bacon and bubbling grease. From a wrinkled paper bag, the woman pulled half an onion, sliced it skin and all, and added it to the mix. Two potatoes, some carrots, and a handful of small green peppers followed. The skillet was brimming. She added salt from a cloth pouch, and pepper from a small tin. She stirred occasionally with her big kitchen knife, obviously pleased with the intoxicating simmer.

Four tin plates appeared from a wooden crate at her feet, and she heaped the concoction on to them. The first she handed to her companion, the next to her guests. Coffee, poured into tin cans, burned their lips but was too delicious not to drink. Lynden and The Duke emptied their plates, seconds were offered, and they emptied them again. When the skillet was scraped to its crusty bottom, she offered the last bit to her guests before taking it herself.

"Thanks for the divvy," The Duke said as he laid their emply plates out for the dogs to lick.

Neither of their hosts replied.

The man went back to sleep under his tree, the woman turned back to her fire. She refilled the skillet with water from a wine jug, added salt, and began to prepare another meal.

* * *

"You always share in a jungle." They were walking toward a concrete irrigation ditch that ran near the yard. "No matter how little you got, if some other hobo's there, you share with him. He'll share back."

The irrigation ditch, three feet wide, was full to the top with clear, swift water. They sat beside it and pulled off their shoes.

"A good jungle used to be like a hotel," The Duke said, dipping his feet, "and professional hobos were the first-class guests. Rules were strict, and if a bo chose not to follow them, he was asked to leave. I did that askin more than once." He grinned.

"You miss that, don't you?" Lynden's feet were dangling in the cool water. He watched the current running between his toes.

"Yeah... I miss it. It's mostly still here—or could be—except for the power running diesel instead of steam. Guys just ain't interested like they once were. What do you figure it would cost to run coast to coast on the cushions... if you were to pay, I mean?"

"A train ticket? Two hundred... three hundred. Maybe a hundred on a bus."

"Time was a guy could travel these rails coast to coast faster than a bus, and not pay a cent. I'm talkin streamline, no backpack, no bedroll, and no going hungry neither. That was forty years ago. Most guys have forgotten how, but a young guy like you, you could do it if you had a mind.

"Good jungles, better than this, were part of it. They had a stove for cooking, wood cut for the fire, even matches. A shaving mirror was nailed to a tree, with a razor hanging by. And tin cans, washed and stuck upside down, were on tree branches for pots and pans. The rules were simple. You left it the way you found it. You shared what you had. You never messed with another man's bindle.

"Say half a dozen guys ditched their train and hit a jungle at the same time. First thing, they'd scrub and scrape their faces, maybe grab a fresh shirt or hat off the clothes tree, then they'd head into town. One guy would go for meat, another'd pick up coffee or spuds. That way no two would be scrounging for the same stuff. They'd hit the bakery, the creamery, the mission, asking nice and being glad for what they got. All your good houses were marked like back at Carlin, remember? That made it easier. Come suppertime your hobos are back at the jungle cooking up a regular 'Blue Plate Special.' I saw times back before the Second World War when poor town folks would come down to eat with us tramps. And I tell you what, we'd always share with em."

"Even if you didn't have enough?" Lynden was remembering the pile of junk he had sorted through at Hubbard's. He hadn't seen a pile of food. Did the gambler give them the last he had, bank account or no?

"Especially then. Giving what you've got plenty of? That's easy. In case you ain't figured it out yet, there ain't nothin easy about being Profesh."

"I'm beginning to get the idea." Lynden had been living with his own personal picture of this world for fifteen years, and its few sharp details had driven all the rest out of focus. Now that the contours and subtleties were becoming clear, he wanted more. Yet he saw that The Duke's reverie had brought with it some melancholy. "You were telling me how it used to work," Lynden tried to pull him back from the pensive place he seemed to be going, "with jungles... and sharing?"

"You might stay in a jungle two hours if you were streamlining. Two weeks if you weren't. Either way, you left things just like you found them. You'd sweep it out with a bunch of brush, wash the cans, fill the jugs, and always scare up some kindling for the next guy. If a yard had more than a couple or three sidings, it had a jungle pretty much just like that. Now, I don't expect there's such a place from hell to breakfast.

"Talking old times gets me all creaky in the joints." The Duke started pulling off his clothes. "Think I'm gonna take a dip."

"In here?"

"Best bath in the country. Last time I was through I ditched a bathing stick around here somewhere." He stripped to his boxers and wobbled through the weeds barefoot. "Here she is." He held up a five-foot tree limb as big around as his arm.

"Me and Hubb figured it out, busted these notches in probably before you were born." He positioned the limb like a bridge over the ditch, nestling the ends into small slots in the concrete. The water rushed by inches below it. "The trick," he said, shucking off his shorts and crouching down, "is to not let go of this timber. Otherwise, you end up watering some guy's cabbage downstream."

In one swift move he grabbed the sturdy stick near its middle, sprang with his thin legs, and launched himself out into the water. Immediately his wrinkled body stretched downstream like a flag. Waves cascaded over his head and shoulders. He stuck his face up, gulped a breath, grinned at Lynden, and went down again. Two more gulps and the surging water had turned him bright pink. He shinnied back up on the bathing stick, balanced a second, and stepped out onto dry land.

"Cleaner than a preacher's dream." He shivered, rubbing himself dry with his hands. "Makes me look like a new man, don't it?"

"If you say so." Lynden turned aside. It was something about the old man's body, so small and pink. So bare.

"Are my eyes going bad, or are you blushing?" The Duke queried, slipping into his shorts. Lynden didn't answer. "I'll turn my back while you take your dip. A guy is entitled to his privacy." He turned around and finished dressing.

Lynden tore off his clothes—not giving himself time to think—grabbed the bathing stick, and jumped in feet first.

The water rammed his first scream right back down his throat. The second was mostly liquid, but on the third try he found his voice. It was a cold-water-on-a-hot-day scream that echoed off the boxcars back in the yard. Ten seconds later he was perched up on the bathing stick like a big, wet bird.

"Feels great, don't it?"

"It feels TERRIBLE!" Lynden shouted through chattering teeth as he jumped to the ground.

"'Excuse me, I didn't quite catch that. You say you're feeling... tolerable?"

"TERRIBLE!"

"Still can't catch what you're saying," The Duke grinned. "Maybe you oughta tell her."

"Her?" Lynden spun around, nose-to-nose with the woman from the camp fire.

"I heard a scream." She took a step back, slowly appraising him with the obvious discernment of someone who knew what she liked. The features of her large immobile face morphed into a broad grin. "Not bad."

"Not bad!" The Duke roared. "That's rich!"

Lynden picked him up. The Duke was laughing too hard to resist. Still naked, Lynden carried his old friend to the edge of the ditch and dunked him in, clothes and all.

* * *

Three hours later they were out on Interstate 70, hitchhiking toward Denver. They'd watched a container freight roll through the yard without stopping—too fast to catch and nowhere good to ride if you did, and a tanker train that was the same. Then word came down that a string of coal cars had derailed and gone aground up near the Moffat Tunnel, blocking the line completely. No east-bounds would get through for at least another day. It was either hitch or stay over in Grand Junction.

"The thing you gotta know about hitching," The Duke said, his thumb cocked toward the empty highway, "is that nobody owes you a ride. You have to work for it." He had switched into his best outfit, and brushed his thinning hair back under his cap.

"Not easy when there aren't any cars." Lynden was sitting with his back against a light post, the afternoon heat making him drowsy. Four vacant lanes stretched east and west in front of him. "Why don't you save your energy until traffic picks up and our chances are better?"

"Because the number of chances ain't important. It's how you treat the ones you get."

Lynden yawned. He drew his legs up and put his head down on his knees. For a while he listened to the hot, hissing sounds of the pavement. When a car sped past, he didn't even raise his head to look.

Soon he was drifting, stepping down into sleep.

Muffled noises.

Foggy pictures.

A train.

His father.

The Tramp.

And laughter. Laughter...

"Hey, Frisco!"

Women's laughter.

An old Volkswagen bus, *a hippie van*, Lynden thought, sat idling in front of him, its double side doors swung open, waiting. The Duke was in the front seat calling his name..

"Wake up, damn it, or we'll leave without you!"

More laughter. A woman and a girl, both smiling.

"Frisco!"

A B.Y.U. decal on the window and a Grateful Dead bumper sticker spelled college students, so the woman behind the wheel was a surprise. "Not like there's much they can teach me at that joint," she was saying when Lynden got in and pulled the doors closed. "If I haven't seen it already, I've seen the previews." She was in her late forties, he guessed, going gray and not trying to hide it. "Carolyn, I said to myself... as long as the alimony's coming in... and my ex is shacking up with some coed... I figure, why not go to college?"

"Hi." The girl in the backseat scooted over, smiling at Lynden. "I'm Millie, Carolyn's roommate. She's old enough to be my mom, but she's cool."

"Hell yes, I'm cool!"

"We live in the same neighborhood back in Denver. We're headed home for the summer and to celebrate my birthday. I just turned twenty-one!" Millie was fair-skinned, dark-haired, and friendly. "As a school, B.Y.U.'s pretty good, and the guys are cute. But *flirt to convert* gets old really fast."

"Yeah," Carolyn called over her shoulder, "the first time somebody mentions magical underwear, it sounds like it might be fun." With one hand she deftly pulled four beers from an ice chest on the bench seat between her and The Duke. With the other she guided the bus back out onto the highway. "Trust us, there's nothing magical about it."

It was all so easy—the miles rolling by, the cold beer, the conversation.

Lynden knew what was coming... they all knew. He tried to ignore the knot growing in his stomach. Small, but growing.

"I would *love* to do what you're doing." He watched Carolyn touch The Duke's shoulder as she talked and drove. "It must feel so good to just... let go." Her hand lingered, as if she was trying to pull the sensation of his freedom up through her fingers.

Millie's blouse fluttered in the breeze from the open windows. "I read *The Dharma Bums*, but not for class, of course." She shrugged. The blouse shifted more, and she didn't seem to mind. "It made me wonder... what would it be like to live the way you do? How would it feel?"

Lynden knew how it felt right then. Sitting in the back seat, pressed shoulder and thigh against a girl he'd never seen until an hour ago.

At Glenwood Springs they stopped for gas and more beer. The girls went to freshen-up.

"What do you think?" The Duke asked, his eyes following Carolyn as she crossed the parking lot. "You think I'm too old for her?"

"She doesn't seem to think so." Lynden considered him. The Duke's hard features, wary and careworn when they first met, looked timeless, rugged. His face, no longer that of an old hobo, was now the face of an outdoorsman burnished to a raw handsome by the years and the miles. "Do you feel too old?"

"Not right now. I might tomorrow, but now I'm feeling like a pup. That Millie isn't too young for you, is she?"

"Too young? No. She's not too anything, except hard to believe. Am I wrong, or does this kind of thing only happen in the movies?"

"Don't matter where it happens... long as it does." The Duke nodded as the girls came back into view. "When I was a kid I couldn't think of much else. Now I'm an old bastard, and I still can't. Only difference is, I do a lot more thinkin these days and a lot less doin."

Lynden opened the van door for Millie. She brushed close as she sat down next to him. When he reached to pull the door closed, he felt his palm sweating against the handle—an old panic poised to ambush. An instant later it was gone.

By nightfall they'd put away a case of beer and most of their inhibitions. The Duke was driving, steering wheel in one hand, other arm around Carolyn, a cold brew tucked between his knees. The radio was playing softly, and the windows were still cranked open. Lynden and Millie, sprawled across the back seat, were talking, murmuring, and kissing in the silences between.

They got to Carolyn's just before midnight. She owned a small tract house on the outskirts of Denver, musty from months of being closed, and stifling hot. Carolyn hurried through the house opening doors and windows and grabbed two portable fans from the garage. "You kids are gonna need this," she said, handing one to Lynden. "Living room's coolest when you're ready to crash." She took The Duke by the hand. "We'll be down the hall."

Lynden put the fan on the coffee table, and aimed it so the air washed gently up and down the couch. Millie turned off the lights. A pearl glow filtered in from a streetlamp.

The whirring of the fan was, for a moment, the only sound.

"I like to make love in the heat," Millie said. She began to undress. Slowly. Standing in front of the fan, she swayed with its oscillations. The thin blouse clung to her damp breasts and then was gone, moist skin glistening in the pale light. "At school there was… no one." She knelt closer to the fan, arms raised, letting the air move against her. Her eyes were closed.

He went to her.

When she stood her pants were gone, then his clothes were gone.

They were on the couch moving together. His hands touching lightly, then firmer, then not touching at all. Just his fingers hovering above the heat of her skin. He could feel her yielding to him, rising to him, pulsing with him.

Kisses then, but more than kisses—offering, indulging, insisting.

Lynden pulled his mouth away, reluctant to leave hers but eager to explore, and moved it to the soft skin of her neck, hot and soft, quivering under his lips.

Her fingers were in his hair, raking through it, clutching, guiding him past her neck, past her shoulder. She cupped her breasts and raised them to him. They were alive beneath his fingers, his tongue. He encircled them with his mouth, drawing them into him, drawing the hardening nipples against his teeth.

Now she urged him, her fingers desperate, down from the roundness of her breasts, down across her belly. In the darkness his lips brushed her navel, muscles moving under it like waves. Further down, and then his face was in her, and the smell of her was everywhere.

She ground against him, hands kneading, then pushing, then beyond her own control, forcing.

Her hands.

His hands.

The Tramp's hands.

Her smell was gone. Sharp tobacco stung his nostrils, the taste assaulted his mouth—pungent, thick, the savage flavor of sweat and lust. In the darkness he saw a shape glittering, a hand, a fist. It was moving at him, driving at him. He struggled to push it away, but the fist held him fast. He couldn't escape it, he couldn't...

"I can't..." He tried to wrench himself from her grasp, her fingers on the back of his head resisting, then reluctantly releasing.

"Frisco... what...?"

"It's not you..." he stammered, "it's..."

"Hey," she was staring at him, "are you okay?"

He was floundering in the half-light, trying to find his clothes.

"Don't go…"

He tried to look at her. Couldn't.

"What the hell are you doing?"

He heard her, and felt hurt rising in her voice, He was powerless.

"Wait a minute—" She grabbed him by the arm, trying to hold on to him.

He turned to pull away.

"You can't just leave." Anger was full in her throat now. "What the FUCK!"

Pulling on his pants had never taken longer. It was impossible to button his shirt. Finally, boots and bag clutched in his trembling hands, he made for the door.

"Frisco?" The Duke, in boxer shorts, was standing in the hallway. Carolyn at his side in panties and bra. "Have you lost your fuckin mind?"

"Millie… I…" She stood before him, as naked in the flesh as he felt in their eyes. "It isn't… you aren't…"

She started to speak, then turned her back on him and ran down the hall, Carolyn at her side.

"Wait, Frisco, don't—" The Duke began, but Lynden did not hear the rest.

He fumbled with the knob, ripped the door open, and fled into the darkness.

Chapter Nine

And oh, the men and women's moans,
Did echo through the air:
Such cries were never heard before
From humans in despair.

Robert Hugh Brooks

Lynden had no idea where he was going. Running was all that mattered.

"No problem too big to run away from?" he shouted to the empty streets. "Bullshit!"

This one was fifteen years too big.

And he was tired of running.

Passing a bench at a corner bus stop he sat down to lace his boots. "Fingers work fine now, don't they?" he screamed, angry at them for no longer trembling. "Everything works now, goddam it! GOD! DAMN! IT!"

"Goddam what?" A voice startled him. The Duke's voice.

"You found me."

"It wasn't hard." The Duke sat down, out of breath.

Lynden wouldn't look at him.

"Why am I'm sitting here instead of stretched-out next to that lady back there?"

Lynden turned, hesitated, then forced himself to speak. "Do you really want to know?"

"I asked, didn't I?"

"I'm a virgin..."

"You're kiddin me."

"All right, I'm kidding. I'm not a virgin. I had my first and only sex when I was eleven years old."

The Duke started to speak, then didn't.

"Think of it. This nice man... this tramp... sees a little kid who misses his dad. Says he'll help find him. And he does... he helps himself."

"Look, Frisco, I—"

"No, wait. You haven't heard the best part. After a few weeks, the tramp dumps him. End of story, right? Only it isn't. That tramp probably forgets the whole thing, but the kid? He never forgets. He wants to. He wants to find a girl like Millie back there and... be normal. But he can't."

"Why not?

"He left me."

"What?"

"You don't understand. I liked what he did... what we did."

"Near as I can tell... that girl back there liked what you were doin. Till you walked out."

"It's not the same."

"Bullshit."

"He was a guy!"

"And you were a lonely little kid. You think that makes what you did... wrong?"

"Maybe."

"Really? What's the big fucking deal?" The Duke looked the question at him. "You go around blowin strangers in bus station bathrooms, do you?"

"No."

"Have you ever?"

"No!" Lynden pulled in his breath, then blew it out nervously. "Except, well, you know."

They sat with that, silently.

"Look, I know what you're thinking." When Lynden spoke, it was as much to himself as to The Duke. "I think the same thing all the time. It's all in my head, right? Well, it is *in my head*. He's in my head, and I can't get him out." Lynden paused, the memories molding his features as The Duke watched. "The first time I was fifteen years old. Her name was Linda. She took me to a tool shed behind her house and wanted me. I knew what to do. But when I tried... *he* got in the way. I mean, in my mind I saw what he and I did together. I couldn't see anything else."

"So, you couldn't do it."

"I can never do it."

The Duke studied him, then stood up and stepped out to the curb. "There's somethin about hobos you need to know. Women are pretty scarce on the freights, always have been. Those that used to ride we called Four Bit Gals, cause they'd lay a guy for fifty cents. I've seen em take on a dozen tramps in a row. They've gotta eat like anybody else.

"But there weren't many of em, and they'd hardly ever team up with a guy. That's why most hobos traveled alone. Still do. Or they travel with a friend. You saw some friends back there at Ogden. What they do is help each other out. Keep each other company."

"You mean they're queer?"

"Yeah," he nodded, "only I ain't so fond of that word. What's queer about guys taking care of each other? Nothing if you ask me."

"Then you've...?"

"Been lonesome?" The Duke stopped him. "Of course I have." They stared at each other, letting the words sink in. "The world's a lonely place, Frisco. And when you're lonely, you take comfort where you can."

"And if you can't? If every time you want somebody... you get punished for it? Where's your comfort then? I don't think I'm a queer. I don't think I'm anything."

"You're a little fucked up, that's all."

"Right, fucked up. Fifteen years ago, some tramp molests me, but I like it. Fine. When I get old enough to think about women, I can't without this tramp getting in the way. Maybe I'm gay, only I don't give a shit about men. Great. So now I'm trying to find this tramp, to... Christ, I don't know what. Because he's the only person that ever... ah, hell. Fucked up? I'd say so."

"And a damn sight too sorry for yourself," The Duke said quietly. "You aren't lookin for a guy, you're lookin for a scapegoat. That tramp ain't it. If he's still alive he's probably just a wrung out old hobo that took himself a prushin once, then let him go. Trouble is... you never let go."

"Oh, I see. I asked for that son-of-a-bitch to do what he did, and then to leave me?"

"I don't know, did you?"

"Fuck you!"

"No thanks. You probably never told anybody about this... figured it would be too embarrassing. Well, that's pure bullshit. You're just afraid somebody'll tell you the truth."

"Which is what?"

"That you're the problem... and that tramp's got nothin to do with it. You've got fifteen years' worth of shit piled on that old man's shoulders, but it ain't his shit, it's yours. That's why you keep him around. He carries the shit, all you do is carry him."

"ALL I do is carry him?"

"Looks that way to me."

"Then you're not only a queer, you're a blind queer." Lynden meant the words to hurt when he said them, but the only pain they inflicted was to himself. "You think I like this?" It wasn't a question as much as a plea. "You think I like what I am?"

"You haven't changed it in fifteen years. What the hell am I supposed to think?"

"What the hell am I supposed to do?"

"Forget the bastard. Or if you can't do that, at least for-give him. That's the only way it's ever gonna end for you."

"End?" Lynden's eyes searched The Duke's. "I can't for-get what that motherfucker did to me, and I won't forgive him. You wouldn't either."

"Maybe I wouldn't," The Duke held his gaze. "But you've got to. You're the only one who can."

Track #9
Ashes Hauled — To have sexual intercourse

What about sex? How important is it?

Important.

You enjoy sex?

Sometimes. Sometimes not. Depends.

On the partner?

Sure. But mostly it depends on me, how much I want it. How much I'm willing to pay.

You buy your sex?

Yeah, and you do, too. It's not just about money. Some things you pay for simply by wanting them.

Pay how?

Speaking words you know you don't mean. The loss of your pride. When you want it, there's no price you won't pay.

Sex is always a transaction then?

They call it intercourse, don't they? Look it up.

Is it worth it?

Beats me. Maybe you start hating yourself for wanting it, or maybe you want it so bad you take it. Either way you're gonna have it, and it ain't free.

Have you ever taken it?

I've done everything in my time but hit an old lady, a lot of it none too pretty. Sex isn't all that pretty when you come down to it.

You don't think sex is beautiful?

No, and you wouldn't either if you ever watched. People sweating on each other, using each other as hard as they can. You talk about taking, that's all sex is.

How about intimacy? Hasn't anyone ever shared themselves with you in that way?

Sure, and me with them. And after it was over, everybody forgot what the fuss was about. At least until the next time we wanted some more.

So, do you still want it?

We all want it. The only difference between us is how much, and at what price.

How much will you pay?

Now? I ain't got much left to pay with.

And the wanting?

It doesn't care squat about what it'll cost me. It never has.

Chapter Ten

If you want to do me a favor
When I lay me down to die,
Plant my bones by the main stem
So I can hear the trains go by.
                                    Unknown

Denver for The Duke had always been the dozen or so city blocks between Larimer Street and Union Station. This was *his* Denver, the rest didn't exist. In Chicago it had been West Madison Street, in Seattle, Pioneer Square—each place a separate city, a separate mecca for the brotherhood of the road. He'd seen times at all of them when a thousand men might come or go on a single day's freights. He'd seen Larimer Street at its peak, and he'd seen it vanish. Yet it was to Larimer Street he guided Lynden, because he didn't know where else to go.

They slept in the doorway of a boarded-up hotel, sharing it with two winos and a hopped-up street kid too loaded to close his eyes. At first light they hit the streets, neither of them sure of anything.

"This used to be old whorehouse row," The Duke said as they walked down Arapahoe toward 20th. He was remembering the rugged houses that once stood there, and the rugged girls that worked them. "A dollar could buy you most anything down here. You ever tried a hooker?"

"You can't be serious."

"Maybe you should. Maybe if you bought and paid for it, you could do what you want."

"What I want," Lynden sounded more tired than angry, "is to forget the whole thing."

They turned at 20th and walked down across Lawrence toward Larimer Street. The old Hotel Henry had stood on that corner, The Victor just a block down. Half a block up had been The Palace where Stu, the one-legged night clerk, had given The Duke and Hubbard a week's free lodging back in the winter of '47.

All of it was gone now, gone to office buildings, warehouses, and vacant lots. But The Duke could still picture the soup line outside Father Divine's up on 24th. He could see his Larimer Street—blocks of pool parlors, beer halls, barber colleges. Every corner had its sky pilots, preaching the word, and its grifters peddling their scams. Every saloon served nickel beer and kept pigs' feet on the bar.

He remembered the hash houses with their chalkboard menus and their "Best Meal in Town" signs over the doors. You had your choice of everything on Larimer Street. For salvation, the Citizen's Mission. For diversion, the Colorado Saloon. And for a new start and a cut of your pay, the Sure-Bet Employment Agency would ship you across town or halfway around the world. Any day of the week, any week of the year you could find a man on Larimer Street who'd been someplace you hadn't. Every stiff had a story to tell and the worst of them was better than the best you'd hear uptown.

But there were no more stories now, no more anything to recognize from those days.

Except Union Station.

They reached Wynkoop Street, turned right, and there it was. Still bigger than made sense, still as grand and gaudy as the first time The Duke had seen it.

Only now it looked like a relic.

He stepped into the street and scrutinized the place, as if he were looking into a mirror.

He didn't realize he'd gotten so old.

"Are we going in?" The Duke heard Lynden's question, but was thinking of the time he and Hubb got twenty bucks apiece just for carrying some high roller's bags to the curb. He was remembering green neon lights inside, dark hard benches, wooden phone booths lined up in a row. Marble slabs partitioned the men's room, partitioned the stall where he'd lain sick for two days with food poisoning, where he might have died if Step and Trainer hadn't found him and carried him to the hospital. One winter he'd slept in the station for weeks, earning nickels shining shoes along with the street kids who plied their trade there.

Out in the lobby was a photo booth, three poses for a quarter. He remembered how this girl from Lake Charles had stolen his heart and his wallet in that booth on a stopover between trains. *Whatever became of her?*

"Are we going in?"

She had real pretty hair, and he was just out of the army, and...

"We're standing in the middle of the street."

...and it was nineteen forty-six.

"Well?"

"Well what?"

"Are we going in?"

"What for?" The Duke lowered his eyes and turned away. "It's just an empty building."

* * *

Lynden knew depression first hand and recognized it in The Duke. He didn't understand the source. "What's wrong? Is it because I ruined it with the girls?"

"What girls?" They had stopped at a place where the sidewalk was covered in blue and gold mosaic tile. "Zaza Theatre" was spelled in green diamond shapes, and green arrows pointed to the edge of the concrete where the Zaza once stood—now a gaping, trash filled hole. "It ain't the girls," The Duke said, staring out into the empty lot, the years and the miles marked more deeply on his face than Lynden had seen before, like ancient stone steps worn and cracked from the tread of too many feet. "It ain't anything."

"Look, I get it. I depress myself most of the time."

"I'm not surprised," The Duke answered flatly. "But it's got nothin to do with you."

Lynden had felt powerless before—with The Tramp, with Derek Zebel, with Millie. And even when, logically, he knew it wasn't true, he'd felt like he was to blame. But this was different. He looked at The Duke, seeing past the cliché of the time-toughened exterior, the wise and world-weary eyes, the *Knight of the Road*. What he saw instead was a tired old man, out of his place and out of his time. *He isn't regretting the loss of Carolyn*, Lynden thought to himself. *He is regretting the loss of almost everything he has ever known.*

And there is nothing I can do.

* * *

It was dusk when they finally walked out to the yard. No trains were moving, no men working the switches. Lynden didn't notice. Catching out or just killing time, he no longer cared what they did. The Duke's mood had infected him too.

They wandered toward the east end where the yard thinned down and almost disappeared. Off to one side, standing on a dead-end spur, were a dozen empty passenger coaches, sleek metal bodies gleaming red and silver in the setting sun. On the first coach was a blue and white nameplate. Crystal Lake.

"What are they doing out here?" Lynden placed his hand against the car. Its warmth felt almost alive.

"They're waiting."

"For what? Power?"

"For a verdict. These here are bad order cars, old ones at that. Some brass hats' probably tryin to figure if they're worth saving. Or maybe they've just been forgotten."

"I don't see anything wrong with them."

"You don't know how to look."

They walked along the cars, past Crystal Lake, Shasta Star, Pacific Cove. Lynden began to notice the flaws—a dark tinted window shot through with cracks, a wheel spring busted. Small things.

"They were built tough, so they look good." The old man gently stroked the car next to him, as if comforting a dying friend. "But inside? Hell, you can feel it. They've got nothing left to give."

At the last coach, Indian Princess, a door was open.

"Why isn't it locked?"

"Maybe somebody fucked up." The Duke sat down on a stack of ties. "Or maybe nobody gives a shit. You go look if you want. I've seen enough for one day."

Lynden hesitated, then tossed his bag down and climbed into the car.

An inferno of hot dead air washed over him.

The light was so dim he couldn't see. But his eyes slowly adjusted.

"Oh my God," he whispered. "Oh my God."

He stood at the head of a narrow passageway piled a foot deep with trash and filth. The wall covering was torn away, and the ceiling hung in jagged shreds. To his right was a sleeping compartment, the berths ripped from the walls, the toilet uprooted and on its side. Everything that could be broken had been, and a mountain of other garbage was thrown in besides.

Worst of all, it looked lived in. It *smelled* lived in.

He walked through the first car, slid back the heavy steel door and went on. Each car in turn was a new disaster. The dome coach had all its seats slashed and the carpet pulled up from the floor. In the club car, lounge chairs were stripped to their wire frames, the bar demolished.

The cars grew hotter as he went, stifling—each filled with thick, dank air that smelled of filth and mold and neglect. But he went on, hoping to find one car, one cabin spared.

The exit door at Crystal Lake was locked.

"Shit!" He'd have to walk all the way back through. He wanted out, now. There was too much ruin, the air was too foul, and suddenly, there was a sense that he was no longer alone.

"Open, you son-of-a-bitch!" He kicked at the door, then threw his shoulder against it. "Open, goddam it or I'll—"

"She ain't going to open, man." He spun around and saw no one. "We got them all locked. And we got *you* locked." He heard snickering.

"I've got a gun!"

"You ain't got nothing."

He thought there were three of them, maybe four.

"We seen you leave your shit with the old dude."

"I've got it with me," he shouted, slipping a hand into his empty pocket.

"Yeah? Okay, you stay here with your gun. When we finish outside, maybe we'll come back and see it."

Laughter. Then they were running.

"No!" He lunged forward, tripped, and fell. For one sickening instant he was glad—he wouldn't have to chase them. He could just hide.

But he couldn't.

He stopped thinking, got up, and ran.

They weren't far ahead of him, dragging things into the aisles, laughing. He charged, fell again, slammed into a door he couldn't see. He had to slow down. "Duke" he yelled, his voice swallowed by the cars.

He careened back through the dome coach, the lounge,

hurrying, listening. The laughter grew faint. It sounded like the raped cars were crying out in pain.

Then silence.

When he got to Indian Princess something was wrong, the air was different. He rushed forward, expecting a knife to slash out from the darkness, expecting a death blow that he'd never see, anything but what he found.

It was the door.

They'd closed it. Locked it from the outside somehow. He threw his full weight against it. No movement, none. He tried again in fury, then in fear.

He pressed his face to the thick glass, straining to see through. He saw—and lunged at the door like a battering ram.

There were four of them, The Duke in the middle. He had a bag in each hand, spinning and swinging as the predators circled him. Four kids, the oldest maybe just in his teens. No, not kids. Four jackals. They were biding their time, wearing him down, enjoying it. Three would taunt from the front while the fourth snuck in behind, each time getting a little closer until The Duke swung back with his bags.

It wouldn't take long.

* * *

The Duke knew this was it. His arms were so tired, and he was getting dizzier with every spin. Noises from the car told him Lynden wouldn't make it, not in time, and these road kids were too tough to handle alone. Nothing but kids. He'd do what he had to, he'd make them pay, but they were going to win.

"You can have the gear," he yelled, but he knew what they wanted.

They wanted his pride.

The circle got closer, closer, until one of them grabbed a bag. The Duke pulled back weakly. Then the other bag

was grabbed, and his arms jerked tight. They had him spread-eagle, yanking him side to side.

A punch to the stomach and he let go.

They grabbed his jacket and pulled it up over his head, covering his eyes, binding his arms. Playing blind-man's bluff they spun him, punched him, pushed him down then wrenched him up again.

Three of them toyed with their prey while the fourth—the oldest and the leader—rifled through the bowling bag and The Duke's valise.

"Look at this junk." He held up the doll mirror and the fist-shaped belt buckle, then tossed them both into the dirt. "We been wastin our time, man. No moola. Guess we outta give it all back." Now he had The Duke's hunting knife in his hand. "Know what I'm thinkin? Maybe we give this back... sharp end first."

They laughed, pinning The Duke tight between them.

The boy with the knife moved in.

The thick train window blasted out in one piece, followed by the toilet Lynden had thrown against it with more force than he knew he possessed. He jumped through. Launching himself at the kids. "No!" he roared and sent them all sprawling in the dirt.

The leader jumped up, knife in hand.

They locked eyes.

Lynden bellowed—a sound that came unbidden and brought with it a rage bottled up for fifteen years.

The leader, terrified by what he saw and heard, withered into a child. He dropped the knife and ran—the others scurrying after him.

Lynden helped his friend to his feet. "Are you okay...?" he asked and wished he hadn't. He could see plain enough.

The old man wasn't just hurt.

He was defeated.

Track #10
Antique — An old timer on the road.

What are you most afraid of?

Most afraid? Dying probably. Some guys say they aren't, but that's just talk. If you aren't afraid of dying, it's because you don't know how to live.

What's your next biggest fear?

That's simple. Not dying.

I don't follow you.

You get busted up, or sick, or just too old to catch out anymore, then where are you? You're not dead, but you aren't living either. That scares the hell out of me.

What if you can't avoid it?

Then you're fucked.

That's it? No other options?

For you, maybe. Not for me.

Any other fears?

One. I'm scared of people.

All people?

Yeah, pretty much. It's not like I'm a coward, I mean I'd kick God in the ass if he gave me a hard time. But that doesn't mean I'm not scared. There's no telling if a guy's gonna nod to me or knife me. In my world, it's safer to be afraid of everybody.

But your world isn't normal.

Neither is yours, and you know that... only you don't want to believe it. A guy walks by you on the street, only he doesn't look you in the eye and you don't look him in the eye. That isn't shyness, brother, that's fear.

So, you think we're always afraid?

Yup. And always trying to fool ourselves into thinking that we aren't.

Chapter Eleven

He gave a gasp, his head sank down,
And open gaped his mouth
His partner hooked his coat and pants,
And caught a rattler south.

Unknown

The river of steel's undercurrents ran deep and were often treacherous.

Invisible from above, they would pull a man down as effortlessly as pull him along.

There *was* tranquility to be had on the surface. The romance of rolling unfettered through the unfurling landscape. The hypnotic magic of motion. The daily discovery of vistas unknown, horizons unseen, life unfiltered. A world only guessed at, and barely comprehended, by those who preferred a roof over their heads to a boxcar floor beneath their feet.

To navigate these undertows, a traveler on this river needed skill and luck, and the acumen earned from the mating of the two. Rules of physics and power made the dangers, if not preventable, at least predictable. Locomotives usually stayed upright on the rails. Cars sat still unless pushed or pulled. And the movements of the freights conformed to patterns of behavior that, if never fully understood, could at least be guessed at.

No such rules applied to the men who prowled the depths of these waters.

* * *

"It happened out on the old Northwestern Pacific. That's a good road the NWP. Good work all up and down, a lot of fine jungles, and the bulls don't give a shit." Step-Down Johnny wondered if they knew what bulls were, these two college kids come down to learn about hobos. What the hell did he care? They asked about his name, he'd tell them.

"Me and some boys were walking through the big tunnel up north of Willits there, and Dirty Face figures he's gonna come in and join us. Dirty Face, that's what us hobos call a locomotive at the head end of a freight train, cause the railroads don't wash em much, and with the windows and tracer light they look kinda like a face." One of the young men noted that on his pad. "Anyway, some of the boys got to running, figured they could beat it on out, but me and old Stockton Tom just laid down by the tracks and let her roll by. Only thing was, one of them sawmill loads came loose on a flatcar back in the train, draggin a timber about yay big alongside." He held up his hands for size.

"She hit Tom first, and bounced I figure, cause she didn't catch me till the hip, right around here." He laid his hand on the flat place under his right pocket, the place where his hip bone had been shaved off clean. "Killed old Tom straight out. Mangled me like a piece of stew meat. The fellas we were with kind of stuck me back together and got me into town. Sawbones did the rest. How's that for your collection?"

"Yes, but about your name?"

Jesus Christ, what are they teaching these punks? "I got my name because after old Dirty Face took my hip, I couldn't jump down from boxcars anymore. I had to step down. See?"

"Then Johnny is your real name?"

"Hell, I don't even remember my real name. Before the

accident it was Sleepin Johnny, cause I was a big sleeper. Seems like I could maybe use a little shut-eye right now. We call it 'pounding-your-ear' in hobo talk, and that's just what I'm fixing to do, soon as you boys clear out of my bedroom."

They were dense, but they got the hint. Step wasn't sure why he'd talked to them. Lonely maybe. Since first light he'd had the jungle all to himself. Rumor said cops were about to make a sweep. Too many guys down at Roper, rumor said. "Fuck a bunch of rumors," was what Step had said, and he'd watched all his company swarm the first drag out for Ogden. Probably the town clowns weren't planning anything, but if they were it'd worked pretty slick. By breakfast time Step-Down Johnny had Roper to himself.

He was glad when the kids came, glad until they re-minded him how dumb kids could be. Having the yard to himself wasn't so bad after all, he decided. He lay down under his favorite tree, fixed his hat right to block the sun, and was just dropping off when he heard a twig snap.

"Coffee's on the fire, wipes are on the tree there, and I'm sleeping," he said without looking up. His guest didn't answer. "Look, if you want to learn about hobos, go ride a train. I ain't got time to—"

"You lied to me."

He knew the voice.

Step raised his head.

Short Arm was sitting next to him. Very close.

"Hey, Spooky. What brings you back so soon?"

"You lied to me."

"Really? I didn't figure I was smart enough to lie any-more."

"Which way did he go?"

"Which way did who go, Spook?" Step sat up slowly, wishing those college kids had stayed a little longer. "I'll bet you mean The Duke, don't you?"

"Which way?"

"Up to Boise, far as I know."

"You said Katy."

"That's right, I did, only Boise's on the way to Katy, ain't it? Or have they moved her since I was up there last?"

"I followed him to Roseville four days ago. K-Falls is one day from Roseville. If he went to Katy, you never would have seen him. Which way did he go?"

Sweat was saturating the front of Step's shirt, "You're right, Spook, I lied to you," he said, working to keep the fear out of his voice. "Me and The Duke was pretty tight once. Hell, we all were, you too. But when you rolled in here the other day, I said to myself Spooks got him some kind of beef with The Duke. And I was right, wasn't I? Now, I ain't seen you in a coon's age, but I see The Duke pretty regular. What's between you two guys I don't know, but I figured, why not give old Duke a chance to settle this thing when he wants to. That's why I give you the bum steer. Truth is, when you asked, I hadn't seen The Duke in better than three months. I swear it."

"Which way did he go?"

"You aren't listening to me, Spook. Like I said—"

"My name is Short Arm."

"Yeah, Short Arm, but you still aren't listening to what—"

"Let's take a walk," Short Arm grabbed his shoulder and forced him to stand.

"What the fuck are you—?"

"I hear a train coming," Short Arm said, pulling him into the yard. "Which way do you think it's going? North, I think. Maybe Pocatello. Which way did The Duke go?"

"Look, you crazy son-of-a-bitch, I told you I don't know. Now let go of me or—"

"I might have been crazy once," the expression on the

scarred face was oddly thoughtful and looked out of place for the moment that it lingered, "but no more. They let me out. I got the papers to prove it. I just don't like people who lie to me. Especially not old friends."

They were out among the cars, Short Arm shoving, then pushing, then dragging Step along, his one good arm much stronger than Step's one good leg. On an empty track between two strings of boxcars they stopped.

"Which way?"

"I don't know. If I did know, I sure as fuck wouldn't tell you!"

A string of cars was being shoved onto the empty siding in front of them. Step could see the lead car, a dozen lengths away, coming at them quiet as death.

Short Arm forced him to his knees, then flat on the ground, his head over the track. "Put your ear to the rail," he ordered, his foot in the small of Step's back. "Listen close. When you hear which way The Duke went... you tell me, okay? I can wait."

"I'm not telling you nothin." The cold steel under Step's ear vibrated more every second. "You're a crazy bastard, Spook... you always were. I see that buckle you're wearing. It don't mean shit. The Johnsons wouldn't have you, even if any of em *were* still alive."

"Which way, Step-Down? You can hear which way, can't you? By now it should be real loud."

It was roaring.

The car was less than a hundred feet away. "I hear this," he yelled. "The Duke's gone someplace you don't know. He *left the road*. You want him, I'll tell you where he is. But get your fuckin boot off my back!"

"He will never leave the road, Step."

The car was almost on him, the foot pinning him in place, helpless.

He uttered a single word.

"Enola."

"Thank you," Short Arm whispered.

Then he stepped down hard on Step-Down-Johnny and watched the car roll by.

* * *

When Hubbard saw the padlock gone from his door, he knew it was pressing his luck to go inside. But his money was in there, three-hundred-and-fifty dollars. That account at the Rocky Mountain Savings and Loan was an easy lie he told, even to friends. You couldn't trust nobody around that much dough.

Either kids busted the lock, or the city maintenance guys. Kids would have messed up some things and swiped his gentlemen's magazines. City guys wouldn't have done much different. Neither of them had a chance of finding his stash. *A guy could dig all day in there and not come close*. The smart play now was to hang out for a few days, watch the place from a safe distance, and if she looked okay, move back in. He could shag over to Ogden and visit Trainer or jungle-up with Step for a while.

There was no reason to risk it.

But there were three-hundred-and-fifty reasons.

He couldn't leave.

"Get the fuck outta my way, cause I'm coming in mad!" he yelled as he swung back the steel door.

"Hello, Hubbard."

Short Arm was standing framed in the doorway, big and ugly and too close.

Hubb's voice and his poker face both failed him.

"You look frightened."

"You scared the piss outta me." Hubbard pushed his way into the cave, his voice back, his composure still lagging. "I thought you was up Oregon way?"

"I was," Short Arm pulled the door closed. "Now I'm here again. Too bad about your lock. I got tired of waiting."

"And I'm tired of people busting into my place. What the hell do you want, anyway? If you're looking for a place to stay, forget it. *No overnight guests...* them's house rules."

"I'm not staying. I'm headed for Harrisburg."

Hubbard stiffened. His buried money no longer seemed important.

"Harrisburg?"

"Step-Down told me."

"Bullshit! He wouldn't have—"

Too late.

"I had him pinned on the tracks." Short Arm's eyes, too narrow and set too deep, seemed to be re-watching the scene as he described it. "Step didn't give it up till right at the end... just before the wheel rolled over him."

"I don't know what the fuck you're talking about." Hubbard lied. He had seen the truth of it in those eyes, and for the first time in memory he was truly terrified.

"No?" Short Arm reached his good hand toward his empty sleeve, and seemed to be scratching something, scratching the hand that wasn't there.

"Look, I got things to do and places to go, so you just get out, all right? I don't want no part of your personal business."

"I know you're scared, Hubbard."

"Hell... you just surprised me is all." Without meaning to he took a step backward.

"Do you think I'm crazy?"

"Course you're crazy... who the hell ain't." Another step backward. For each pace Hubbard retreated, Short Arm took one forward.

"I always liked you."

"Bullshit."

"Next to The Duke, you were probably my best friend."

"Then it must have been me that was crazy." Hubbard stopped. He'd had poker games like this. If he let himself

get backed into a corner, he'd lose his whole stake.

He wasn't in that corner, not yet. "Tell me something, old friend. How'd you lose that arm?"

"Dirty Face took it."

"Yeah?" Hubbard began side-stepping toward the door. "Old Dirty Face, he can be a mean customer."

"He's mean... but I beat him. I got my arm back."

"You what?"

"Would you like to see it?"

Hubbard was within a few feet of the entrance. One step, two at the most, and he'd be out.

"You *want* to see it, don't you?" The tramp he'd known as Spooky offered again, a grotesque smile on his grotesque face.

"Sure... you crazy son-of-a-bitch!"

Hubbard lunged for the door.

And tripped.

"You never could bluff." Short Arm was standing over him, reaching for his sleeve. "I can see how scared you are. You're shakin like some yard bull's about to bust your head. You got the bull horrors, Hubbard?"

"Fuck you."

"Don't be afraid. I like you, but I'll have to kill you anyway. Don't worry... it'll only take a second."

Hubbard thought about kicking out at him, knocking him off balance, tripping him maybe. But violence wasn't his style. He'd stick with the bluff.

"Go piss up a rope!"

Short Arm laughed, then reached his good hand into his empty sleeve.

It only took a second.

Track #11
Red Light — To throw from a moving train.

Have you ever killed a man?

I don't think I'll answer that.

You have then. In cold blood?

That's a stupid term for it. I'll give you cold blood. Next time you're downtown, look at the people sitting in those office windows. That's murder, cold and sure. The only thing it ain't is quick.

That's not what I'm talking about.

The hell it isn't. You think killing has to be with a knife or a gun? That isn't cold blood, it's hot. I met a steeplejack once—used to work high steel. Skyscrapers. Before starting a job, his bosses knew how many men were going die on it. They *knew*. "This is a one-and-a-half man building," they'd say, "and this is a three man." It doesn't get any colder than that.

But it's not one man killing another.

Really? What is it when they send a guy down into a mine that ain't safe? What do you call black lung, and brown lung, and all that chemical crap guys are dying from?

You're not answering my question.

What do you want to know?

About you. Have you ever killed anyone?

Yes.

Why?

Because I had to.

Why?

I didn't have a choice.

Chapter Twelve

He must know hell, lest he should guess,
That all his weary tramp is o'er,
A hell of hunger and distress,
Where he, cold, naked, and footsore,
Alone and ill must wander still,
Through endless roads for evermore.
                              Arturo Giovannitti

They spent most of three days in Denver, holed up in a four-dollar room at the Hotel New Columbia. Three days drunk, living by their senses, shutting down their emotions. The Duke never ventured farther than the john down the hall. Lynden hit the pavement a few times for crackers and more wine.

They drank till they puked, then slept, then got up and drank more.

Mostly it was a quiet drunk, no narration required for the personal dramas they each replayed for themselves again and again—Lynden's disintegration with Millie, The Duke's disgrace at the hands of the road kids.

From their window they could see most of Denver. For hours they just sat, watching it. Street sounds rolled up to them, a clean breeze from the Rockies moving gently through the curtains along with the noise. At night they heard freights. The highballs blasting out across the plains, the locals, the drags. Dim light from the hotel sign lit their room, dusk until sun-up. It was better than darkness, easier to hide in.

When they finally caught out for Kansas City, it was as much from boredom as anything else. "Fucking cheap hotel rooms," The Duke kept mumbling most of the last day they were there. "Fucking Denver."

"Fucking Denver," Lynden agreed and they each forced down another slug. They were working too hard at staying drunk. The wine was no longer enough.

Time to leave.

They stumbled down to the Larimer yards, fell into a boxcar, and passed out. The Duke had gotten them on the right train somehow, but he missed the time by half a day. They woke up hot, cotton-mouthed, only just pulling out of the yard.

"We're fucked, Frisco," The Duke mumbled. "She sat here the whole damned night."

"So?" Lynden's tongue felt twice its normal size, and sticky, and tasted of cheap wine and day-old vomit.

"I figured we'd be waking up somewhere near K.C. That's why I didn't stop for grub. And we don't have no water."

"I don't care." The taste on his tongue brought a surge from his stomach that he fought to keep down. "I don't want to eat or drink anything... ever again."

Suburbs and factories slithered past, the blur that was Denver fading behind them as the eastbound began to pick up speed. Dropping in and out of consciousness, Lynden's aching eyes soon saw wheat fields reaching endlessly toward razor-sharp horizon lines, painfully bright. Grain was everywhere—golden, auburn, rust, sand—its colors swirling and rippling together, the landscape rolling like a great brown sea.

Sick as he was, Lynden rolled with it.

"There's only two ways to ride a freight," The Duke had told him the night before, or was it the night before that? "Ride drunk, or ride sober, but don't ever catch out if you're anywheres between. It'll kill you."

Now Lynden understood. All morning his body throbbed with every noise. Even the softest creaks of the wooden floor, the groans of metal walls, seemed to happen right inside his head. The loud sounds hurt so much they blinded him. The only hangover he'd ever experienced, he had self-treated with dim lights, cold compresses, and a day's quiet rest in bed.

This was murder.

At every crossing or stretch of bad road, the train threw him sideways, bouncing him off the wall, lifting him off the floor. The Duke was lying flat, moaning. Lynden tried, but his head felt like a rotting melon fit to burst. He crouched in a corner, eyes pressed tight to his knees, hands clamped over his ears.

It can't last forever, he told himself. Then he prayed to be forgiven, to no God he knew, for whatever it was he had done to deserve this.

Then he gave up praying.

By noon the temperature in the car was upwards of a hundred degrees. Shakes had given way to sweats, then to stomach cramps so bad that for relief he had to hang his ass out the door.

It was thirst, intense and unwelcome, that told him the hell was starting to end.

Then hunger.

The train began to slow.

"Any chance of finding some food along here?" he shouted, wincing at the shrillness of his own voice.

The Duke scraped some dirt from his face and rolled over.

"No."

"How far to Kansas City?"

"All day, and most of the night probably. Ain't you dead yet?"

"What?"

"Last I heard, you were wishin somebody'd kill ya. I liked to a done it myself. How you feelin?"

"Fucked. Thirsty... and kinda hungry, though. You?"

"Same. Except for the hungry part. My gut feels like I ate a cactus."

The train jerked, slowing more, and the hot smell of brake shoes billowed around them.

Lynden crawled to the door and stuck his head out. A water tower rose above the prairie in the distance. "Town coming." There was a name painted on the water tank, but his eyes were too blurry to make it out.

"Don't even think it, Frisco." The Duke pulled himself to a sitting position, bracing himself with both arms so as not to fall back down. "These bull locals don't run like hot-shots. Maybe they stop ten minutes, maybe the whole fucking day."

"I could keep an eye on the power and turn back if it starts to move."

"And you could also get your ass ditched. Chances are there ain't even a store open."

"You wouldn't say no to a cold drink, would you?"

"Maybe. The crummy's only a few cars back, ain't it?" He made no effort to look and waited for Lynden to confirm it for him. "They always got water in a caboose. I'll go beg us some if you want. But don't be thinking about that town."

"I don't want water." Lynden retied his boots and stood up, feeling dizzy but less so than he feared. "I want something really cold, orange juice maybe. And I want some cookies, and a baloney sandwich on white bread."

"Jesus, I thought you were sick." The Duke struggled to his feet and stuck his head out the door. "It's ain't worth it, Frisco." He pulled his head back in. "You're in no shape to run, hell, a mile each way. And that's what it's gonna take."

"I can do it."

"Bullshit."

"Don't worry. I'll make it back."

The Duke grimaced, then leaned unsteadily out the door to spit. "Maybe I'm afraid you won't."

"You? Afraid?"

"You saw me with those punks. Fuck yes... I'm afraid." The words seemed to exhaust him, draining what little energy he had left. "Now—you doin this crazy shit—cause I can't do it myself? Fuck you and your orange juice! I shoulda stayed in Denver and stayed drunk."

Lynden stared at him. "Is that the wine talking, or are you serious?"

"I'm a played out old tramp is what I am." The Duke leaned against the door frame. "If you're getting off, take your gear. I ain't gonna watch it."

The train lurched to a stop, cars squeezing together.

The silence was paralyzing.

"This train's not leaving without me." Lynden slid out the door, not waiting for a reply.

He'd gone less than a car's length when he heard his bowling bag hit the ground behind him.

* * *

Just run, Lynden told himself, *don't think.* For the first ten car lengths he pulled it off, ignoring the pain in his head and the twitching muscles in his stomach. But they wouldn't stay ignored. He tried an old backpacker's trick, concentrating on the pains completely to forget everything else.

It worked.

It also kept his mind off The Duke.

By twenty cars he'd found a pace he could handle, breathing settled, arms swinging, sweat cooling his sides and back. The air lines blasted as the power was cut loose. *No hurry*, he thought, counting each car as he passed it, counting the steps it took. He could see the town now—grain elevator, a few trees, the greeting sign where Highway 40 slowed into Main Street.

If the store is *closed, I'll shit.* But it wouldn't be closed, not this time of day. *Unless it's Sunday?* He had no idea.

A dirt road ran parallel to the tracks. He crossed over to it, glad for an even surface to run on. Across the highway was the town's single block of store fronts. Far down the tracks, he saw exhaust columns from the disconnected power units.

There'd be plenty of time.

* * *

Bad as The Duke's eyes were, they followed Lynden as he left the road, crossed a little patch of grass that gave the town a park, and stopped to catch his breath on Main Street. *Fucking greenhorns.* He didn't want to watch. He wanted the power to hook on, so they'd pull out and leave the kid behind, leave it all behind.

Only he couldn't help himself. *Fucking orange juice!* He jerked his head in, and went to the far end of the car, disgusted.

A minute later he was back at the door, shading his eyes again, staring into the sun, watching for Lynden.

* * *

The sign over the window said Wheatland Grocery. The sign in the door said Closed. *Shit!* He stuck his face against the glass. Empty. Stripped. No food, no nothing. *What do these people eat?*

He sprinted back across the street, forcing calm to settle over him, willing his breathing to slow.

There had to be another store. If he took his time, he could... there! A woman with a shopping bag was at the far end of the block. He raced toward her and there it was, Maxwell's Corner Market—the best disguised grocery store he'd ever seen.

His first impulse was to burst in and start grabbing things off the shelves. *Plenty of time*, he told himself. *No hurry.* He tucked in his shirt, pushed back his hair, took a deep breath as he stepped through the door.

"Good afternoon." The girl at the counter gave a self-conscious tug at her bangs as she greeted him.

"Good afternoon." Lynden wondered how his breath smelled, then remembered that taste in his mouth and knew.

"Nice da-a-y," she said, with the flattest "a" he'd ever heard. What he didn't hear was the power units returning.

"Yes, nice." He covered his mouth and moved past her into the store.

He had never noticed how much food there was in a grocery store, even a small one. Aisles of food, stacks of it. He was suddenly so hungry he wanted everything. He picked up the first can he could reach—tomato paste— and studied it for thirty seconds before realizing what it was. *Focus, got to focus. Orange juice.* He found it, picked out the biggest bottle they had. *Cookies.* No problem, they had a whole shelf full. He wanted the little square ones with the chocolate chips and the rippled tops.

They didn't have them.

They had to have them.

Two minutes of looking, and he finally grabbed some Oreos.

Bologna, cheese, white bread, apples. The apples took a minute to pick out—he was from California apple country, they weren't.

"Will this be a-a-all for you?" the girl asked when he dumped his armload on the counter. She slipped the words out past a piece of chewing gum and tugged at her hair again.

"Yes, all." He nodded, starting to worry about the time.

"Unless you've got any chocolate bars?"

"We keep the chocolate behind the counter. My favorite's Hershey semi-sweet. I believe I'd eat Hershey a-a-all day long if it wasn't for my complexion." She blushed just enough for her battle scars to show.

"I'll try your favorite, two bars."

She added them to the pile and began tallying his order on a hand crank adding machine. Between each clunk of the handle, he listened for some noise from outside, some clue about the train.

Nothing.

"Six fifty-two." He handed her a twenty. "Six fifty-two out of twenty." She opened the cash drawer and silently counted change into her hand. "Six fifty-two, fifty-three, fifty-four, fifty-five, sixty-five, seventy-five, seven dollars." She sighed. Lynden sucked in his breath. "Eight," handing him a bill, "nine, ten, and ten is twenty."

But there was still a bill in her hand.

"Somethin ain't right." She snatched the money back before he could stop her.

This time Lynden helped her count.

When he pulled the screen-door closed behind him she was still saying, "Tha-a-nk you," and primping her hair.

The first thing he saw were the engines back with the train. The second was a sign that said 'Cold Beer to Go.' Even hung-over it sounded too good to pass up.

He burst through the tavern door with three bucks in his hand. "A six-pack, quick." He slapped the money down. The old woman at the bar reached back, brought a six-pack of long necks out of the cooler, and took his money without once looking away from her soap opera. Lynden grabbed the beer and was gone—in and out in less than thirty seconds.

He hit the street running, a sack of groceries under one arm, a six-pack under the other.

The freight was hooked-up and ready. He could see the engineer's elbow in the lead unit window, and back down the tracks he saw the train stretching to the horizon.

In no time he was across the highway, through the park, and onto the dirt road. Dust flew up from his feet, bottles clattered, groceries flattened under his arm.

Where the road ended, he re-crossed to the tracks, running alongside the train again.

He could stop.

He could catch it now for sure, even if he didn't get back to their car.

But I don't just want to catch it, he realized, *I want to beat it.* And suddenly it wasn't about running anymore, it was about proving something—to The Duke, to The Tramp, to Millie, to all of them.

Lynden knew it was stupid, but he sped up anyway.

He wasn't trying to prove he was smart.

He'd covered less than half the distance back to the boxcar when he felt his energy go, drained out in a rush like water from the bottom of a busted bucket. His stomach knotted, his head began to roar. Every few strides the groceries would slip, or the beer, or he'd stumble into the train and almost fall. Their car was impossibly far away.

The train came to life.

Air hissed next to him, couplers strained. The cars began to move.

Shit! There was no way, but he wouldn't give up.

Then he slipped, sprawling to the gravel.

He wanted to scream, but didn't have the strength.

A flatcar was rolling up. He got to his feet, threw himself and his load onto it. The car pulled forward a few yards, jerked, then stopped.

For one silent instant he wasn't sure.

Fuck it!

He was on the ground again, lurching forward, beer

bottles and groceries nearly escaping his grasp. This time it was either get to his car or miss the train. Win—or lose completely.

Ten cars, twenty, the train jerked again. He ignored it. Twenty-five cars. His vision blurred, and the pounding in his ears drowned out the world of noise.

Then a sound broke through.

He looked up.

"Run, Frisco! Run you crazy son-of-a-bitch!" The Duke raced toward him. "You did it, boy! Goddam, you did it!"

"Our car?" Lynden gasped. "Where's our car?"

"Right here." The train was still stopped, but they could hear the couplers beginning to stretch, which meant it could move any second. The Duke tossed their bags in the open door. "I went back to the crummy and tried to stall em," he panted, pulled himself into the car, and reached down to give Lynden a hand. "Worked for a minute, but the shack got wise. Fuck him. You made it anyway!"

Lynden flopped on the floor.

The car began to roll.

He passed a beer to The Duke, grabbed one for himself. "To me... goddam it!"

They clinked bottles, twisted caps, and shot beer and foam all over themselves.

* * *

Kansas City was just waking up when they rolled in the next morning.

"What would you say to a shower and some hot eats?" The Duke led them out of the yard, across a railroad bridge over the Kansas River, and past the Stock Exchange toward 12th Street. "There's a Y up here that ain't half bad, and a greasy-spoon next door that's outstanding. I don't mean to be spendin your money, but I'm hungry enough and filthy enough that I'd beat you over the head for it if you said no."

"No."

"Screw you."

Lynden had never been to a YMCA, but he followed his friend's lead. He paid for a night for both of them in the hobo equivalent of a five-star hotel.

"Doesn't anybody ever clean this place?" They were undressing in the broken-down bathroom, sitting on the sinks because the benches were all busted. Lynden had just stepped barefoot on the floor and felt the soap slime oozing up between his toes.

"Clean it?" The Duke laughed. "The sign says Christian, it don't say Clean." He stepped into the shower. "Leastways they got plenty of hot water."

"Yeah, and if we run out of soap, we can just scrape it up off the floor."

"That's the idea."

Half an hour later they walked into Sam's Café, clean and hungry. A booth by the door was open, and they'd hardly sat down when two steaming cups of coffee appeared.

"That was fast." Lynden had his back to the street, counting the crowd.

"Fast, not fancy... that's Sam's. Food's good though. Get the chicken. It's the special of the day."

"We don't even have menus."

"Don't need em. Chicken is always the special of the day. Trust me."

They ordered two specials, and almost instantly the food appeared.

"How do they do that?"

"You don't want to know. Just eat."

Chicken-pot-pie, lots of it, with biscuits, vegetables, and home fries on the side.

When Lynden pushed his plate away, every bite gone, he sat back to look around. The place was full of people

he'd come to recognize, people he'd seen all his life but never noticed. Working stiffs mostly—construction guys, retired civil servants, winos just coming off a drunk, or just coming onto one. *Guys like The Duke*, he thought. Then he remembered how he'd looked in the YMCA mirror.

Guys like himself.

"Quite a place, ain't it?" The Duke was watching him watch everyone else.

"It's a comfortable place, but I'm not sure why."

"Because they put good food on the table cheap, and they let you eat it in peace. There isn't some waiter tugging on your sleeve every second asking 'Is everything as you wish?' If it wasn't, you wouldn't be eatin it."

"You're right." Lynden smiled at the old man. He was sounding like he had when they first met.

"Of course, I'm right," The Duke set his fork down, warming to his topic. "The best joint I ever ate in was just like this, only better. The Blue Light Café she was called, right outside of Pasco, Washington, right near the yards. They had soup for a nickel, served right out of the can, and bunks in the back for guys to sleep."

"Sounds perfect." Lynden couldn't figure out if it was the shower and food making him feel so good, or The Duke, or all three. Or maybe it was Sam's Café and the Y next door, and the sense he had, so unfamiliar, of being completely at home.

"It was A-number-one! Mulligan stew served up on tin plates, Tokay wine on tap. Every bum from here to Sunday knew the Blue Light. It was just about the most—"

"Just about the most what?"

The Duke was looking past him and into the street. "Wait here," he ordered. He got up, walked straight to the door, took one step outside then ducked back in. He returned to the booth just as their waitress brought the check.

"Is the alley door open?" The Duke asked, grasping her arm and catching her off guard. "Is it?"

"Sure," she pulled away from him, "but if you're thinking about skipping out, think again."

Lynden dug for his wallet. "I'll pay, don't worry." She eyed his money, then disappeared with their dirty dishes. "Will you sit down and tell me what's going on? You're acting like a nut case."

"Maybe I am, but I've got my reasons," The Duke spoke carefully, deliberately. "There's no time to explain now," he looked Lynden straight in the eye, "but I'll tell you everything, as soon as I know."

"Now what?"

"I ain't sure yet. And until I am, I'm keepin you out of it."

"I don't *want* to be kept out of it," Lynden protested.

"And I don't want you getting hurt. This ain't negotiable. Meet me at Union Station at six o'clock. Take my gear."

"You're not kidding, are you?"

"If I'm not there, don't wait." The Duke stood up, checked the street, and made for the rear door. He stopped, came back. "You never heard of me, understand?"

"No. I don't understand."

The old man leaned close and grabbed Lynden's shoulder. "Convince me you never heard of me." He squeezed until it ached.

"All right, I never heard of you. Don't do this. Please."

The Duke released his grip. "Sorry if I hurt you." He patted the spot he'd been grabbing. "You'll be okay, Frisco. You will."

He turned to the back of the café, and in a moment was gone.

Track #12
Blowed-in-the-glass — Genuine.

Do you miss the old days?

Hell, yes. This country was bigger then. A guy could stretch out. And the road was bigger. Every kind of bum had a place on it. Everybody knew the score.

Why has it changed?

Because people change. They get to thinking they want something better than what they've got. Everything new: new house, new car, new city. But nothing's really new... just different. Sharing mulligan by a fire hasn't changed in a million years. There's just fewer guys sharing now than before.

Have you changed?

I'm older. I don't move as quick as I once did. I'm not as hungry as I once was.

Hungry?

For everything. Food, love, open spaces. Hell, I had an appetite in those days. I'd take in enough for ten men and still want more. Now there isn't so much left, leastways not much that I care about. Except the open spaces. I'll still take all of them I can find.

How do you feel about getting old?

Feel's got nothing to do with it. You have one thing when you come into this world, and that's your own self. Until you're twenty, twenty-five maybe, you're picking stuff up all the time, like putting money in the bank. Then for a good long spell you've got all you want. The account's full. But sooner or later things turn around on you. It's time to start paying out... a little every day. Then, before you know it, you've got nothing left to pay with. It doesn't matter how rich you get, or how much you know, one day you'll be tapped out. Balance zero. That's getting old.

Would you go back? Would you do it all over again?

This train only runs one way, friend, and there's no getting off. I wouldn't go back, even if I could.

Why?

Because I've ended up exactly where I was supposed to... sitting in this jungle, talking to you.

Chapter Thirteen

Many a man's been murdered by the railroad,
By the railroad, by the railroad;
Many a man's been murdered by the railroad,
And laid in his lonesome grave.

Unknown

"Frisco?"

Lynden was asleep in a back corner of the Union Station lobby. He'd been there since four—just him, the ticket agent, and a janitor with a big, quiet broom. Three people in a lobby the size of a football field. *I'll just blend right in with the crowd* he'd thought and scrunched down in an orange plastic chair to scan the cavernous, cobwebbed ceiling, to read and reread the outdated travel posters, and to wait.

All the obvious things had occurred to him. The Duke was in trouble. The Duke was running, or was he running out? But he wouldn't have left his gear. And why run out, why now? Why had his father run? Why had The Tramp run away with him, then abandoned him? Suddenly his own personal escape clause began to take on new meaning. There's no problem too big to run away from. Words to live by? Maybe for more people than he'd thought.

But he'll be here. He's profesh, and he gave his word. That's all I need.

It was all he'd let himself consider.

When six o'clock, then seven, then seven-thirty had passed, it was getting hard to ignore what might be coming. *There are more ways of running than with your feet.* He took refuge where so many had before. He willed himself to sleep.

"Frisco?"

There was a hand on his shoulder, shaking him.

"Frisco, that you?"

He opened his eyes. "Duke?" Then turned around. "Bill!"

"Keep your voice down," Trainer whispered. "You awake enough to listen?"

"Where's The Duke?"

"Damn it, Frisco, keep it down!" Trainer was serious, and scared. "The Duke don't want nobody knowing he's here, and me neither. It ain't safe."

"But where is he?"

"Platform seven. Just walk down the main hall there and slip into seven when nobody's looking. We got her unlocked from the inside."

"What about you?"

"I'll be there directly. Go on now, he's waiting." Trainer turned and vanished out the front door.

Lynden walked down the main concourse. Slipping out of sight would be easy. He was the only person there.

Of the dozen gates, only number twelve was in regular use for departures and arrivals. The others looked like they'd been closed for years.

At number seven he pushed against the tall metal doors. They groaned, then swung open. He ducked inside, and before he could catch them, they clunked shut behind him. Their echoes ricocheted repeatedly off the cold concourse walls.

He walked down a flight of wide steel steps, down another flight, through a broken wooden door, and outside onto the platform—eerie in the evening's half-glow. Red signal lights shone on all the tracks. Nothing coming, nothing expected.

Lynden had seen the arrival/departure board. One train in from Denver at 8:30. That same train out for Chicago at 9:05. He wondered if anyone would be on it.

A flash of color caught his eye—skyscraper windows blazing in the setting sun. When he looked down The Duke was by his side.

"Glad you made it, Frisco."

"I'm glad you made it. What's going on? Why's Trainer here?"

"This ain't the place to talk. Follow me." He guided Lynden to what looked like an abandoned metal tool shed, Trainer Bill and Rusty were already inside.

"I would have brung you straight down," Trainer said, "but we wanted to make sure I wasn't being followed."

"By who?" Lynden stared at The Duke. "Short Arm? Was it Short Arm you saw today?"

The Duke shook his head. "I saw Trainer, and that meant somethin was up. He ain't been this far from Pig Hollow in better than five years."

"And?"

"He came out here to warn us."

"That Short Arm means to kill you," Trainer said, "and he knows which way you're headed. Chances are he's in K.C. right now. I ain't as quick as I used to be, and he had a day's start on me."

"Then we were wrong about Harrisburg?"

Trainer and The Duke looked at each other. "We lied about Harrisburg, Frisco. Stay cool a minute and just listen. Hubbard and Step fed Short Arm a story that I was making for K Falls. The last anybody knew he was headed up that way looking for me."

"And Harrisburg was to keep us running away instead of after him?"

The Duke nodded.

"Did you ever mean to tell me?"

"I don't know. None of that matters now."

"It does to me! I—"

"Step and Hubbard are dead, Frisco." Trainer got up and glanced nervously out the door. "We found Step next to the tracks. An accident, the bull called it, but that weren't no accident. Somebody held him under that train."

"You mean a train...?"

"Took his head clean off." Trainer nodded. "And if you ask me, he got to lay there and watch it coming."

Lynden didn't want to ask. "Hubbard?"

"Gut-shot. He was stretched out on his back when we found him, deader'n shit. His shirt had this hole in it 'bout the size of a four-bit piece. We rolled him over." Trainer hesitated. "We rolled him over and there wasn't nothing left below his rib cage."

"Jesus. You're sure it was Short Arm?"

"Left his moniker both places. He wants The Duke to know he's coming."

"Why Hubbard? And how'd he get a gun that close? Hubb might not have been much of a gambler, but he didn't strike me as a fool."

"He done it because Step and Hubb pulled the double-cross." Trainer laid it out. "Somehow Short Arm got wise."

"And the way he did it," The Duke added, "is Short Arm's big secret. That's why he wants to kill me. One of the reasons anyway."

"You know?"

"He showed it to me." The old hobo sat down, as if surrendering to the weight of the story he was about to tell. "I hadn't seen Spook in, hell, a long time. Like I told you, I thought he was dead. But I roll into this Colton jungle a couple a weeks back, and there he is. 'Hey, old friend,' he says to me, 'I was hopin we'd meet up. I've got somethin to show you. I think you're gonna like it. Sit yourself down.'

"I figure I owe him after what happened with his arm, so I sit down and watch. He and this nice-looking Mexican kid are playing cards. The kid's wearing new clothes, stiff blue jeans and a plaid shirt with the box creases still pressed in. Got a pocket full of money like he just came off a job, but he don't speak English too good. Spook winks over at me and starts making fun of the guy. He *wants* that kid to thump him.

"It's like I'm watchin a train wreck happening right in front of me, seeing every detail, and there ain't a damn thing I can do to stop it.

"The kid don't want to hit a one-armed guy, but Spook keeps after him until the kid gets mad and lets one fly. There goes Spook, flat on his ass. Right away the Mexican kid reaches down to help him up. Next thing I know, that kid comes flying backwards, a big smoking hole in his middle.

"'Ain't she somethin?' Spook asks, holding up this little double barrel, maybe a foot long. Then he slips it nose first up inside his empty sleeve and hooks it some way so it hangs there.

"'You took my arm, Duke,' he tells me, 'but I got it back, and I forgive you. Let's shake.' Quicker'n shit he whips that little sawed-off out and lays it up against my face.

"Then he laughs.

"'Check his pockets,' he orders me. I do. The kid was wearing a money belt, but it was mostly blown away. 'Cook us some dinner,' Spook says, and I do that too. He starts talkin some madness about the Johnsons, about how he's gonna bring em back, bring back the buckle just like the old days. And he wants me to join up with him. 'Ain't nobody left to fight us now,' he says, 'and if they do my short-arm can handle em. That's my name now... Short Arm Johnson.'

"I cook up some coffee, and when it's good and hot I throw a cup right in his face. He squeezes off a shot and blasts the crap out of this bush I dove under. By the time he reloaded I was on a train and gone. Been runnin since."

"And you better keep running." Trainer nodded. "You, too, Frisco. I'm sure as hell gonna."

"You?"

"Only reason I'm alive right now is because I was up getting my relief check when he rolled through Pig Hollow. He's a crazy bastard. Always was. I don't figure he'll stop looking for any of us who used to be Profesh. Until we're all dead."

"Or he is," The Duke added. "I know him. He won't stop."

Lynden couldn't believe what he was hearing. "We're going to the police... right now. Maybe they won't believe you guys, but they'll believe me... I'll make sure they do. He's killing people for Christ sake."

"He's killing bums, fruit tramps, and old men," The Duke said. "You go to the law if you want, but don't expect Trainer and me to back you. Odds are they'd lock us up and let Short Arm run free."

"You really believe that?"

"We know it," Trainer said, resigned to a truth that Lynden was only beginning to accept. "They'd just as soon pin those murders on us as anybody. I'm heading for Canada. Duke, how about you?"

"I ain't exactly decided yet, but Canada's no good for me, or you neither, Bill. We stay on the rails long enough and you know he'll find us. He's using the same tracks and ridin the same cars as us, so our paths are gonna cross sooner or later. I figure we've got two choices. Either we find him first, or we quit."

"Who are you trying to kid?" Trainer picked up his bindle and moved toward the door. "We ain't about to kill

Short Arm, even if we could. It ain't who we are."

"I know... but that's no protection against a twelve gauge."

"And we ain't neither of us gonna leave the road. Hell, I don't ride much anymore, but I still couldn't give up the life. Wouldn't know what to do with myself, and you wouldn't neither."

"I know that, too." The Duke reached out and shook Trainer's hand. "Canada, eh? Could be I'll see you up there."

"You do that. And Frisco," Bill extended his hand, "if I don't see you again, it's been a pleasure. You got the makings of a good tramp. But if I was you... I'd go home." He scooped Rusty into his arms and stepped out the door. "Canadian Pacific, here I come."

"Watch your ass, Bill," The Duke called after him.

Trainer waved over his shoulder but did not turn around.

* * *

Darkness filled the tool shed, its contents vague silhouettes in the shadows. Lynden and The Duke sat face-to-face, barely able to see each other's outlines.

"Do you think he'll make it?"

"Trainer? I don't know. If Short Arm isn't after him, maybe. Otherwise, Canada ain't near big enough."

"But Short Arm is only one man. By himself he—"

"He can find anybody if they stay near the high steel, and that's the only life Trainer knows. These freights let us ride, Frisco. They don't let us go. And Canada's only got one set a tracks, same as here. Us tramps live in a small world, smaller than you'd believe."

Long silences separated their words.

"You've been lying to protect me, haven't you?" Lynden didn't wait for an answer. "The story about Harrisburg and about how the bum got shot in Colton. You made those up. Why?"

"Maybe I was just covering my own ass."

"I don't believe that."

"Maybe I knew from the start that Short Arm was probably gonna get me. Maybe I didn't want him gettin you, too." The Duke and his voice dissolved in the blackness. "Pride, I guess."

There was a longer pause.

One piece of unfinished business still hung in the air between them.

"My tramp," Lynden said finally, "you didn't know him, did you? And Short Arm probably doesn't know him either."

"That fella who took you? I knew some guys that coulda been him. I know he hurt you. And I know it hurt when he let you go. But you're better off that he did. Trust me on this, you didn't want that life."

"And I didn't want the life I got."

"Most don't, or think they don't. There's no secret to it, Frisco. We're all of us on a train. It don't run smooth, it don't run easy, and it don't run one minute longer than it's meant to. You gonna ride it, or let it ride you? That's all the choice we really get."

Track #13
On the Plush — Living above the average.

What do you like most about your life?

That's hard to say. I don't ever think about liking my life.

Okay, pick just one thing.

Coffee brewing in the jungle. I like that. It isn't much for taste, but the smell is really something.

Anything else?

Sure, lots of things. There's a way the sun shines through a boxcar door sometimes, just when it's going down, that makes the whole world look like it's burning. That's a sight. When the weather's good, I like riding the tops. It's risky as hell… no safety rail, but nothing blocking your view either. You can see so much. I like being able to see. And I like the moon.

Why the moon?

Feels like it's keeping me company, I guess.

What are some other things?

Catching fish bare-handed, that's a good one. A bottle of wine on a cold night. Making women smile. I have always liked making women smile.

If there was one thing you couldn't do without, what would it be?

Besides eating, you mean? That's simple. Trains. I wouldn't be anything without them.

You'd still be you.

I'd still be alive maybe, but without the freights I'd be some other guy. It's like the animals they keep in zoos. Wild animals they call them, but that's a lot of crap. They stopped being wild as soon as they went into a cage. They're still alive, but they aren't what they'd like to be.

And more than anything, you'd like to be who you are.

Yeah... yeah, I would. Without the freights that wouldn't be possible.

Are the freights like a drug for you?

Not like a drug, but like sunlight. I could live without it, but who wants to live in the dark.

Why don't more people ride?

Why don't more people do any one thing? Hell, I like trains, and I like riding them, but I couldn't work for a railroad no matter what they paid me. Some guys though, they'd give anything to pull track time for a paycheck.

What's the difference?

Riding free would ruin it for them. Getting paid would ruin it for me.

Chapter Fourteen

But I'll shoulder my pack in the morning, boys
And I'm going because I must
For it's so-long to all when you answer the call
Of the wanderlust.

Robert Service

The Amtrak for Chicago was an hour late pulling in. Lynden and The Duke watched it from their hiding place. Suddenly it was clear what they had to do.

"Frisco, you game for one more ride?"

"Could Short Arm catch a streamline?"

"Not with one arm, he couldn't."

"Could I?"

"Damn rights."

They snuck out and hid behind a backhoe parked near the mainline tracks. From there the whole loading platform was illuminated before them.

"We ain't got but one chance, and that's when she's just pullin out of the station. Move too quick and we'll get busted for sure. Wait too long, and we'll get our arms ripped off trying to grab her. Understand?"

He did understand—not just the old hobo's warning, but everything behind it. The Duke, the last Profesh, was about to catch the fastest, hardest, most dangerous thing on rails. Short Arm no longer mattered. Nothing mattered but that Amtrak for Chicago.

Lynden stared at his friend. Suddenly he was seeing more than just one old man. He was seeing Step-Down-

Johnny, Hubbard, Trainer Bill—all the fading knights of the road, all waiting to run for this final train, this final ride across the great American night.

The Duke talked quietly in their hiding place, of bulls and blinds, and of holding down streamliners on every road in the country. "You probably never heard of a *blind*. It was a space at the end of the old mail cars, a cozy little outside nook where nobody on the train—like a conductor—could see you.

"These new streamliners ain't got real blinds, not like the old ones, but where the cars couple together is almost as good. There's usually a little wooden platform, no bigger'n a stair step, to stand on. A guy that knows what he's doin can catch out there and ride between the cars, as long as he don't get seen. They won't usually stop a freight to throw off a hobo, but they'll sure as hell stop a streamliner.

"Gettin on's the easy part. It's stayin on that's hard. You can't ride too long on that platform... old timers called it *the death woods.* Fall asleep standin there, and you grease the tracks for sure."

Lynden was aware, as he listened, that everything around him—everything he could see, and hear, and feel—was growing sharper, crisper, as if the blurry focus of all that had come before was drawing down to the perfect clarity of these few moments, these sensations. A voice speaking truths to keep him alive. A night suspended from all reality except what was before his eyes. The train.

"If we're good enough, we can snag one of those blinds, then deck her... climb up and ride the tops. I seen guys killed tryin it. Seen em throwed off and scraped off. Even saw a guy freeze up there once. You deck a streamliner, Frisco, there's nothin you can't ride.

"We'll shoot for the first blind. The second will do, or the third maybe. After that she's got too much speed.

Don't worry about passengers seein you. Train windows are tinted, and with the lights on inside nobody can see out worth a damn. Daylight's a different story, but we'll worry about that in the morning."

"You think we'll stay on it that long?"

"Yeah... if we're on it at all."

The Amtrak's musical horn sang out, its tracer light flashed on.

It began to move.

This train didn't ease forward like a freight, it blasted forward. The Duke leapt out to meet it, then stopped and pointed. Next to the first blind a door was open. A conductor lingered there, gazing out into the night. They watched him go by.

The second blind was clear.

They ran.

Unseeing eyes stared through tinted windows; unseeing passengers eased back in reclining seats.

In the dining car, dinner was still being served on white linen. Drinks flowed freely in the club car.

And outside, at the second blind, two men were risking everything—not just their lives in the moment, but the legacy of a brotherhood whose freedom knew no limits, and the faint hope that such freedom would not be lost forever—for the honor of a ride.

It was a fast catch, frantic, and at the same time beautiful. Desperately they threw themselves at the train, no thoughts of danger or dying. No thought of anything but getting on. As a man they hit the blind, as a man they jumped.

Clinging to thin steel they were whisked away.

* * *

All is darkness, then suddenly a westbound streamliner roars by on the next track. Lights from its cars flash out pictures of the two men. Flash: hanging by one hand,

Lynden slipping. The Duke yelling. Flash: the old hobo springs like an acrobat as he scales the end of the car. Flash: he is out of sight, but not gone. He's on top reaching down for Lynden.

Flash: the blind is empty.

The westbound passes.

Two hobos make their catch.

Chapter Fifteen

Outside I heard the thunder come and go
And glimpsed the golden squares of passing trains,
Or felt the cumbrous freight train rambling slow;
And yet that life was sweet for all its pains.
                                            Harry Kemp

Lying side by side, cleaving to the train's slick top and to each other, they sped away from the city. Wind and diesel fumes sailed over their backs. An electrical storm out of the south erupted overhead, sending bolts of brilliant lightning and curtains of rain tearing through the night sky. Plunging into a tunnel of dense forest, a lightning flash revealed every tree, then seemed to fragment into multitudes of fireflies blinking and darting in living light-waves that glittered through the woodland. At a crossing the train's horn rang out, and a sparkling bioluminescent sea radiated in every direction.

In one hand Lynden clutched a thin steel railing, in the other he clutched The Duke. An hour passed, or two hours, or maybe only minutes. *You're wet and tired, but it's all right—just hang on.* His hand cramped, his body shivered. *Just hang on.*

His head nodded, then snapped up. *I could sleep. I could sleep, no problem. Except I'd fall, and I'd drag The Duke down with me. Don't sleep!*

Noises faded.

"Wake up," The Duke shouted. "Train's slowing down. I think a station's coming."

"God, I was asleep."

"Yeah, and it's my turn next. But first we gotta get past this station."

"What do we do?"

"If we're lucky, we don't get caught." He moved his head close to Lynden's. "We're too damn good to get caught!" he yelled.

In his voice Lynden detected no trace of the dejected old man from Denver; in his face, even in the darkness, he discerned no hint of that defeat.

Instead, what he heard, what he saw, was joy.

As the depot's brightly lit platform appeared, they slid to the train's dark side. At the last moment they swung out and dropped off into the darkness. Lynden hit the ground wrong, pitched forward, and landed on his face. A few yards away from him The Duke was sitting in the dirt rubbing his shoulder.

"You okay?"

"Ain't sure. Give me a second."

"What did we do wrong?"

The Duke got to his feet. "We fell on our butts." He hurried over and gave Lynden a hand up. "But I ain't through yet. How about you?"

"*Hell* no."

They crept close to the train shed, crouched, and waited.

In a few minutes a strange quiet blanketed the train and the platform. Without any effort to conceal himself The Duke stood up and ran. Lynden sprinted at his side. Together they flashed into the halo of platform lights, streaked past a startled baggage handler, and hit the train running as it began to move.

Through the night they rode, sliding off, sprinting, struggling to get themselves and their bags back on—at Marcelline, La Plata, Fort Madison, a handful of other stops—towns and counties disappearing beneath the streamliner's hungry wheels.

Though Lynden didn't sleep again, his body cried out for it. He let The Duke collapse each time they clambered back onboard, clutching the hobo's thin jacket to keep him from sliding off.

The tracer light from a passing freight revealed his companion's face. Lynden had seen it frightened at Pig Hollow and beaten in Denver. Here, exhausted and asleep, the expression on the old Profesh's face surrendered to simple, satisfied peace.

* * *

"Station coming." Just after dawn, their train slowed again. Lynden shook The Duke to life. "Galesburg... I think."

"Galesburg?" The Duke raised his head and twisted painfully. "Yeah, we gotta ditch. Ain't no riding streamline when the sun's up. If we get seen, we'll get busted for sure."

"I don't want it to stop," Lynden said, and knew it sounded crazy. "This ride... I don't want it to end. Not ever."

"Of course, you don't," The Duke looked him in the eye. "I seen it last night. You've got the bug." When the old man straightened his back, his face went white with pain. "I don't want it to stop either, Frisco. I never want it to stop... never have. But I'm spent. If it wasn't for you, I'd have rolled off this sucker hours ago, and been glad for it. You're gonna have to help me... I'm too damn stiff to move."

Lynden stood on the roof of the rocking car and looked toward the station. "I'll slide you over." Taking the old man's hand, he eased him down into the blind.

"Let's ride her in if we can," The Duke shouted. "I ain't up to runnin."

Lynden shook his head. "People on the platform. We gotta ditch or they'll see us."

They watched as the station drew near. Lynden

dropped down first, almost falling again. The Duke followed, stumbled, but Lynden caught him.

"Just a few more yards." Lynden looped his arm under The Duke's shoulders. They ducked behind some boxcars, skirted the station house, then hurried as best they could across a parking lot and out onto the street.

It was a long while before The Duke could speak. He sat on the curb sucking air, wincing at each breath.

"We gotta talk, Frisco."

Lynden waited patiently beside him.

"Unless I keep outrunning him, like last night, Short Arm's gonna find me." He stated it as a simple fact. "And I ain't built for speed anymore. Drag freights, bull locals, sure... but my days on the blinds are done."

"What if I stay with you?" Lynden heard himself say it, words that no one had ever said to him, and an offer he had never made to anyone before. "We could stay ahead of him. Didn't we just snag a streamliner?"

"Sure, but there's no *we* in this deal."

"I don't follow."

"Look around." The old man cast his gaze out towards the tracks. "I hardly recognize the world these rails run through nowadays. This life ain't for you. Hell, it ain't even for me anymore, only it's all I know."

"That's right, you *do* know it. Better than anyone. Listen... I don't understand how it happened, but I've changed out here. I've spent my whole life trying to make a place for myself, one where nobody could let me down or leave me behind. Last night I found it up on the roof of that train. With you." He let the words, and what they meant, linger between them. "Right here is exactly where I'm supposed to be."

The Duke gazed at him, a new appreciation in his eyes, and a thousand-mile stare. "I'm sorry," he said, not unkindly—he could see ahead what Lynden could not, "but the *here* you think you're lookin for don't exist anymore. There's damn few open boxcars now, soon there won't be any. Remember that hotshot container train we missed in Grand Junction… all closed up and goin to beat hell? That's the future, and there ain't no room for a hobo in it. Bulls already got cameras watching the big yards, before long, it will be all of em. And most towns won't abide a jungle these days, even a good one. It's only gonna get worse."

"But look at what we just did… what we've been doing since Roseville. Sure, things have changed since the old days, but it's still the life."

"*My* life, Frisco… not yours. And it rolled out from under me when I wasn't lookin, like somebody forgot to set the brake. All this stuff we been doin since we met up? We ain't been ridin trains, we been ridin shadows of what was."

"How can you say that?"

"Cause I knew it when it could *be* a life. I wish I could give you that. Twenty years ago, ten even, this might have been the game for you. I'm guessin that's what you felt last night… what might have been. I'd have gladly shared the road with you in those days and been proud to call you Profesh. Hell, I am proud. But your future's somewheres else. Mine is too… what's left."

They sat in long silence, side-by-side there on the curb, the truth in the old man's words holding them immobile, each for his own reasons. Both had arrived at an ending, with no idea what came next.

"Looks like I've got to quit my wanderin ways," The Duke said finally, speaking words he never thought he'd say. "If I don't stay off the rails Short Arm'll catch me sure."

"That's the only way to stay clear of him?"

"Yeah. And even then, there's no guarantees. He's a crafty son-of-a-bitch."

"How about this," Lynden spoke from his heart, bypassing his head entirely. "Let's buy Greyhound tickets and head back to California. My apartment's just sitting empty. You could bunk with me for a while... as long as you wanted."

The Duke considered for a moment, then shook his head. "I've never had a finer offer. But you've got your own life to lead. Seems to me it's time you got started."

"Past time," Lynden acknowledged the truth of it, "but there's no reason you can't come along."

"In case you ain't noticed," The Duke raised an eyebrow, and with it a knowing smile, "I ain't the come-along type. Even if I was, you didn't do all this to find a tramp. You came out here to get rid of one."

"And you think I have?"

"I think you can... if you give yourself a chance. Maybe find some little computer gal and just cut loose," he said. "One time's all it'll take."

Lynden blushed in spite of himself, in spite of what they had been through together. "What about you?"

The Duke got slowly to his feet. "I might be gettin too old to ride, but I ain't too old to work. I'll find something."

"Where?"

"Who knows? Down south maybe. Virginia's where I'm from, down in the Cumberland Valley there. I'll bet you didn't know that."

"No... I didn't." Lynden's voice cracked, surprising him. "I hardly know a thing about you... not really." He brushed a grimy hand across his eyes.

The old man held his young companion's gaze.

"You know everything that matters, Frisco. At least everything that matters to me."

Track #15
Throw the guts — One has given all he has

What about things that you can't do?

What things?

You tell me.

There's nothing I can't do. Nothing I want, anyway.

Nothing? You never came up against a train that was too fast, a fence that was too tall?

Sure, but that doesn't mean much. You can always walk around a fence. You can always wait for another train.

But what if you couldn't?

I don't get what you're driving at.

What's the one thing you've wanted to do most in your life?

Ride. Just ride.

And if you couldn't?

I don't know.

Would you do something else? Would you try to change?

Change what? The stuff I'm made of? How am I supposed to do that?

Other people have done it.

Fine, go talk to them.

Painters lose their eyesight, runners lose their legs. They change, they adapt.

Bullshit. They're still painting, they're still running, you just can't see them doing it.

They can still imagine, you mean. But it's only in their minds.

Only? Anybody can move their legs, but if their mind

isn't hungry for running it doesn't mean crap. If they *have* that hunger, then they're always running, legs or not.

People can't change their dreams then?

You've got it backwards. It's our dreams that change us... and they don't ask our permission.

So, we're slaves to our dreams?

Yeah, if we're lucky enough to have dreams at all.

Is that luck, or is it a curse?

Both maybe. Sounds more like a question for a philosopher than a hobo.

Fair enough. Here's a question for a hobo. If tomorrow you couldn't ride trains anymore, what then?

But I can.

Pretend.

What... that I can't ride trains? Okay. If tomorrow I couldn't ride trains any more... then I'd ride them anyway.

Chapter Sixteen

In my extensive travels,
To the corners of the earth,
I have learned to analyze a man,
His failings and his worth.

John S. Hoare, Jr.

"Will you let me buy you a bus ticket?" Since they met, whenever they needed something Lynden had offered to do the buying without hesitation. He didn't know what The Duke did for money, or if he even had any. Like in a jungle, he figured the old man would share when and if the need arose. "I imagine it's a long walk to the Cumberland Valley."

"Longer on an empty stomach," said The Duke, patting his own to make the point. "You've been damn generous with your dough, Frisco, and if I ain't said so before, I appreciate it. Must be good money in those computers. I'd be obliged for help with that ticket, but what do you say I stake us to some breakfast first... if there's time before The Grey Dog rolls?"

"You're buying?" Lynden feigned surprise. "If I wasn't hungry before, I am now."

* * *

The ticket counter at the Greyhound Bus station wasn't open yet, but the Shamrock Bar and Grill across the street had a *Come On In* sign hanging askew in the tinted-glass front door. A row of battered pick-up trucks with shabby trailers was lined up out front.

"Carny joints," The Duke observed, indicating them with a nod. "Wonder if they're comin or goin?"

The Shamrock smelled strongly of cigarettes and faintly of stale beer. A row of booths ran down one side, a long bar with a dozen customers hunched over morning drinks ran down the other. All but the two back booths were empty. "Carnies." The Duke motioned and said something else, but it never reached Lynden for all the shouting from the carnival crew.

They ordered breakfast. When the waitress left, a clumsy silence crowded in between them. Lynden found himself wishing that the bus station had been open.

"Anxious to get movin, aren't you?" The Duke was watching him. "I'm the same damn way. Once I make up my mind to go—and it usually don't take much makin—I can't wait to get to it."

"I know," Lynden was looking within himself as he spoke. "I don't want to leave... you, but I want to leave. That's not how my mind usually works."

"It's cause your mind ain't a computer, Frisco."

"Yeah, I'm starting to figure that out."

The silence again, less clumsy now.

Lynden let his thoughts drift. He'd hardly been gone more than a week, yet his old life seemed impossibly distant. How would he go about piecing it back together? Before leaving Data Dynamics he'd noticed a girl in shipping. Maybe he imagined it, but she had seemed to notice him back. "Find some little computer gal," The Duke had said, "and cut loose."

Maybe her. Maybe he'd give her a call.

The Duke broke his concentration. "I'll be right back. Gotta wash up before the chow comes." Lynden nodded. He'd almost remembered her name.

The food came and he dove in, not waiting for his tablemate.

"Sorry I took so long." The Duke looked fresh when he returned, fresher than a wash-up in a restroom sink would account for. "I think I got us some good news."

"News?"

"You in a real big hurry to get home?"

Lynden thought about the girl in shipping. Karen? Or was it Colleen?

"No... not real big."

"Great." The Duke forked a clump of hash browns. "I just got us jobs!"

*　*　*

The Tri-State Expositions and Carnival consisted of six trailer joints, a handful of set-ups, and one liberally dented Airstream house-trailer. "We got two joints still hung-up at Mankato," Jerry explained. "Legal trouble, if you know what I mean." Jerry ran the glass pitch. His other job was breaking in the new men. Lynden, The Duke, and a wary dog called Slum were bouncing toward the fairgrounds in Jerry's Studebaker pick-up, listening to his version of how things worked.

"You're the new marks, so everybody's your boss." Smelling of weeks' old sweat, Jerry had the worst case of acne Lynden had ever seen, his face a minefield of burst or bursting craters. He poked at them as he talked or dug at the crops of blackheads sprouting in his ears.

"Tom's your first boss. You watch your PDQ's around him. Tom owns the joints." They'd met Tom back at The Shamrock. Big, pushing forty but trying to look younger, dirty blond hair limp to his shoulders, and a too-tight rock band tee shirt stretched over more belly than bicep. Tom was the only one of the crew who hadn't shaken their hands.

"If you want to know, Mike's the real boss of this show. He owns the privilege, and he used to own the joints. Tom beat him out of em playing stud in the gyp top down at winter quarters. Tom's my brother and Mike's my daddy. Only not really. Daddy just takes care of us, so that's what we call him. Sometimes if the rubes wanna get feisty with Tom or me... them thinkin we're Mike's kin can back em off, if you know what I mean."

Lynden understood perfectly.

Mike looked like the Devil. Black hair slicked back, mustache and sideburns sharpened to points, at least six foot six and switch blade thin. He had sharp cheek bones and sharp cowboy boots. "You'll do," was all he said when they were introduced, his voice part southern charm, part Satan.

"Them two joints in Mankato, that's Tom's doing," Jerry continued. "He's got Arkansas plates on the trailers, Florida plates on the trucks, and the two marks he's got driving have phony IDs out of Oklahoma. What's a cop gonna say when he sees all that? Tom ain't real smart.

"Then there's Old Dan. He ain't that old, but that's what we call him. Runs the best Cigarette Shoot I ever seen. He don't say nothin but Buffalo most of the time. I seen him work the tip all day for a quarter a shot, but soon as somebody gets their fur up, Old Dan just says Buffalo and nothing else. Ain't nobody will mess with a crazy man, if you know what I mean."

There was Charlie Ben who ran the Pop-Toss. His rotten teeth moved when he talked. The Covelo sisters had the Grab-Joint. "That's carny talk for refreshment stand," Jerry explained. "The Covelos are pushing seventy, but up till ten years ago they had a Geek Show with the Kuschner Brothers Big Top. They'd still be geekin, only the crowd didn't like it when two old ladies started eating live frogs and spiders and stuff. A geek's gotta be young... that's show business, ain't it?

"And there's Clara... Tom's girl. Or leastways he thinks so. She used to hook a little on the side, but Tom don't like nobody knowing that. Tom don't like nothin."

Clara was twenty years old, if that. Short, tight, well formed in places men like—a body built to be admired. Back at The Shamrock she'd seen Lynden watching her. "My name's Clara." She pulled her hair back into a ponytail, appraising him as she effortlessly snapped a rubber band around it. "Looks like you're on."

"My friend and I are. Frisco's my name. Pleased to meet you."

"Yeah, me too." She reached out and shook his hand. He hadn't expected that, or the ease with which she did it.

Parked on the shoulder up ahead was a battered Lincoln Continental with Tri-State stenciled across the trunk. Mike was standing on the roof.

"Don't none of us read much," Jerry explained, taking the exit Mike waved him toward. "Daddy goes ahead and points so we know where to turn. One time we were headed for Des Moines, and he was standing up on some overpass, but I missed him. Got halfway to Kansas City before he caught me."

In a few minutes the Lincoln roared past and turned onto a dirt road. They followed it into the fairgrounds, snaking past rodeo bleachers and tent pavilions and ranks of shiny new farm equipment staged for review. Pick-up trucks and horse trailers were everywhere, and pens full of 4-H kids grooming animals several times their size.

A serious man wearing a broad brimmed white Stetson and an impatient expression pulled a dusty golf cart up to Mike's car. "That'll be Mr. Director," Jerry snickered, "come to dicker on the privilege... that's what we gotta pay to play this crummy fair. Bastard will skim his cut right off the top, but any trouble starts... he'll be the first to run us outta town, if you know what I mean."

The midway was a grassy clearing bordered by tall elms. "When we're done, you ain't gonna know this place."

Jerry swung his trailer into position. "You guys ever worked carny before?"

"I worked em before you were born," The Duke answered, "and Frisco knows the ropes... he can do anything."

"We'll see." Jerry eyed them.

Mike, Tom, and Clara were nowhere to be seen, so Jerry ran things, directing them all morning as the empty field was gradually transformed. "You *have* worked carny before," he said to The Duke at one point. Then he looked at Lynden and shook his head.

It wasn't until lunch break that the friends had a chance to talk alone. "Sorry I sprung it on you like that." The Duke made sure no one else could hear. "But Tom wouldn't hire just me. Probably figured I was too old. You don't mind, do you?"

"No... I don't mind." Lynden shrugged, remembering Clara's handshake and forgetting his eagerness to be on his way. "How long will you need me to stay?"

"A couple a days... three at most. By that time, I oughta be in good with em. Jerry ain't so bad... leastways I've known worse. And Mike seems right enough. Tom... he could be trouble. But a lot less trouble than Short Arm."

"Didn't these carnies used to travel by train?"

"Yeah, until they traded rails for rubber tires. Who knows? Maybe I could do the same."

Jerry was heading toward them. "How about Clara?" Lynden asked, keeping his voice low. "You think what Jerry said was true?"

"About her hooking, you mean?"

"Yeah."

"I don't know. What do you think?"

Lynden shrugged his shoulders. He didn't know exactly what he was thinking, only that he couldn't stop thinking it.

* * *

The trailer joints were all in place ready to be stocked. Next came the set-ups—flimsy corrals of rope, wood, and canvas to contain the Glass Pitch, Pop Toss, Hoop Throw, and a few other games. Jerry saved the Glass Pitch for last.

"Bring them crates over here... and don't you dare drop em!" Once the crates were opened and in position, Jerry went to work, Slum watched, as if he were helping, wagging his tail each time a new item was placed. A mountain of green, orange, and pale blue glassware began to take shape. Jerry had special ways of doing it, special places for everything. Wide bowls with shallow lips perched near the top, deep flat-bottomed goblets anchored the bottom. He balanced tiers of tinted glass on top of one another, never leaving much flat surface showing or a niche where a dime might lodge.

When he was done, Lynden and The Duke applauded at his unlikely artistry.

"You all go and clean up your joints. I'm gonna take me a nap."

"Hold on a minute." The Duke stopped him. "What's our percentage?"

"Twenty-five for you, twenty-five for Tom, and fifty for Daddy... cause he owns the privilege. Daddy don't mind if you palm some but take too much and he'll catch you sure. One way or another Daddy takes care of everybody, if you know what I mean."

* * *

Jerry had assigned them to run side-by-side games in an ancient wooden trailer joint. They helped him swing open the sagging side wall and prop it into place, releasing a wave of stifling, stagnant air, and revealing a chaos of torn cardboard boxes and tattered stuffed animals. "This used to belong to Barnham," he said, offering no proof.

"It'll probably be worth somethin someday, if it don't rattle apart goin down the road. New marks always start here. Most of em finish here. We'll see about you two."

When Jerry left, Lynden's carny education began.

"First off, you know that all these games are crooked."

"I've had my suspicions, but…"

"But nothin. Every one of them is fixed, right down to the floorboards. Your bigger shows need to run straight these days… cause the law's watching. A jerkwater outfit like this? They wouldn't know how *not* to cheat."

As they were cleaning out the dart joint and blowing up balloons, The Duke explained. "There's numbers from one to twenty, sposed to be pinned at random behind all these balloons on the dartboard. Like the sign there says, pop a balloon with thirteen or higher behind it, win a big prize. Only, there ain't but one number anywhere in this joint that's thirteen or higher, and since Jerry says I'll be runnin this joint, that'll stay right here in my shirt pocket. If the law comes along or I want to stir up the crowd, next time somebody pops a balloon I'll swap numbers on the sly… instant winner."

"It's that simple?"

"Most cheats are. Folks ain't usually playin to win the big prize anyway… they could just buy one if they really wanted it. They're playing for a *chance* to win. Work the crowd right, shout em up good, and they'll go away happy. You watch."

"That's awful."

"Yeah… maybe." The Duke didn't seem to disagree. "If your conscience is bothering you, that Bumper Car you're gonna run tomorrow ain't fixed… exactly. The marks push a little car down the track, it bounces back, and wherever it stops, that's their prize. Land on the right square and they win a big one. Land on all those other squares and they get one of these slum prizes." The Duke reached his hand into a bag full of cheap rubber lizards. "That game isn't crooked, but it takes a miracle to hit the right square. Is that any better than cheating?"

"The Duck-Dip, String-Pull, Cigarette-Shoot?" Lynden looked around the midway at the games being assembled. "All of them?"

The Duke nodded. "Take Jerry's Glass Pitch. Even if they do get a dime to stick, which ain't likely, the mark wins an ashtray that cost these carnies a nickel. People like to win, sure. What carnies know and marks don't... is that *what* they win doesn't much matter. Every time they play, they're gonna win a slum prize. Every time they try again, it's our job to help em believe they got a shot at winning the big one. Just like Jerry said, it's *show business*."

* * *

For a dollar fifty, the Ladies Auxiliary served dinner—corn bread, ham, hashed potatoes, fresh green beans, and all the coffee you could drink—in the fairground's cook shack, a long, screened building with Formica top tables and a painted concrete floor. Farmers, 4-H'ers, and carnies taking a break from setup filled the place.

"It's probably best we don't say much just yet," The Duke cautioned before they entered. "Folks would always rather talk than listen, so all we need to do is give em a chance. Once they've told us all about themselves, they'll feel like they know us, if you—"

"—know what I mean?" Lynden's Jerry imitation was spot on. "You bet."

They sat with the other carnies. Immediately Tom singled them out.

"You said you'd worked carny before. Where?"

"West." The Duke looked up from his plate. "Oregon, California. You ever get out that way?"

"Hell, no," Tom blustered. "That country's full of perverts."

The two new hires nodded, and Tom's mouth took off. He had big plans, big ideas that had nothing to do with this gypo outfit. He was going to open a real business, a "Bookade" he called it, proud of the name he had made up on his own.

"I know a guy up in Chicago that's got one something like it. Bastard's so rich he could buy these carnies by the dozen. You know what he pays for books? Buck, buck-and-a-half. You know what he sells them for? Ten, fifteen. I even saw one from Denmark that sold for twenty dollars. The real money's in the movies, though. Get about twenty of those projector booths, two movies each, and at two-bits for ninety seconds, that's what I'm talking about. No perverts though. Nothing will ruin a dirty bookstore quicker. Who's gonna spend a quarter with some pervert watching him?"

Tom didn't stop until the cook shack was nearly empty "I got whiskey in my trailer," he said finally. "It ain't worth wasting on these carnies. Come on, let's have a belt."

When they got up to leave, Jerry, who had been sitting silently next to them the whole time, got up, too. Tom glared him back down.

A field in back of the main pavilion had sprouted a small city of house-trailers and campers. Dogs barked and pulled at their ropes, radios blared, wash hung on makeshift lines. Tom's Airstream was one of the oldest rigs, windows blocked with cardboard, sides dented and scarred. It rocked and groaned under Tom's weight as he mounted the sagging metal stair.

There was a small dark living room, a smaller kitchen area, and a few paces down the narrow hall, a bedroom with one bare light bulb and a large bed stretching wall-to-wall. In the middle of the bed, a book open on her lap, sat Clara.

"This here's ten-dollar whiskey," Tom announced,

reaching into the one small closet and pulling out a pint bottle. Clara raised her large brown eyes from her book, saw who was there, and self-consciously moved up to the head of the bed.

No one but Lynden noticed her movement.

Tom held up the bottle and took a long, noisy gulp, making sure they were all watching. "Damn that's good!" He wiped his mouth. "You better appreciate good liquor. I ain't wasting this."

"Nothin better than a good drink of whiskey." The Duke took the bottle and raised it to his lips. One quick nip and he handed it back. "Mighty good. Mighty damn good."

"You too, Frisco. Don't drain it."

Lynden took the bottle. He'd never held one before and was surprised at how light it felt in his hand. As he raised it to his lips, Tom warned, "Just one pull."

Clara was watching. Lynden sensed her gaze on him.

He tilted the bottle, felt the fire run straight down his throat and into his eyes. "Good," he exhaled. "Thanks."

Tom snatched the bottle, took another quick shot to establish ownership, then set it in the closet. When his hand came back, it was not empty.

"This here's my protection." He raised a short-nosed revolver above his head. "I gave twenty-five bucks for it up in De Kalb. Box of shells, too. Either of you know about guns?"

"I've handled them," The Duke said. "That there's a real beauty. Twenty-five bucks? Hell, that's a fifty-dollar piece, at least."

"You hear?" Tom turned on Clara. "Fifty bucks, he says!" Clara didn't even look up at him.

The Duke listened as Tom began to brag about the gun, and how he'd gotten the best of the seller. Lynden pretended to follow the conversation, but his focus was on the girl. She kept her bare feet tucked close under, reading

her book as if no one else was there. Each time he looked at her she became prettier.

He tried not to avert his eyes—but *not* to get caught staring—hopeful that she would look up again.

She didn't.

She also didn't turn a single page.

* * *

When they got back to the joints, Jerry was waiting.

"You all been over to Tom's trailer, I guess."

"Yes sir, that we have."

"He give you some of that cheap whiskey out of the closet?"

The Duke took a chance. "Sure did. Me and Frisco were just saying how that's the worst drink of whiskey we ever had. You didn't miss much."

Jerry grinned. "Tom don't know it, but I been in that closet lots of times. His whiskey's so cheap it's hardly worth stealing. Hey, either of you guys like a smoke?" He pulled papers and tobacco from his shirt pocket.

"Thanks, but I gave it up," said The Duke as Lynden shook his head. "What about that pistol?"

"His pop gun?" Jerry effortlessly rolled a cigarette, a process he had obviously practiced to perfection, and lit it. "Yeah, he's pretty proud of that, ain't he."

"He ever use it on anybody?"

"Tom!" He picked a piece of tobacco off his tongue, took another drag. "That guy's so yellow he wouldn't shoot a can for fear it'd shoot him back. Tom's all wind." He exhaled, squinted at them through the smoke, and twisted his nose. "Kind of a foul smellin wind, if you know what I mean."

"What's Clara think of him?" Lynden asked, ignoring a warning glance from The Duke.

"She don't like him no better than I do." The answer came too quickly for casual conversation. "Mike and her daddy used to work big carny in the old days. Her daddy died a couple of years back, so Clara come in with us. She's done high school... the whole shot. That girl doesn't miss a lick, no matter what Tom says. He talks tough, but he's more scared of her than anybody."

"They married?"

"Are you kidding?" Jerry spat the words. "They rode the carousel, sure, but when it gets down to signing papers, she ain't married and she ain't gonna be."

"Why does she stay with him, then?"

"You'd have to ask her that... wouldn't you." Jerry crushed out the cigarette. "I'm hitting the sack. We start at seven."

He left them without saying goodnight.

"I think you touched a tender spot."

"About Clara? You mean he and Clara...?"

"I figure he'd like it that way. And I figure you would too... if you got the chance."

"You saw me watching her?"

"And I saw her watchin you. I'd stay out of it, Frisco. No matter how much they might trash-talk each other, these carnies stick together. You get too friendly with Clara and they'll come down on you for sure... and on me."

"Have you forgotten who you're talking to?" Lynden knew he didn't need to mention the incident with Millie. "I wouldn't screw things up for you, even if I thought I could."

"Don't be makin promises you can't keep."

"That's one promise I can't seem to break." A gust of wind rattled the elms and they stopped to listen. His attraction to Clara, unanticipated but not unwelcome, was becoming stronger than his fear. "If trouble did start, over Clara I mean, what do you think Tom would do?"

"Tom's a crude, blow-hard, son-of-a-bitch, and probably as big a coward as I've ever seen. But you mess with his girl," The Duke met his eyes, "he'll shoot you."

Track #16
Square — To abandon the road.

What do you think of compromise?

It's giving up something to get something, just like blackmail.

How do you mean?

Say a guy doesn't like his boss, or his job, or the people he works with. What he ought to do is quit and look for a better deal somewhere else. But he's making good money at this job, and he's got a wife and a couple of young ones, and a mortgage. So, what's he do? He takes the money, and he puts up with the crap.

Is that bad?

Not just bad... it's habit-forming. The first couple of years that guy might be okay, because he knows he doesn't like it. But what happens if he's there for ten or fifteen maybe, and they give him a promotion and his own office, and put him on the expense account? You know what happens... he starts telling himself that he *does* like it.

Couldn't that be true?

Could be. But what if it isn't? And what if he knows it isn't?

Is a compromise like that ever worth it?

Maybe. It depends on what you're giving up, and what you're getting. I've seen guys give up their lives for something or someone they believed in. That's the biggest compromise there is.

Isn't that refusing to compromise?

Refusing to compromise is saying, "Me first, and screw the rest."

Then you think compromise is good?

I didn't say that. Dying is never good. Lying to yourself is never good. But everything has a price. Friendship, security, loyalty, they'll all cost you. And freedom? That one costs the most. What's a guy willing to pay for his freedom? Does he even know what his freedom is? It's not the same for everybody.

No?

Rattling around on freights all your life doesn't make you free, any more than sitting at a desk makes you a prisoner. Every guy makes himself free the best way he can, or he puts himself in a cage. It's up to him.

With or without compromises?

That's up to him, too. We all get what we pay for. If it's freedom we're buying... then we better be willing to pay the price.

You know a lot about compromises.

I know what my freedom is. I also know what it cost me.

Chapter Seventeen

But there's one thing that we're loving more
than money, grub, or booze
Or even decent folks what speaks us fair,
And that's the grand old privilege to chuck
our luck and choose,
Any road at any time for anywhere.

Unknown

By ten o'clock next morning all the joints were stocked, cleaned, and ready. Ride jockeys were firing up their huge metal monsters, pitchmen were trying their spiels on invisible marks. Lynden, alone in his Bumper Car joint, was fighting a mild case of stage fright.

"Loosen up," Jerry ordered, moving from game to game passing out change belts.

"I'm loose."

"Sure you are." Jerry shook his head. "Since you obviously ain't done this before—in spite of what your buddy let on—here's how you make change. Keep six bits in your hand all the time. When a mark gives you a dollar bill, slip him that six bits quick as you can. That makes them feel like they ain't really spending it, and sometimes they'll slip you a five or a ten by mistake."

"And if they do... I'm supposed to keep it?"

"I hope to shout. Where you been all your life?"

"You wouldn't believe me."

A thin plywood wall separated Lynden's bumper car from The Duke's Balloon Game. As soon as Jerry was gone,

The Duke stuck his head around. "You figure he knows?"

"What, that I'm a rookie? I figure everybody knows."

"Yeah, you're probably right." The last of Lynden's confidence vanished and it must have been written all over his face because The Duke continued, "Listen, Frisco, do your job, make them some money, and that's all they're gonna care about. This is strictly a percentage deal... they get three quarters to your one. That ain't bad, unless you don't get any."

"Got it."

"Watch the other guys, listen up, and work the crowd. I'll be right here if you need me." The Duke's head slipped back out of sight.

Then, from his end of the trailer, the old man's voice rang out, "Quarter to play, quarter to win! A winner every time here at the Balloon Game!"

People gathered around.

All the other games were pulling crowds. Charlie Ben was juggling plastic rings at the Pop Toss. Jerry hovered protectively over his glass mountain. Old Dan's raspy monotone barked out from the Cigarette Shoot. Next to him Clara stood behind her galvanized pond, a cluster of little kids drawn to the glint and the guilelessness of her smile—and to the flotilla of bright, yellow, plastic ducklings bobbing innocently.

Lynden's was the only joint still empty.

He cleared his throat, and, louder than he meant to, shouted, "Quarter to play, quarter to win." But it was barely loud enough to be heard over the midway noise. "A winner every time here at the Bumper Car!" A moment later a boy in overalls leaned on the elbow board.

"How do you play, mister?" The boy eyed the race car and the stuffed animals on the shelves.

"Quarter to play, quarter to win," Lynden repeated.

The boy just stared.

"Push the car against the bumper down there." Lynden gave the car a shove. "It bounces back and wherever it stops, that's your prize. It's easy."

"How much does it cost, mister?"

"Quarter to play, quarter to win, young fella."

The boy handed over a tightly wadded dollar bill, and Lynden handed back three moist quarters.

"Give her a push!"

The car raced forward, bounced, and sailed back. It stopped on a square full of contorted rubber snakes. "We have a winner here!" Lynden shouted, presenting the boy with his slum prize.

The boy looked at it, then looked at Lynden. "Thanks, mister." He walked off with the new toy clutched tightly in his hand.

How many people came by in the next fourteen hours, how many quarters he took, and how many rubber snakes he gave away, Lynden didn't know. Standing in the old wooden trailer, he was elevated a few feet above the throng, like standing on the bank of a human river watching it flow past. But too many were passing.

"Tell em you just gave out a big prize." The Duke poked his head around the partition. "Make a big stink about it, like you're happy as hell and can't wait to do it again. That'll keep em comin."

"Ah, too bad," Lynden consoled a customer who'd just missed the winning spot. "Not ten minutes ago a little girl came close on her first turn, just like you. Darn if she didn't win the second time."

It worked. The mark made a second, a third, even a fourth try, hoping to match that little girl's luck.

Was it luck these people hungered after, he wondered? When they looked up past him, at the rows of ratty teddy bears and blow-up vinyl baseball bats, did they really *want* those things—junk they could have bought in a five-

209

and-dime—or was it letting themselves want the prize that mattered? The farmers and field hands, the kids with cotton candy, the housewives and husbands—their families huddled around them—hanging back at a safe distance to appear aloof if anyone was watching but coming close enough to taste the deliciously ridiculous desire, and feel the thrill that came with it.

A shot at winning the big one, The Duke had called it.

Maybe that's all any of us want, Lynden thought.

It's not the winning, it's the hope that we might.

And at his Bumper Car game, hope only cost a quarter.

* * *

It was afternoon when Tom came by. "You ain't palming, are you?"

"Want to search my pockets?" Lynden heard the attitude in his own voice and was glad it was there. Tom was an asshole.

When he was gone, The Duke poked his head around. "What's that all about?"

"Palming, I guess."

"Or about last night. Tom may be stupid. I don't figure he's blind."

Jerry came by to relieve them for lunch. "Pick up something from the Covelos, and tell em you're carny so they give you a deal."

Lynden took the first break, but instead of going for food he wandered toward the Duck Dip.

"I heard you working the tip—the crowd—like a real pro," Clara said. She had just given a big prize to a little girl, and Lynden watched her expertly slide the winning-numbered duck back into her apron, instead of into the pond with all the losers. "Not bad for your first day."

"You knew?"

"I'm pretty good at reading guys," she scanned him, "and I could tell right off that you aren't carny. I haven't figured out what you are yet, but I will."

"You just might." Lynden considered her in return. "About last night. I'm sorry we marched in on you like that."

"Don't be. I was sorry when you left." She leaned forward to whisper something, but drew back when she saw her boyfriend approach.

"What are you doing here?" Tom demanded and put his face close to Lynden's.

"He's looking for you," Clara answered. "The law's been snooping around his joint."

"Let him tell it!"

"Two deputies," Lynden lied. "They looked pretty curious. I thought you should know."

"I didn't see no deputies! Why didn't you tell Jerry?"

"Because you're the boss, honey," Clara broke in. "You want the help answering to Jerry instead of you?"

"I want this guy back in his joint!" Red-faced, Tom stormed away, unaware of the smile between his girlfriend and his newest hire.

* * *

The temperature inside Lynden's Bumper Car game had climbed into triple digits by late afternoon. Everything within the old wooden trailer—the sawdust-filled stuffed animals, the stained satin drapes, the sad hand-lettered signs promising *A Winner Every Time!*—seemed to be wilting along with the first-time carny barker. Smells of spilled beer, corn dogs, and livestock pens hung thickly over the straw-strewn fairgrounds, all of it layered in the dust of a world where the dirt might be hidden but was constantly disturbed. Daylight slipped into dusk, the heat lifted, and for a few minutes the midway was almost empty. Lynden felt his drenched shirt cooling. He stretched his back, caught his breath, and rested his voice.

Darkness fell.

Rides glittered and whirred.

The carny became a different planet when the sun went down. Teenage boys prowling for living prizes, older toughs as eager to win a fist fight as a stuffed toy. Ride jockeys cranked up the speed to crank up the screams.

The carnies pitched as if their day had just begun.

Lynden hustled, watched, and shouted as the hours streamed past. He tossed an occasional question to The Duke, and received a cross look from a prowling Tom.

And from Clara, a glance. More than one.

The whole day, hardly a single big prize had been won. When three sheriff's deputies strolled through just before midnight, every joint suddenly had a winner, except for Lynden's—the only game in the show that wasn't rigged.

* * *

When the midway finally closed, Lynden and The Duke bedded down on the floor of the Balloon Joint, but they were too tired to sleep.

"What do you think we made today?" Lynden asked quietly, lying on his back, staring at the dark ceiling and the faint outlines of the balloons and stuffed animals hanging above them.

"Twenty bucks each, twenty-five maybe. You did all right. If that computer business goes south... and you never know, it might," The Duke tried to sound serious, but couldn't keep the smile out of his voice, "you've got yourself a promising future as a carny. Fame and fortune could be yours!"

"Fame and fortune... and all the cotton candy I can eat." Lynden was finally easing toward sleep, drowsily enjoying the joke. "Sign me up."

Outside the joint they heard footsteps approaching. "Buffalo." It was Old Dan. He leaned against their trailer, they heard a bottle gurgling, then the footsteps faded.

"I saw you over at Clara's joint. She seems like a pretty

nice gal."

"Sure, I guess..." Lynden, fully awake again, knew that his attempt at disinterest fell flat.

"Tom didn't look so happy to see you two talkin."

"Like you said, Tom's a son-of-a-bitch."

"And Clara's his girl. You aren't forgettin that?"

Lynden didn't answer.

* * *

The Duke lay awake in the dim, musty joint, letting his thoughts drift and listening to the sound of Lynden's breathing deepen and slow as his young friend slipped into the perfect sleep of exhaustion. *Would he ever know such sleep again? Do the old ever know it?*

Working carny was simple enough, he thought, and hadn't changed much since he'd first tried his hand at it as a kid. If things didn't pan out with this bunch, there were plenty of gypo shows like it wandering around the country. He'd always be able to find a job. Hell, maybe he'd buy his own joint one day. He'd fix it up proper, keep the paint fresh and the prizes clean and classy. People would know, just from looking, that it was different, that *he* was different. If he ever crossed paths with Trainer Bill again, maybe Trainer could join up and give him a hand. So long as they went easy on the drink, and learned to leave the housewives alone, they'd do just fine.

The trick was to not screw up. A couple of months with this outfit and Short Arm wouldn't matter anymore. Yeah, the freights would be off limits, but if he worked steady and didn't blow it all, he could easily save three or four hundred bucks in no time. Enough to give a man options.

If he didn't screw up.

Which meant sucking up to Tom.

The Duke knew he could abide the bragging and the bullshit, jungles were full of it.

He knew he could keep his mouth shut if he had to. You

couldn't survive as Profesh without knowing when to pull your punches.

Survive? Is that what he'd spent his life trying to do? Just survive?

The Duke looked over at Lynden sleeping beside him, and as quickly as it had come, the carnival fantasy slipped away.

"Goodnight, Frisco."

He closed his eyes and soon was dreaming of a bright green Burlington Northern triple-header crossing the Columbia River Bridge between Portland and Vancouver.

It crossed that bridge, in exquisite detail, all night long.

* * *

Lynden woke at sunrise. The Duke was already gone. He stayed gone until just before opening time.

"Where the hell have you been?"

"Busy. I've got a deal cookin'."

Though the midway was twice as mobbed as the first day, Lynden noticed something going on at The Duke's joint. Several times Jerry whispered a quick word. Charlie Ben came by the booth, and Old Dan. Finally, Mike came, stayed a long time. He was smiling when he left.

Jerry came back when it was time for lunch but told Lynden to work through. "Let your buddy bring you something," he ordered, stepping into The Duke's booth before Lynden could protest.

"I need your money, Frisco." The Duke, in a hurry, was holding out his hand.

"Bring me a couple of hot dogs, and something cold to—"

"Forget lunch. I need *all* your money."

"What?"

"You gotta trust me. I'll explain later."

"That's all I've got left! Almost two hundred bucks!"

"Yeah, I know. It'll have to do."

"This is crazy." Lynden handed over the cash.

"You don't know the half of it." The Duke grinned. "If I get a chance, I'll grab you some eats, but I've got lots to do and not much time to do it." He was gone.

Tom rushed past the Bumper Car, and stopped at the Balloon Game, confronting Jerry. Lynden thought he looked madder than usual, or scared. Maybe both. "Where's the old man?"

Lynden couldn't see Jerry, but he could hear him. "I ain't his keeper."

"He's up to something, ain't he?"

"Maybe."

"Don't give me that! I know what he's planning, and I know he don't want me in because he heard about the joints. Well, you tell him *I'm in*. You got that?"

Lynden couldn't hear Jerry's reply, but heard Tom grunt, "All right then!" as he stomped away. Lynden glanced toward the Duck Dip, hoping to catch another look from Clara. Instead, one of the ancient Covelo sisters was running the game, strutting what stuff she had left, and wearing a tank top that revealed too much of it.

The Duke got back an hour later with two cold hot dogs and a Coke that was mostly ice melt. "Eat hearty, Frisco. Your money's at work."

Jerry leaned forward. "Tom knows... he's in. You got it all set?"

"That I do." The Duke gave a quick nod and a wink, but not to Jerry.

He was looking at Lynden.

* * *

It was twilight. Lynden looked up and saw Clara, back at her booth, watching him. She was in the middle of dipping ducks. He was making change.

They both stopped.

He thought he saw a question in her eyes.

Track #17

Hobo Fever — A passion for riding trains; or a malady for which travel is the only treatment, death the only cure.

Do you ever feel guilty about the life you have chosen?

Guilty, how? Have I done some things I wish I hadn't? Sure. Am I gonna do some more? Probably. I'm not a saint, I'm a hobo.

Do you ever feel guilty about *that*?

Should I? You think, because of the choices I've made, and the stuff that I *don't* have—home, family, a future beyond my next ride—that I owe somebody my guilt?

You see guilt as a debt?

I sure as hell don't see it as a gift, though we're always trying to give it to each other, aren't we? You're trying to give me some now. Of course it's a debt, and once you take it on you're paying interest forever. If I ain't got a real mortgage, why would I want that one?

If not a debt to somebody else, how about to yourself? Do you ever regret the path you've taken? Riding trains isn't just what you do, it's who you are, and who you want to be. But doesn't that intense wanting—to the exclusion of everything else—exact a toll?

Nobody rides for free, if that's what you mean. But I get what you're driving at, only you're on the wrong track. It ain't about guilt. Or if it ever was, that's so long ago that I can't remember.

If not guilt, then what?

I don't know the word for it. I can tell you that sometimes I *do* hate myself... for wanting this life so much. Surprised? Not the life, mind you... the urge to live it.

That's one powerful son-of-a-bitch. Powerful or not, a man can fight an urge. I never did. I followed it. I still do... every day.

Some people, maybe most, think more of themselves for *not* following their passion.

Sure, because it makes what they ended up doing seem like a sacrifice. And everybody knows that sacrifice is noble.

So, they should feel guilty for making a sacrifice?

Should they? No. Do they? You'd have to ask them. Maybe that's another reason I hate myself sometimes... because I stopped caring about their answers.

You prefer not knowing?

Prefer's got nothing to do with it. What I know—*all* I know—is who I am. That doesn't mean I always like myself... far from it. But I ain't gonna summon up a single seconds' worth of guilt wishing I was somebody else.

Chapter Eighteen

*My heart is warm with the friends I make
And better friends I'll not be knowing,
Yet there isn't a train I wouldn't take,
No matter where it's going*
Edna St. Vincent Millay

Lynden folded his arms and leaned against the Balloon Game, the midway empty and their joint buttoned-up for the night.

"All right, what's this about?"

"I don't suppose you've ever heard of—" The Duke began, but Jerry burst in and interrupted.

"You guys, give me your change belts," he said, excited. Then, to The Duke, "I'll be right back." As quickly as he had come, he hurried away.

"What the hell's going on?"

"—the gyp top," the old hobo continued. "You ever heard of it?"

"That's some kind of gambling, right?"

"Carny gambling. I've seen gyp tops big as a casino, and small as a deck of cards. Most every show's got em."

"And?"

"I'm playing in one tonight... with your dough. Fact of the matter is, I set it up."

Lynden considered him. "That was Hubbard's territory, wasn't it? You never mentioned being a gambler before. If you need money, I'll—"

"It ain't about the money. Look, Frisco... Short Arm

may be too much for me, but Tom's one bastard I *know* I can handle. Everybody's kissing his ass right now, but I'm fixing to make it smart a bit. When I'm through, he'll be the one kissin ass. Either that, or taking a hike."

"What's he done to get you so stirred up? I thought the plan was to lay low for a while and try to make a place for yourself here. This doesn't sound like laying low."

"It's what he *ain't* done." There was surprising conviction in the old man's voice. "Living the life I've lived, I'm used to being invisible… kind of like it, actually. I *ain't* used to being disrespected, or seeing my friends treated that way, neither. Maybe I'm not on the rails right now, but I'm still Profesh."

"What do you mean, *right now*?" Lynden gazed at him but didn't wait for an answer. "I'd like nothing better than to see Tom taken down a notch or two," he admitted, and allowed a momentary thought of what that might mean for Clara, and for himself, "but not if it means you getting shot in the process."

"Nobody's getting shot. Not if everybody plays their part."

"Their part in what? I still don't know what the hell you're planning."

"I'm gonna win the carny joints from Tom, just like he won them from Mike. Really Mike's gonna win em, I'm just the setup man. Word got out that I'm a sucker at cards and that I've got a fat wad of cash to lose."

"My cash?"

"Yeah, only I ain't gonna lose it. That's the setup. Tom can't gamble worth shit, but Mike got liquored up one night and lost the joints to him. Ever since, Tom's stayed clear of the gyp top because he knows he'll lose them back."

"But he's too greedy to pass up a sucker?"

"That's what we're countin on."

"We?"

"I had some help." The Duke smiled. "I was wrong about these carnies stickin together. They don't like Tom no better'n I do."

"That's not too hard to believe... but the rest of it sounds crazy." Lynden fixed his old friend with a stare that was as earnest as his voice. "What if you lose the money? And what about Tom's gun?"

"That's where you come in. First—like I told you—I ain't gonna lose. Everybody's agreed to give me back my losings and let me keep my winnings."

"And that revolver Tom's so proud of?"

"He won't even think of using it till he wises up. By then we're long gone."

"We're... leaving?" Lynden remembered that last look from Clara, and the question in her eyes. Did she know?

"Hell, yes, we're leavin! Tom's a prick, but he ain't a complete idiot. He'll probably eat crow for these carnies, cause he's got no place else to go. But after tonight, if we stick around, he'll find a way to get back at us. Assholes always find a way."

"And my part in all of this is... what?"

"Hold onto my gear and wait for me right here at the joints."

"Tell me there's more to it than that."

"Course there is." The Duke ignored the tone of disbelief in his young friend's voice. "If trouble starts, I'll come runnin. Jerry left the keys in his pick-up, so we've got a getaway car. Not that we're gonna need it."

"What if you don't come?"

"I got that figured, too. By four o'clock, if I'm not here, you beat it down to the freight yards and wait under the bridge at the east end. There's a hot shot rolling for Cicero around five, and we gotta be on it. That is... if you're up for one last ride."

"Of course I am, but—look—I'm not leaving here without you, gun or no gun."

"And I don't want you to. But if something goes sideways, wait for me at the Cicero Mission down by the West Chicago yards. I'll get there quick as I can."

"I don't like it." Lynden shook his head. "And I've got a feeling there's something you're not telling me." As he said it, he was seeing that question in Clara's eyes. "Let's just get out of here. Let's catch that ride now. Whatever you're really doing this for, it's not worth it."

"It *is* worth it, even if you can't see that right now. Frisco, I *need* to do this. It's like you runnin for those stupid beers back in Kansas." He smiled at the memory. "It didn't make any sense, but you did it anyway. And I want to do a favor for a friend," he added, "while I still can."

"Favor?"

"No time to explain, but trust me... you'll understand."

"Understand? What are you—?"

Jerry ran up, out of breath. "Game's all set. Tom's having it in his own damn trailer, tilted the mattress up against the bedroom wall to make room. He insisted, if you know what I mean!"

"When do we start?"

"They're waiting on you."

"Duke, listen to me." Lynden stepped out to block their path. "Let's just go—"

"We will. You to whatever lies ahead for you, and me back to where I belong, back to the road."

"But—"

"It's all that matters." He gripped Lynden's hand. "Do like I told you. Be on that train."

* * *

The gyp top was a card table crowded into the bedroom of Tom's Airstream. Jerry and The Duke found a single chair vacant when they arrived.

"This can't be the high-roller you was telling me about!"

Tom blustered, his earlier efforts to impress the newcomer with his gun and his liquor an inconvenient memory he needed to expunge. "First he mooches my good booze off of me without so much as a thank you. Now you expect I'm gonna sit at the same table with this... hobo?"

"Evenin folks," The Duke saluted. Mike was in the game and Old Dan and Charlie Ben. The Covelo sisters each had a chair. Tom sat with his back to the wall, Clara standing right behind him. The Duke nodded to her.

"Duke," Mike saluted back. "We hear you came to play some cards."

"I've been known to play. Always carry a stake just in case." He patted his jacket pocket.

"Sit down and play then!" Tom blurted. "And you get outta here," he yelled at Jerry. "I can't stand you hanging around while I'm trying to think!"

Jerry tensed, but The Duke held his eye and he backed away, slamming the door after him.

"Game's five draw. No wild cards, no limit, and guts to open. Any questions?"

The Duke settled slowly into his seat, stalling for time. "What's maximum draw?"

"Planning on getting some bad cards?" Mike asked. Everyone at the table smiled.

"That's never the plan," The Duke shrugged, "but—"

"Draw's three," Tom cut him off. "Anything else?" The Duke shook his head and Tom shuffled.

As the cards flew around, The Duke pulled a neat bundle of new five-dollar bills from a jacket pocket and laid it carefully on the table in front of him. Then he brought out another just like it. "I like to bet mostly in fives."

Everyone was watching The Duke's hands.

"Fives keep things easier," he said, pulling a third bundle from his jacket. "Of course, a fella can play with tens," another bundle came out, "but the money goes too damn quick. You folks have any problem with keeping the minimum bet at five?" A fifth bundle was now sitting on the table in front of him. Tom lost his place dealing, and before anyone could protest he grabbed all the cards back.

"Five's okay by me," Mike said, impressed. Around the table, each of the others agreed. Tom was the last.

"You ready to stop showing off and play some poker?" Tom was shuffling again, abusing the cards as if the misdeal was their fault. Everyone nodded. Everyone but The Duke. "What's your problem now old man?"

He had two problems, neither of which Tom could know about. Earlier that day, using twenty brand new five-dollar bills from the bank, and eighty brand new one-dollar bills to tuck under them, he'd built his Missouri Bankroll. "That's what they call it," he'd told Jerry, "because Missouri's the Show Me state. You show em five hundred when you've really only got two." The first problem was to keep Tom from discovering the subterfuge. Of the two hundred he started with, there was only a hundred and fifty in front of him now. That was the second problem. He hadn't told Jerry that part, the kid wouldn't have liked where the other fifty went.

They were all in on the bankroll scheme.

Tom fell for it just like they'd planned.

"I don't play with spectators," The Duke said cordially, flashing a tight-lipped smile. "It's not that I don't trust you, but that's one of my ironclad rules. If somebody wants to watch, I don't want to play."

"She ain't hurting nothing!" Tom snapped. Clara was the only spectator.

"I didn't say she was." The Duke's hand moved toward his money.

"It's my trailer. I say she stays!"

"Fine." He slipped a bundle into his pocket. Another bundle followed. If it was going to work, it had to be now.

"What's she hanging around for anyway?" Mike spoke up. "You just ran Jerry out of here, I say she goes, too. Wasn't she standing over your shoulder the night I lost the joints? Maybe I was too stewed to care then, but I'm stone sober now. You hear what I'm saying?"

"It's my trailer, damn it."

"And it's your big mouth that's always running," Mike shot back. "Now get that girl out of here... or I will."

Tom glared at Mike, then at The Duke. Finally, he turned on Clara. "Get out! I don't want you hanging on me, so don't come back till the game's over, you hear?"

Clara stepped from behind Tom's chair and threaded her way toward the door.

Her eyes met The Duke's for an instant as she left.

"Can we play?" Tom demanded. Everyone nodded.

The Duke eased back in his chair.

The hard part was over.

* * *

When he first saw her coming toward him out of the shadows, Lynden wasn't sure Clara was real. He'd been thinking about wanting to say goodbye, wanting it very much. Then, there she was, conjured out of his longing.

"Nice night," she said, walking up close. "Mind if I keep you company?"

"I don't mind." Lynden could smell the carnival on her, and perfume, and a deeper, denser scent like just tilled earth, new mown grass—but not like them at all. Her scent. "You're out late."

"And by myself." She glanced around the darkened midway as if seeing it with new eyes. "Tom never lets me out of his sight unless I'm working my joint... hardly even then."

"I guess he really... cares about you?" He meant it as a statement, but it came out as a question.

"About controlling me, yeah. I can't tell if it's because

he actually feels something, or he just doesn't want to risk losing me to somebody who does."

They had started walking as they talked, and at the Ferris wheel, quiet and still for the night, they stepped through the gate. He steadied the unstable gondola as she got in, and they sat side-by-side, rocking gently and letting words take their time.

"Do you care about him?" Lynden encouraged the rocking with gentle nudges from his legs, and he could feel, through the movement of the car, that next to him Clara was doing the same.

"I like being looked after... if that's what you mean." There was no self-reproach in her voice, just self-aware-ness. "When you've done without, and been alone, having a place to be safe and people to watch out for you feels pretty good. Maybe that sounds cheap, but it's the truth."

"It doesn't sound cheap." They rocked the car in unison some more, sharing the motion. "But at least for tonight, I'm glad Tom *isn't* watching out for you."

"Me, too." More rocking. "We've got your friend to thank for that."

"My friend?"

"You know... The Duke. He asked if I would, and I said sure, only he'd have to take care of Tom some way."

"Asked you to do what?"

"Give you a date." Clara turned and looked at him, and there it was again, that question in her eyes. Only now, he thought he understood. "I told him twenty was enough, but he gave me fifty dollars. Said he'd like to give me more if he had it."

"He paid you to have sex with me?" The rocking stopped. "Who the hell does he think I am? Jesus, who do *you* think I am?"

"He told me you'd say something like this." Lynden could see her considering him, not judging but trying to understand. "He told me some other things, too. Talk about caring—that guy cares about you—probably more than you know."

"And this is how he shows it? By buying me—what did you call it—a *date*?" He spat the word at her, the taste of it toxic on his tongue.

"It doesn't matter what you call it, Frisco." She continued to gaze at him, curious but not unkind. "He told me this is how you'd be, only I didn't hardly believe him. What are you afraid of?"

Lynden didn't answer and wouldn't look at her. Couldn't.

She reached up to touch his face.

He jerked away.

"Listen, whatever it is you're worried about, don't be. I've been tricking off and on since I was fourteen, so there's nothing I haven't seen. Don't be scared of me."

"Scared?" He snapped his head around and glared at her now. "Of you?" There was a surprising fierceness in his voice, and in his eyes. "What makes you think you've got the power to scare me?" He'd seen that kind of power—when Derek Zebel cornered him in the bathroom, when The Tramp took him, abused him, and discarded him—and this girl didn't have it. "I'm not scared of you." He couldn't lash out at the men in his head, so he lashed out at her. "I'm disgusted..." He let it hang, attempting to drive the insult home with a look to match. Instead, his face carried an anguish his features could not hide, stealing the power from the word.

"I've been called some salty things," if his verbal slap connected, she didn't show it, "but that's a new one. Your friend told me you had some kind of hang-up... but disgusting? Maybe I'm no prom queen but disgusting I'm not. Whatever it is, Frisco, you've got it bad."

"Go away." He did not look at her as he said it.

"Sure, if that's what you really mean. I'm yours for the next couple of hours, that's how long the old man said we'd have. I'll do anything you want, just say the word."

"I want you to leave." He forced himself to look anywhere but at Clara.

She stood up, started to go, then sat back down and faced him, willing him to face her.

"Look. I'd bet money you've got a stack of stroke books hidden in a closet somewhere. I know Tom does. What makes you think I'm less fun than some book? I'm better. I'm real."

He expected to see pity in her eyes, or rejection. Instead, he just saw a girl.

"Don't get me wrong," she held his gaze, "if we were in love that would be different. But we're not. You need something. I've got it."

"You're serious... aren't you?"

"As serious as I get. Listen." She touched his arm. This time he sensed neither threat nor exposure, nor risk. It was just a touch. And it felt different. It felt good. He didn't draw back. "I won't make you do anything, and I won't stop you unless you hurt me. But you won't hurt me. I can tell."

"What The Duke said... it's true." He flashed on images of Millie, of her hurt, of his shame. "I can't..."

"So what? Let me share a secret. The trying is usually the most fun anyway. I'd just as soon spend a few hours working up to it as doing it. But you decide. If you want, we can just talk."

Lynden was silent for a long time, and she sat silently beside him.

"Did The Duke tell you anything else?"

She thought a minute. "Something about a tramp," she said, "about me helping you get a tramp off your back. You know what that means?"

"Yeah..." He paused, letting what it *did* mean settle in.

"Yeah, I do." Another pause, an interlude perfectly balanced between everything that had come before and all that would follow. "You're right... that old man cares about me more than I know."

With no more words to say, they rose together.

The empty gondola rocked gently behind them as they slipped hand-in-hand into the welcoming embrace of the night—no time for the sweethearts that might have been, but time enough for lovers.

* * *

At a quarter past four he was waiting under a street bridge near the east end of the Galesburg yards. No light tower cast its silver glow there, and the moon was obscured by thick summer clouds. He sat on his bag and held The Duke's valise loosely between his legs. Already he'd seen three power units slide past, then back again.

The Chicago freight was built and ready.

From deep within the yard a horn cried out. Three times it blew.

The lead locomotive's tracer light flashed to life, its wandering beam painting the darkness before it. Lynden stood and watched the train approach, heard the engines grow louder, saw the dark steel snake move toward him in the night. He walked to the top of the bridge one last time.

No one.

It was happening too fast, all of it. He skidded down the steep embankment, then hurried across a handful of tracks to the main line. He didn't want to hurry. The engines had gone past already, and cars were swaying lazily by. He stood and watched them go, twenty or more.

I won't do it.

An empty threat. The Duke had made him promise.

A Great Northern boxcar rolled up, both its doors open. The catch was easy, even with two bags to carry. In a moment he was standing in the open doorway watching the street bridge and the night slip by.

No exhilaration came with this catch, no thrill. No Duke. Only emptiness in an empty boxcar.

Up ahead in the darkness, another shadow. Another street bridge spanned the yard.

Had he been waiting at the wrong one?

Up on the bridge, a pickup stopped.

A figure emerged.

Someone running.

There was a hint of movement on the embankment, a flash of something out across the tracks.

"I'm here!" Lynden yelled to be heard over the train noise. "I waited at the wrong bridge!"

"That you, Frisco?"

"Here! I'm right here!"

"Thought you were gonna leave without me!" The Duke saw him, and in a moment the old hobo was running beside the car.

"Never."

"Damn rights!" The Profesh, the last of his kind, shouted in reply. He was running with the train—running for the joy of it—though he could have gotten on easily. "When we get to Chicago, I'm buyin. I won two hundred bucks!" He waved a fistful of cash in the air. "You and Clara... everything okay?"

"Damn rights!" Lynden pumped his fist and howled, as he never had, at the magnificence of it all—the perfection of this moment, in this place, with this man.

There was a siding ahead, and an old-style switch with a tall pipe standard.

The Duke was running full speed when he hit it.

Chapter Nineteen

He could hear the roar of the big six-wheel,
As the drivers pounded the polished steel,
And the screech of the flanges on the rail
As she beat it west o'er the desert trail.
Unknown

Three weeks later Lynden was on a Conrail hot shot from Pittsburgh to Harrisburg. He rode the front porch of a bulk feed car watching the afternoon sky darken, threatening rain.

He rode alone.

The Duke had warned him, on one of their first rides together, that a freight car can buck violently at any time. Was it the concussion, the events of that night, or not wanting to remember that fractured his recollection?

The concussion was part of it.

Even so, he wished that some pieces of his memory were not so intact.

His mind's eye watched, in slow motion, as The Duke's body cracked and folded and broke itself against the switch-pole.

He had reached out, his compulsion to help so powerful it overrode the futility of his act.

The train had lurched, throwing him off his feet, smashing his head into the boxcar wall.

* * *

It was hours before he came to.

He was in the boxcar.

The train was still moving.

His hair was matted with drying blood, the feel of it sticky, and surprising when he tried to run his fingers through. He struggled to get his legs under him. Couldn't. A clouded kaleidoscope had hijacked his ability to see, everything around him was fragmented, foggy, unfocused. When he closed his eyes, slipping out of consciousness again, what he saw there was perfectly lucid. There was the switch sign. There was The Duke smashing into it face first. He reached out to help, heard himself screaming, and woke up.

It was well past noon when his freight stopped in the Cicero yards on Chicago's west side. His legs barely holding him, he slipped to the ground, pulled his and The Duke's bags with him, and managed to wobble forward.

A single thought drove him. He had to go back.

How he found the right train on the right track back to Galesburg he didn't know. Instinct. Luck. It didn't matter. In less than an hour he was in a boxcar heading west. He collapsed, surrendering himself to tormented sleep.

* * *

Had his train not jerked repeatedly when it slowed to enter the Galesburg yard, he might have missed it. Instead, he opened his eyes, crawled to the edge of the boxcar, and lowered himself down. Ignoring the pain in his head, and the pounding on his spine that sent shock waves down his arms and legs, he stumbled back up the tracks toward the yard limit, dragging the bags with him. He barely recognized the first overpass, and he was almost unconscious again when he reached the second. He started running awkwardly, crazily—his movements as disjointed as his thinking—as if the accident had just happened.

As if The Duke would still be lying there hurt, needing help.

Needing him.

When he came to the switch, his vision snapped... it became excruciatingly clear.

The Duke's body was gone.

Evidence of his death was everywhere—blood covering the ground, the steel switch standard bent half over, the outline of a body in bloodstained earth.

The Duke had crashed to a stop there, lain there, bleeding out.

Alone.

No one beside him—as Lynden knew he should have been—for those last moments.

He'd died there.

A bolt shot through Lynden's spine and brain. It doubled him over, forced him to the ground. He lay in the bloody dust, begging for The Duke to come back. For the pain to stop. For death.

Begging.

Instead of death, what came to him was an eastbound freight.

The engineer blasted. Suddenly Lynden focused. "The Cicero Mission, near the west Chicago yards," he mumbled. The Duke had been adamant. If something went wrong, if they got separated, that was where they would meet.

This freight was a local, barely moving... it would take all night to get to Chicago. When an open boxcar came up, reflexes guided his legs and arms, instinct overcame his pain. A clumsy catch, and dangerous with his bag in one hand and The Duke's in the other, but he managed it.

Energy spent, he cast himself onto the boxcar floor, his bowling bag the only cushion for his throbbing head.

The Duke's battered valise clutched to his chest.

* * *

Three days after arriving in west Chicago, Lynden finally walked into the Cicero Mission—three days spent lying in a Cook County Hospital bed with twelve stitches in his head. A brakie had found him in the west Chicago yard, knew immediately by his appearance and his youth that he didn't belong there, and called an ambulance. An old bum would not have been so lucky. Most unusual of all, there were credit cards in his wallet. No cash—all that had gone to the poker game, and to Clara.

The desk clerk at the rescue mission, a man who, from his missing teeth and gaunt cheeks looked as likely to be an overnight guest as an employee, was no stranger to being the last stop on a hopeless search for someone who was lost. "Sorry, chum... I ain't seen your friend. From what you say happened, seems like he woulda been hard to miss. You checked around the yards? Maybe somebody there..." Lynden had checked, but he knew there was no chance. The Duke never made it that far.

He charged a ticket on the first bus out for Galesburg.

The hospital and police station revealed nothing. He tried the Galesburg Morgue. The coroner, a fat, thick-veined man in a white smock that needed washing, was glad to see him. "I think we've got your old tramp."

"He was not a *tramp*." Lynden resented the insult to his friend, and the bitter reminder it stirred from his own past.

"If you say so. I've seen plenty that are. Thought the county would have to bury this fellow, just like all those others. He was floating in a farm pond south of town. From the looks of his liver, I'd say your friend enjoyed his drink."

"No... he didn't," Lynden remembered their three-day bender in Denver, "not like you mean."

"Guess he fell off the wagon," said the big man, undeterred. "He was full of booze when I opened him up."

Inside a room that smelled of death and the chemicals used to mask and manage it, a green plastic drape covered a corpse. "This your friend?" The coroner folded the sheet back, revealing a head and torso. The thing in front of them—puffed like a cushion, incision lines in place of seams—did not look human. Not even dead human. It might have been The Duke's size. Maybe his age. It was not him.

Lynden shook his head.

The coroner reached down and shaped the thing's face with his fingers. "You sure? Chances of two like this turning up at the same time are awfully damn slim. Of course, not every old bum that dies makes it to the morgue. Some crawl off into a ditch, and nature does the rest. But maybe you just can't let yourself recognize him." He was not ready to let it go. "We found a birthmark on his left gluteal that you might have—"

"I'm sure."

* * *

Lynden searched the freight yards, carefully checking the bushes and ditches at the east end. He found a patch of flattened grass. It was covered in dark stains that might have been blood. If it *was* blood, there had been a lot of it, enough to confirm what he already knew.

He asked all the car-knockers and brakies he could find. "I know that bent-up switch you're talkin about," one told him. "Took two of us, using a come-along and a lotta muscle, to pull it straight again. If you're tellin me that a man running into it did *that*... I'm tellin you he didn't survive it. Hell, I know I couldn't have."

He was in Galesburg, the last place he'd seen The Duke, the last place he'd seen Clara. He stayed for nearly a week, spending most of his days in a cheap downtown hotel. To rest, he told himself. To let his strength return.

He knew that was a lie.

As he lay in his room with the lights out and window open listening to the passing freights, or sat silent over breakfast at The Shamrock—at the same table he'd

shared with The Duke on the morning they'd met Clara—
his memories of those final hours before the accident held
him, immobile, pinned in place by lingering emotions he
couldn't avoid and didn't want to. They acted on him like
familiar music heard from a passing car at night, fading,
but vivid enough to touch his heart. He knew he'd never
have them back, either the moments or the people.

He knew that.

But he could not bring himself to leave.

* * *

"Hoover? I thought you logged out for good." The voice
on the other end of the phone—a Data Dynamics coder
named Perkins who sometimes shared cold pizza with
him—was the only person at the company he knew well
enough to call. "When you split, the Double Dildo went
limp. Zebel about shit."

"He'll get over it." Lynden was in a phone booth across
from his hotel. There was no phone in his room, the toilet
was down the hall, and the bed no longer seemed to fit
him. It was time. "Pricks like him usually do." He heard
The Duke and the road in his voice and liked the contrast
with the way Perkins sounded on the other end.

"No, they don't... they get promoted. He's at HQ in
Seattle now. Go figure."

Derek Zebel, who had cornered him in the men's room
and grabbed his crotch, was climbing the corporate ladder. *What would The Duke have thought*? He imagined
something like, *Assholes always sniff each other out.* That
brought a smile, the first he'd let himself enjoy since the
accident.

Perkins launched into a verbal data dump about their
project, all of it familiar, all of it meaningless—unless
Lynden was willing to engage his brain that way again.
Perkins didn't ask where he had been. He didn't ask why
he had left. Only as an afterthought, when the program-

mer had downloaded everything he had to say, did he ask the question Lynden thought he wanted to hear. The reason he had called.

"So—dude—when are you coming back?"

There was no doubt that they would rehire him, he was too good at what he did. He knew it, they knew it. Yet hearing Perkins' feeble invitation to return—as sincere as he was likely to get from anyone at the company—left him feeling nothing.

"Soon."

Already he had a plane ticket in his pocket. It was what he and The Duke had agreed to that last night—that Lynden would return west and put his old life back together, only better. The Duke would return to the road—and he had. Running for a train was the last thing he had ever done. Even though his friend was dead, Lynden felt an obligation to follow through with his part of the bargain.

He was scheduled to fly out the next morning.

Yet *soon* was all he could bring himself to say.

* * *

Instead of taking a cab to the airport, when the sun was still rising on his last day in Galesburg, he took to his feet and trusted them to guide him. As he walked through the still quiet streets, in his bowling bag he carried The Duke's things along with his own.

It didn't matter if he missed the plane, he could take another when he was ready. It didn't matter if he blew the cost of the ticket. In his old life earning money had never been a problem, spending it never a priority. His paychecks would sit, uncashed, on his dresser for months until someone from accounting pestered him to deposit them.

He didn't know where he was going, only that it wouldn't be home. Not yet.

At the first street bridge across the tracks, the bridge where he had waited for The Duke just ten days earlier, he ran into a pair of tramps.

A binge the night before had blown all their money, and they were debating drowsily how to get more cash. Lynden sat quietly with them—close enough to hear, removed enough not to intrude—savoring the flavor of their words. They decided to head down to Peoria and put the touch on an ex-sister-in-law. As they got up to leave two more arrived. The new tramps had some food, so the old tramps stayed.

He spent the rest of the day there, watching the men come and go, watching the trains.

An eastbound began rolling toward him at sunset, three power units on the head end, followed by tankers and piggy backs, gondolas and grainers—a mixed consist train—and a third of the way back, a Soo Line boxcar with an open door.

He didn't plan it.

He didn't resist.

The feel of the gravel beneath his boots as he sprinted forward, his trajectory merging perfectly with the train's. The leap into the car—breaking free, not only from the ground, but from the ropes of sorrow and self-pity that had bound him even after the concussion cleared.

As he stood in the open doorway, the pulsing of wheels and rails coming up through his legs became an injection of energy, and of life returning, from The Illinois Central's mainline into his own.

His train pulled near the site of the accident. Lynden forced himself to face it. The switch standard had been mostly bent back into shape, just as the car-knocker said, and looked no more or less damaged than anything else in the yard, its trauma now hidden in the cold steel of its memory. Repaired, but not the same.

Never the same.

* * *

"These freights let us ride, Frisco," The Duke had told him once. "They don't let us go." It sounded like fate when he heard it—impossible to defy, inexorable. But as the miles rolled beneath him in the days that followed, and the cities—Cincinnati, Detroit, Buffalo—he began to wonder. Yes, the freights would not let his old friend go. But that hold, like a death-grip on a gondola ladder, was The Duke's to release, not the train's. Maybe he maintained it was beyond his power, that it was fate, as a way to avoid facing that choice. Or was the current truly so strong and irresistible on this river of steel that, once swept up in it, you could never again find your way to shore?

Lynden could feel the pull, and the freedom that came when he gave himself over to it.

In any yard that still had a jungle, he would linger with the hobos for an hour or two, maybe a day, cooking with them over an open fire, passing bottles of wine. It was their company he sought, the rhythms of their speech, the way they lived. None of them were The Duke. Yet in ways—a turn of phrase, a manner of movement, a glance from eyes that had seen a million miles—they were *exactly* The Duke.

At the Collingwood yard just outside Cleveland, he ran into an old friend. "Us tramps live in a small world," The Duke had explained, "smaller than you'd believe." So small that if you stayed on the rails long enough, you were bound to run into everyone you knew.

"Rusty took sick before I made it to Canada," Trainer Bill told him, no more surprised at their chance reunion than if they'd been neighbors meeting on a street corner. "By the time I found a vet who would help, it was too late. Now I don't much care if Short Arm does find me. It's The Duke he's after anyway."

"The Duke is dead." There was no gentle way to break news so raw—so hard to accept—let alone tell it to The Duke's longtime friend.

Trainer cursed when he heard the part about the switch. "Bastard knew better than to run alongside that train."

They shared a quiet dinner, tossing twigs into their small fire, grateful for the scant light it shed, bright enough to see what needed seeing, dim enough to disguise their grief. Another tramp approached, but sensing the gravity of the moment, he left them to their solace.

"Where you headed next, Trainer?" Lynden asked at last. "Do you think Pig Hollow might be safe for you again... now that The Duke's gone? Maybe Short Arm has lost interest."

"Maybe, but without Hubb and Step around... it's me that's lost interest. I'd be missing Rusty, anyway. He was a pup back there you know. I never thought about him dying. Always figured it would be me that went first." He poked up the flames, but not too high. "Damn dog."

"Do you have family somewhere?"

He shook his head. "All dead. Step, Hubb, The Duke. Ain't got no family left. I've been on my own my whole life, but I never remember feeling lonely before. Not like this. Don't know where I'm goin. Don't much give a shit."

"You still thinking about Canada?"

"Maybe." Trainer looked at him, a look so forlorn that Lynden had to avert his eyes. "What about you going with me? I used to be Profesh too, you know. I could show you some things. We could... team up?"

"Thanks..." They both understood that it wasn't a request to partner, but a plea to postpone, if only for a while, the worst of the loneliness that lay ahead. Knowing that no such reprieve was possible didn't make the answer any easier for Lynden to give, or for Trainer Bill to receive.

"I appreciate it, but The Duke told me I needed to get on with my life... not on with his."

Bill stared at him a moment, then gazed back into the fire. "Damn dog."

Trainer was still sitting there, mumbling, when Lynden dropped off to sleep.

When he woke in the morning, the old hobo was gone.

* * *

In Pittsburg, a day later, a thin gray rain was falling—mist hugging the ground—as his freight for Altoona eased out of the main yard. He was standing in the shelter of his boxcar, looking out toward the river, when sidings full of dead freight equipment began to emerge from the fog. A whole separate yard slowly revealed itself, every section of rail crammed full of derelict rolling stock. Wabash, Milwaukee Road, Penn Central they said. Soo Line, Grand Trunk, Apalachicola. Hundreds of them, rusting on the rails.

He grabbed his bag and swung down from the train.

Scarred by accidents, slashed by derails, branded on their sides with the words "Bad Order," the once distinctive colors of a dozen proud freight lines blended into a muted mosaic of neglect. He wandered through the shrouded wreckage, through strings of ravaged cars so cannibalized that their remains weren't worth hauling away as scrap.

Beyond the forgotten cars were scores of power units marshalled in uniform, desolate rows. Motors scavenged, horns gone mute. Carcasses. Lynden had come to see them as more than mere machines. In a world whose singular purpose was movement, they were a force of nature, no less elemental than the winds or the tides. If the hand of God was to be found anywhere on the rails, it was on their throttles. Humble yard switchers shunting endlessly back and forth. Short-haul diesels lugging locals day after day over the same tired tracks. And the huge, long haul diesel-electrics—six thousand barely harnessed horses, so powerful that the ground shook under their passing.

All had earned his respect.

None had escaped this graceless iron graveyard.

He stopped to rest on the wide front step of a huge Union Pacific diesel, its side panels removed and power plant ripped out. The massive locomotives were crowded together there. Fog had settled low. He heard footsteps slowly approaching. Out of this mist-filled slot canyon of steel a shape came toward him.

"Ol Dirty face... he don't mind if you sit on him a spell."

The man had been big once. But like the machines around him he was hollowed out, a failing tree whose heartwood had succumbed to age, disease, neglect. His weathered exterior, tempered by time, was just strong enough to keep him from tumbling over. Frame bent, gate uneven, "Bad Order," was written on him as clearly as it was scrawled on the abandoned rolling stock he shuffled past.

"I don't guess he'd mind if two of us sat." Lynden made room on the step. "I figure he's carried heavier loads."

"That he has." The man steadied himself on the grab iron, and eased down onto the metal tread, his frail body meeting it as gently as two freight cars perfectly coupling. "I live hereabouts... so I can call on my old friends when I want." He patted the step affectionately. "You?"

"Just a visit. I saw," Lynden gestured to take it all in, "this... from my boxcar door. I needed to see more."

"*Needed*, you say?" A smile broke across the face that Lynden could now see had been broken before. "That would make you a rare sort of a hobo. Most of em just roll on by."

"I'm not a hobo—of any sort—not really." Lynden returned the smile. "I'm just a visitor here. Come to pay my respects to Mr. Dirty Face. And to make a new friend.

Frisco's my name. I mean... Lynden. Lynden Hoover." He extended his hand.

"Pleased to meet you, Mister... Lynden Hoover," the man said with a curious look, and a hand was offered in return, the knuckles thick, fingers twisted, but the grip still firm. "Peculiar thing about some visits..." He began to pull himself upright again, ready to resume his slow sojourn, and leaned on Lynden's arm for help. "A fella never knows exactly how long they're gonna last." Standing now, he took a deep breath, settling himself, gathering his strength. "Fare you well... Mr. Frisco." He nodded, and turned to continue on his way.

"Thanks—and I'll do that—but like I said, it's Lynden." Maybe the old man had forgotten.

"There's what we call ourselves... then there's who we are," the stranger said as he began to shuffle away.

Lynden also rose, his ear had caught another train approaching out on the main line. "By the way—in case I should pass this way again, and want to pay my respects to our old friend here—what do you call yourself?"

"Most use Eli..." the man said over his shoulder, his fig-ure merging into the mist as he spoke. "You can use my given name, if you'd druther—" There was more, but it was lost to the blasting horn of the freight Lynden hoped to catch, the sound surprisingly loud and close.

The name and the man disappeared into the fog.

* * *

That afternoon his train rolled past Greensburg, Ebensburg, and a dozen small villages in between. It was fast, smooth—quarter-mile long sections of welded rib-bon rail having replaced the old, short segments. Absent the repeating double-drumbeat of wheels over flexing track joints and the rocking and the pounding that came with them, the sensation in his boxcar was not of riding but of flying—banking, diving, soaring through the damp

Pennsylvania twilight.

The crew changed at Altoona, and he switched to a bulk grain car with a clear front porch. From there he could see more.

He rode, captivated by the hundred-car train curving along the contours of the river's valley—thunderheads reeled toward him, turning evening into night. His train slowed at Lewiston, and the town slipped quietly past beneath the darkening sky.

Then, lightening.

A single bolt. Another. Many. It ripped everywhere from the blackness, cutting jagged slashes of brilliance that imprinted themselves into Lynden's vision and remained even when he closed his eyes.

The clouds released torrents of rain that quickly overfilled the culverts, flooded the ditches and streams. He could see the deluge overlay the landscape with its dense, gray drapery.

On the banks of the Susquehanna, train and storm and rider became one.

Lightning burst so near that its explosion dwarfed all other sounds. Flashes sprayed the whole drenched world with blue-white fire. It struck out over the river, stabbing a bridge, a house, a town, then blasted right next to the train again, knocking the wind out of Lynden like a blow to his chest.

The air smelled of electricity, rain, and rails. Thunder shook the earth.

These freights don't let us go, The Duke said, but this one proved his old friend wrong. In its purity and power it possessed him even as it liberated him. No enticement to stay, this was a gesture of recognition, demanding nothing, giving everything. He was equal to the ride, it said. The rails were his if he wanted them and would be even if he never rode again.

As the train slowed, rain turned to drizzle. Out across the wide Susquehanna, the lights of Harrisburg came into view. *The Enola Yard*. Lynden remembered a time when that had been his goal. A time when The Duke was still alive.

Though Lynden now knew that the destination had been false—a ruse to keep an old Profesh and his young friend out of harm's way—the motive was true.

Finally at Enola, he thought.

That journey, begun so long ago, had come to an end.

He stepped off the freight as easily as a man leaving a streetcar, an aviator returning to earth. The ground felt both foreign and familiar beneath his feet. The sound of the train had been so deep in his hearing for so long that he sensed its receding like an emptying pitcher must sense itself filling with nothing. The smells—of journal grease and diesel fuel and cold iron—were so known to him that he could effortlessly discern their differences.

From behind a clump of trees, came the familiar orange glow of a jungle fire. Lynden hurried toward it. Within that circle of warmth, he knew he'd find some company, and a place to pass the night.

Just short of the flickering light, he stopped. He could head straight into town for some hot food and a dry place to sleep. But the crackling of the fire, the sound of it, changed his mind.

He moved a few steps closer.

There were two figures in the fire's light. One lay passed out on the ground, a mostly empty wine bottle beside him. Head and upper body covered by black plastic, legs sprawled in a puddle. Lynden knew the type and had jungled-up with more than one. Enough wine and they could sleep through anything.

The other figure was hovering over the bottle-bum. A bear of a man, well past six-feet tall.

Red plaid hunting jacket.

Right sleeve hanging loose at his side.

No hand below the cuff.

Thick hair covering his head and chin.

And a face Lynden had not seen in fifteen years.

He watched as Short Arm, his Tramp, stalked around the fire, pausing every few steps to look at the drunk. A predator circling its prey. He kicked the bum, hard. The bum moaned.

Lynden saw him stroke the hanging sleeve—the sleeve that wasn't empty.

The gun would flash, the body would jerk. The bottle-bum would die.

"Evening." He stepped into the firelight.

"Get out!" Short Arm spun to face him, a human man-trap ready to spring, and reached reflexively for his sleeve.

"Thought you might want some company for dinner." Lynden walked close to the fire and nudged a sack of groceries with his toe. Next to it was a half-empty box of shotgun shells.

"Get out, I told you!"

"I don't think I will." He was acting on instinct, his words fathering themselves. But when he heard them, he understood. This wasn't about violence. It wasn't about being afraid. It wasn't even about the revenge he'd wanted and had been sure he would never get. It was about control. About denying it to this monster who had exerted it over him when he was a boy, and whose specter had continued to exert it all the years since. "Looks like there's plenty of grub for all three of us." He nodded toward the unconscious bum. "This one is still alive... isn't he?"

"N...no" the big man stammered, looking for the fear he expected to see in the stranger, and seeing none. "You get outta here, before I—"

"*No?* You don't want to share your food with me? Or...

no, he isn't alive?" Lynden ignored the threat. "Doesn't look to me like you've killed him yet. I don't see any blood."

Short Arm gaped at him, confused. "Who are you? I don't know you."

"Sure you do." Lynden dropped his bowling bag and moved closer, quickly—so close and quick that Short Arm involuntarily took a step back. There was the smell Lynden remembered. Sweet tobacco, sour sweat, and something else familiar. The scent of fear. But this time the fear wasn't his. "We're old friends. We took a trip together once."

"No we never... I don't know you." It wasn't denial, it was disbelief. "I don't know nothin you're talkin about."

"Some coincidence, isn't it? You and me... ending up here?" The face he stared into—scarred and accustomed to scowling—did not wear bewilderment well. "You know what a coincidence is, don't you? It's like a train showing up just when you need it. Or a lonely little boy standing by the tracks at exactly the wrong time and trusting exactly the wrong tramp. Or two old hobos, who used to ride together, running into each other at the Colton yards."

"Who ARE you?" The bewilderment was immobilizing him. Lynden could see it and pushed it.

"I'm a kid you took for a prushin fifteen years ago. You don't remember me?"

"You're not making no sense!" Short arm's eyes looked frantic, uncomprehending. "You're crazy!"

"No, you're crazy... Spooky. That was your name, wasn't it? But you changed it. To Johnson."

It was panic—not his usual malice—that caused Short Arm's hand to move clumsily toward his empty sleeve.

Lynden, knowing what the hand was reaching for, anticipated its movement, its arc, and grabbed it.

"This is for that guy you killed in Colton." He jerked the big man's arm behind his back. "And for Step" He cranked the arm higher. "And for Hubbard." So high that Short Arm

"WHO ARE YOU?" Stunned, robbed of strength, his resistance was momentarily broken.

"A friend." Lynden pulled off his belt, looped one end around Short Arm's neck like a dog collar, and strapped his hand behind his back with the other. "A friend of The Duke's."

"The Duke?"

"He's dead." Lynden cinched the belt tighter, then wrenched his captive around so they stood face-to-face. Control. Complete control. "You didn't get him. I got you."

Short Arm stopped struggling.

"The Duke was my friend once." His breathing slowed. His features relaxed. The panic left his eyes. "We were partners."

"I know that."

"Did he tell you that we *both* wore the buckle?" The bewilderment was gone, and guile had taken its place. "No... he would have been ashamed to tell you that. He was Profesh, and he had his secrets... just like I do." Short Arm couldn't wait to reveal his best secret to his captor.

"Don't lie to me. It won't work."

"We went on runs together, him and me." Short Arm smiled as he said it and thought to himself that very soon he would be able to kill this crazy stranger. "The last time I saw him he still had the buckle... same as mine. He showed me in Colton."

"This buckle?" Lynden, without averting his eyes, dug in his bag, brought out the buckle and shoved it in Short Arm's face. "Somebody gave him this."

"I gave it to him," Short Arm said with a laugh. "Back before he took my arm. But he lied about that, didn't he? That's not right... lying to your friends."

"You don't know anything about it." Lynden tried not to think about the lies The Duke had told him. But Short

Arm had awakened the memory. "He *was* Profesh."

"That's right, he was. And he was a Johnson... just like me."

Lynden's fist moved on its own, not asking his permission, and he felt lips splitting beneath his knuckles as he connected with Short Arm's mouth.

The big man fell backwards, but rolled over and sprang to his feet, blood adding color to his yellow-toothed grin.

"Hit me again."

Lynden closed his fingers around the Johnson buckle and drove his fist into Short Arm's face.

"Maybe I *did* take you for a prushin," Short Arm's smile grew wider as he started to work his hand free, circling the fire to keep his efforts hidden. Pulling against the belt was choking him, but it didn't matter. He could stand choking. "Sure, I did," his words becoming a snarl. He could see that the kid was punching himself tired, each blow a transfusion of energy that weakened his attacker as it strengthened him. It was like being strapped down in the hospital again, like wanting to scratch his missing arm. Only now, he wanted to scratch the trigger and watch this punk's head come apart. "I remember," his wrist was bleeding, his skin tearing, "I fucked you in the face," he felt blood dripping on his fingers, "and fucked you in the ass." The belt was digging into his flesh. "But you weren't worth shit, so I threw you away!"

Short Arm stumbled to his knees.

His hand came free.

He swung it to the gun, felt the stock, felt the triggers.

As Lynden kicked at his empty sleeve and made the shotgun shudder in Short Arm's grip—both barrels exploding before he could release the hook—the last member of The Johnson Family's final thought was *This ain't right!*

Smoke and blood burst from his jacket.

He flew sideways, twisted, torn open, clawing at the hole where his shoulder had been.

Blood and screams poured out of him.

Lynden watched and did nothing.

The blood slowed.

The screams stopped.

Short Arm was dead.

Lynden stood in the jungle. It was quiet now, the shotgun blast having erased all other sound. He could hear himself inhaling and exhaling. Each breath he took was a breath that Short Arm would not—a new tally of being written on a slate that for Lynden had been wiped clean, and that for Short Arm would remain forever blank.

Deep breaths that sounded fresh in his ears, felt fresh in his lungs, fresh and altogether new, as if he had never breathed so deeply before. Breaths, he understood, that but for chance and a well-placed kick at an empty sleeve, might never have been his at all.

He smelled green willow smoking on the fire, and gunpowder lingering in the air.

He smelled the after-scent of the rain.

The adrenaline coursing through him, like the passing storm that had washed the countryside, began to recede as the seconds ticked past and his breathing slowed. The force of its surge left him spent. Spent, but clean.

His vision, dialed back from the razor-like clarity his survival had demanded, took on a deeper focus. Lynden looked around him. So much more than his ride had ended in this jungle. The fire burned as it had before, heedless of what had transpired within its circle of light. Nothing but the flames moved, not even the unconscious bum he'd rescued.

His eyes came to rest on the bare, bloody ground, and on Short Arm's twisted, motionless body. He had taken this man's life.

But not just a man, and not just his childhood tormentor. *He's a Johnson, I'm Profesh...* The Duke had told him in Pig Hollow. *It doesn't matter what you say—nothing has changed.*

It had changed now.

Johnson and Profesh, the last of their kind.

He had killed one, been unable to save the other.

He alone had survived.

There would be time for the weight of it all to settle on him.

Now it was time to go.

Lynden picked up his bag, the feel of its scant but precious contents—The Duke's knife, the buckle, which he had wiped off an placed inside, his own meager road clothes—a distillation of all he had lost, all he had gained.

"You'd better be moving, friend." He walked over, knelt down and gently shook the body beneath the plastic, not sure that the bum could hear him. "Time to wake up," he shook harder, "the bulls will be here soon."

The body jerked. An arm emerged. Lynden saw a hand, and a flash of firelight on the long steel blade it gripped.

Then he heard the voice.

"Frisco..."

And saw the face.

"I... woulda killed him," The Duke stammered. Grotesque scabs and bruises covered most of his head— one eye swollen shut, front teeth gone. His left hand was in a sling at his chest, his right gripping a butcher knife. "I was playin dead... waiting for the right time."

"I went back for you..." Lynden's words tumbled over each other. "That night—I got knocked out—I was in the hospital for days... but I went back."

"I knew you'd try." The Duke grasped Lynden's hand and struggled to sit up, to focus. He looked at the fire and the body next to it. "You got him for me."

"I got him for both of us," Lynden said simply. "I killed him."

"What he said..." Talking sapped what little energy the old hobo could muster. "It's true... I wore the buckle sometimes. But I wasn't no Johnson... not like him." He collapsed against his young friend. "You gotta believe me."

"I believe you."

Lynden held him there in the quiet, the murmur of far-off trains and rattle of labored breathing the only sounds.

"Let's get you to a doctor."

"I musta tore somethin loose inside when I hit that switch." The Duke coughed. "Up until a couple a days ago I could walk a bit. Now I ain't goin anywhere unless somebody carries me. I can't even crawl."

"All right then, I'll go for help."

"The hell you will. There's a dead body here, Frisco. Who they gonna pin it on... a kid with busted knuckles or a busted up old man? Go fetch me that gun."

"You can't be serious."

"Somebody musta heard that shot." A siren, distant but distinct, had joined the night sounds. "You can't be here when the bulls come. Just bring me the goddam gun."

"No... I won't."

"Think..." The effort of speaking was exhausting him. "I'm at the end of my road. They can't do nothin to me. But with that son-of-a bitch dead, you're at the beginning of yours. He already fucked up your past. Don't let him—or saving some old hobo—fuck up your future."

"I am not going to lose you again."

"No... you're not... but I ain't letting you get tangled up in this mess. I'll be easy to track down—county hospital, I figure—at least till I heal up. That's better'n you being in a cell. Now... get me that sawed-off."

There was no arguing the logic.

"When they get you situated somewhere, I'll find you."

Lynden eased him back down onto the ground. "I'll make them let me see you, even if you get arrested." He walked over and picked up the shotgun. The barrel was warm to the touch, the end of it smeared with Short Arm's gore. "I'll tell them I'm family—"

"You tell them you're my son." The Duke reached up, took Lynden's hand and held it for a moment, just held it. The siren was closer, too close. "You gotta get outta here."

The Duke released his grasp, took the gun.

"I'll tell them," Lynden began to back away. "I'll tell them you're my father."

He looked at the old man there by the fire, broken but proud, the shotgun clutched to his chest, the flames casting shadows that played across his face like twilight through a moving boxcar door.

Lynden turned and hurried out into the yard.

He ducked behind one string of cars, climbed over the couplings of another.

The siren had almost arrived, flashes of red light joined its wailing.

He heard the shotgun bark.

* * *

The Duke had outfoxed him one last time.

He *could* crawl—as far as that box of shells. The old Professional had lived his life exactly as he wanted. Why would his end be any different?

Lynden stood motionless in the darkness—silent for the lost years and the found days.

For the final moments.

For his friend.

The Last Track
Hold it down — Ride a long way.

Do you ever think about the future?

Not much. Would that change it?

Do you care if anyone remembers who you were? How you lived? What you did?

Not really.

Then what have you lived for?

Myself, I guess.

Will your life have meant anything when you're gone?

I'm not going anywhere.

You *will* die.

So I hear.

And your way of life, will it die?

When I go, it goes.

But there will be other hobos. People will ride as long as there are trains, won't they?

Sure... but not the way I did. Nobody will ever look at boxcars the way I look at them or feel rides the way I feel them. Don't get me wrong, I'm nothing special. I'm a hobo. But I might just as well be a brass-hat or a pencil-pusher, or whatever you want. I'd still be the last of my kind... just like you are the last of yours.

You're saying that there *is* no future?

Not once we close our eyes, and we're all gonna close em.

Yet, when someone asks—when someone like me shows interest—you still teach, don't you? How to catch a moving train, how to build a jungle fire, how to stay alive out here on the road? If there's no future, why bother?

Habit.

I think it's more than that. I think you want to leave something of yourself that continues on when you can't... not a mark on a wall, but a mark on the world.

You know—after all this talk—looks like you're getting the picture. Maybe I am, too. I ain't surviving... period. But my way of life? It might. Maybe I teach because I *do* hope it keeps rolling after I'm gone. I was taught by an old Profesh, hobo royalty. He treated me royal, that's for sure. Seems like I oughta pass it along.

Returning a favor?

Not returning it... living it.

Epilogue

Somewhere a hobo is waiting. He sits on an old wooden box, a small fire of twigs and branches burning between his outstretched legs. As he blows on cupped hands, the steam of his breath and the smoke of his fire rise to mingle with the morning vapors. His pants are gray and loose, his shoes brown and shapeless. The fire's heat draws the scent of leather, earth, and grass from his garments, and these smells combine with the fire's own fragrance to make a rich, sustaining aroma—a nourishment for his particular hunger. His quick breaths drink in the odors, nostrils stinging from the sharp morning air.

All night he has waited by the fire, standing every few minutes to hold his coat open, capture the fire's energy, and stave off the cold. Hugging the coat tightly around him, he presses the trapped heat into his skin.

Now the sun is up. Its warmth is stretching across his shoulders, sinking through his jacket and through his back, clear into his bones. Waiting will be easier now.

A sound breaks the morning stillness, singular and unearthly as it echoes toward him. Again it comes—the sure, clear blowing of a southbound freight.

His freight.

He knows every train that has ever run. Before he saw his first engine or heard his first whistle, he knew. Gleaming rails have stretched through the landscape of his life, through his dry lands and his mountains, through his cities, through his seasons dark and light. He has followed them willingly, mastered them, owned them. He has also been their slave.

The hobo has no face, no age, no name. He has a need, an appetite never satisfied. Every moment that he's not on a train, he is waiting for a chance to catch one. Every moment that he's sitting still, he is waiting for a chance to go.

Slowly the engines rumble past, jets of black smoke and brilliant sparks pouring from their stacks. He kicks out his fire. An open boxcar rolls up and the ceremony, sacred in his world, begins again. He breaks into a run, grabs the door, leaps. A maneuver, natural for him, that has cost men their arms, their legs, and their lives.

For *this* hobo the ritual is essential. Essential as breathing.

The End

Author's Note

Catching a freight guarantees nothing but a departure. Beginning a story is the same. In both cases you may think you know where you're going, but where either will actually take you is only revealed as the tale or the trip unfolds. You found a bit of hobo lore and language as you traveled these rails, a sampling of hobo poetry and philosophy, and hopefully something more. But you were riding in times now long past, and much that was once widely known of these men and their world has slipped from our collective memory, perhaps to be lost forever.

Yet, a surprising amount has been written about this brotherhood of travelers who emerged with the coming of the great iron roads, and who held dominion over them for more than a century. If you choose to venture a little further down those roads, please consider these three books to help you on your way.

No one has chronicled the heyday of hobo life better than Roger A. Bruns in *Knights of the Road, A Hobo History*.

Ted Conover's *Rolling Nowhere* is a top-notch, first-person narrative from the very era and some of the same rail lines traveled in this book. Hubb and Step could easily have jungled up with Ted at the Roper Yards.

And the extraordinary photographs in Michael Mather's *Riding the Rails* will get you closer to these men than anything short of sharing a boxcar with them.

Life on the rails has changed since I last caught out some forty years ago. Always illegal, it was dangerous to ride then, and is even more so now. As Hubbard said, "Old

Dirty Face, he can be a mean customer." Please heed those words if the call of the road becomes too great to resist. No need to catch the westbound before your time.

Author's Bio

Ed Davis is the author of the novella *In All Things*, a fictionalized account of his training year as a psychiatric technician at the country's largest institution for the developmentally disabled. His travel collection, *Road Stories*, details adventures from skid rows to the Sierras, an African hospital to ancient Inca ruins high in the Andes. His death row thriller, *A Matter of Time*, was written in real time, in twenty-four hours, as the last day of the hero's life unfolds.

His work has appeared in *Gris-Gris*, *New English Review*, *Potato Soup Journal*, *The Penmen Review*, *Rougarou*, and *The Umbrella Factory Magazine*. A runner, backpacker, and master's level discus thrower, Ed and his wife Jan live in Northern California, not far from Jack London's Beauty Ranch.